T0106099

KEMMERER

KEMMERER

Robert W. Callis

iUniverse, Inc.
New York   Bloomington

KEMMERER

This is a work of fiction. All of the characters, names, incidents, organizations, and dialogue in this novel are either the products of the author's imagination or are used fictitiously.

iUniverse books may be ordered through booksellers or by contacting:

iUniverse
1663 Liberty Drive
Bloomington, IN 47403
www.iuniverse.com
1-800-Authors (1-800-288-4677)

Because of the dynamic nature of the Internet, any Web addresses or links contained in this book may have changed since publication and may no longer be valid. The views expressed in this work are solely those of the author and do not necessarily reflect the views of the publisher, and the publisher hereby disclaims any responsibility for them.

ISBN: 978-1-4502-4065-9 (sc)
ISBN: 978-1-4502-4066-6 (ebk)

Printed in the United States of America

iUniverse rev. date: 08/31/2010

This book is dedicated to David M. Nelson of Kemmerer, Wyoming. The son of a Wyoming pioneer family, David is a man who is truly larger than life. He taught me most of what I know and understand about the West and all that I know about the great state of Wyoming.

PROLOGUE

The morning sun glistened off the light cover of snow that had fallen the previous evening. Except for the occasional spray of snow blown by the ever present wind, nothing moved on the high plains desert. A jackrabbit cautiously poked his nose out from under a large sagebrush that was flush against the rock wall of the small box canyon and sniffed the air carefully. For several minutes, the rabbit sat motionless, checking for any sign or smell of danger. Finally the rabbit was satisfied that no danger was present and proceeded to hop among the sagebrush, looking for his next meal. The rabbit's fur was brown and white allowing him to blend in with his snow-covered surroundings, giving him a natural camouflage to protect him from discovery by his many enemies. When the rabbit paused, only his tracks in the snow were apparent. Suddenly the rabbit caught a movement out of the corner of his eye. He froze and remained motionless to avoid detection. It was too late. The hawk struck savagely, and in less than a second the hawk and his prey were gone. All that remained were the tracks of the rabbit and a few specks of bright red blood contrasting with the clean white snow.

CHAPTER ONE

A cold rainy drizzle fell in the early morning darkness, reminding everyone that this was April in the Midwest. Carson Andrews dodged to avoid the water dripping off the small canopy over the front door to the coffee shop. Inside he breathed in the smell of coffee brewing and the warm damp smell that comes from steam heat and lots of damp clothing and raincoats. The tall, lanky Andrews waited briefly in line, got his usual large latte and waited by the door for Willie, his friend and co-worker, who was late as usual.

Carson sipped his latte and sighed. He and Willie Nelson had started working for International Consulting within thirty days of each other. After three years they were both still systems analysts, but with more seniority and less of the grunt work. They both lived in Oak Park, a Chicago suburb, which was close to work by train, affordable, and not too dangerous. Each morning they met at this coffee shop and rode to work together. Often they did not ride home together because of the erratic schedules their projects tended to develop. Carson enjoyed the early morning train ride in and the chance to talk to Willie. They had both attended Eastern Illinois University but had not known each other in college. Since meeting at work, they had become good friends, often assisting each other with assigned projects.

Glancing at his watch, Carson started for the door

to make sure he wouldn't miss the train. The station was only a block away, but the commuter train waited for no one. Suddenly the door burst open and in rushed Willie. Willie was of medium height with a slight build, a light, freckled face and wild red hair that never stayed combed. It was obvious that he left his apartment in a hurry as his hair was uncombed and his necktie hung loosely around the collar of his unbuttoned shirt. Both his suit and his trench coat looked like they had spent the night rolled up in a ball. Neatness was not Willie's long suit. Carson was an exact contrast. He was tall, about six foot four inches, with black hair, dark brown eyes and a slender frame that was very erect. His suits hug on him like they were tailor-made, when in fact they were off the rack. His suits were from carefully observed sales at Nordstrom's and other top of the line department stores. Carson was a consummate bargain hunter. While in college he had worked part-time at a department store, and he knew the ins and outs of retail. Any clerk he ran into at a store during a sale was overmatched. Carson managed to get deals where none had existed. He negotiated with confidence, and when he returned an item, he either left with a better item or an improvement on his credit card.

"I know, I know, I'm late," whined Willie as he followed Carson out of the warm coffee shop into the cold rain that awaited them. They dashed to the train where they scrambled to find seats together. After they were seated and had deposited their coats and briefcases on the empty seats across from them, Carson pulled the extra cup he had stored under his coffee cup and carefully poured half his coffee into the spare cup for Willie.

"One of these days I'm going to be gone when you finally show up," said Carson. "What is it with you? Is your alarm clock broken?"

"I just couldn't seem to roll out of bed. It was nice and warm and when I looked outside and saw the rain and cold, I decided to catch a few more winks."

"Hah," said Carson, "you haven't been on time to anything in three years, including our trip to Vegas last month."

"I wish I'd missed that trip completely," replied Willie. "That trip cost me almost $700, which was a huge hit to the Willie Nelson retirement fund." Willie's real name was Wilhelm Nelson, but since his days in junior high school it had been Willie Nelson.

"I assume you can come up with your share of the cash for our camping trip to Door County?" asked Carson. Carson, Willie, and their friend and co-worker Fast Freddy Connor had decided to try something different and to get away from the city for a while. They had come up with a camping trip to Door County, Wisconsin, for a week. It was cheap, there were state parks with camping areas, lots of beaches, and lots of young people, including females, and it was only about five hours away from Oak Park.

"Uh, how much is that going to run?" asked Willie.

"Your share, according to what we discussed last week-end , is about $250," replied Carson. We're renting a tent, we have the campsite reserved, and we need food, camp supplies, and your share of gas and tolls. You did remember to borrow your brother's sleeping bag?"

"Yeah, I got it from him two weeks ago. It's under my bed in my apartment."

Carson had come up with the idea of the trip and had organized a list. Some of the gear was from Boy Scout camping days and dug out of long neglected boxes and a few items like a Coleman lantern, were actually new. Carson had figured out that a tent could be rented and his gear was mostly already packed and stacked in the trunk of his old Chevrolet.

After a few minutes of silence, except for the clacking noise of the train as it swayed from side to side on the commuter tracks, Willie checked his Palm Pilot and groaned, "Oh God, I'm stuck working on the Midwest Trust project with Marty Beth and Lillian."

"And this is a surprise because?" responded Carson. Willie was famous among the analyst group for being very uncomfortable around any females. He was also notorious for having a very short memory. More than once, the Palm Pilot with its tiny electronic brain had saved him from humiliation, embarrassment, and numerous potential reprimands.

The Midwest Trust project was huge. The old and very staid trust company had hired International Consulting to review their organization and procedures and to recommend changes that would improve efficiency and profitability without adversely affecting the wealthy clientele of the firm. For the analysts, this kind of work was very boring, and working in a very conservative place like Midwest Trust was even more boring.

"There's nothing wrong with Mary Beth and Lillian," said Carson. "They're pretty good analysts and I heard last week that they're behind in their project and were looking for more help. Tell you what, I'll see if I can get Fast Freddy to come with me and we'll zip over and have lunch with you."

Looking relieved, Willie muttered, "Thanks," and went back to work on his latte.

Growing up in Illinois, Carson was used to the overcast skies, the rain, the wind, and the penetrating cold that seemed to last all winter and most of the spring. The only difference was the winter froze the rain into snow and it was definitely colder. He had grown up in downstate Illinois and while he was used to the weather, the city of Chicago was still new to him after three years of living there. No matter how hard he tried he still could not get comfortable with the crowds of people, the traffic, and the congestion. Still he enjoyed the city. He was a clothes hound and scoured all the shops and departments stores for bargains. He also liked the small, out-of-the-way restaurants. For the most part, he liked his job, although he didn't plan to be an analyst forever.

Carson and Willie left the train and walked the eight blocks from the Ogilvie Transportation Center to the glass and steel skyscraper that was the home of International Consulting or "ICE" as the analysts and most of the other employees referred to it. Unlike Willie, who had to walk four more blocks to the ancient stone tower that housed

Midwest Trust, Carson was working on a project in the ICE building.

International Consulting was one of the largest business consulting firms in the world. They had offices in every major city around the globe and had a well deserved reputation for being aggressive and effective. They were also expensive. Their clients got what they asked for, but at a price. After purchasing stock under the company's employee stock plan, Carson had read the annual report and determined that the company must bill his time at about five times what they paid him. Nonetheless, he had been very happy to get a job with a respected company like Ice when he graduated from college, a time when many of his college buddies had been scrambling for jobs.

After getting settled in his spartan cubicle, Carson e-mailed Freddy to arrange to meet him and go have lunch with Willie. The response was immediate, which meant Freddy was living up to his nickname. Fast Freddy did everything in a hurry. Some things he was good at and they went very well. Some things he was not good at, and they went from bad to worse because they were done in such a hurry. Freddy talked fast, he ate fast and for the most part, he worked fast. He was about medium height and build, had a dark complexion with jet black hair that was always slicked back with some sort of mystery hair grease that smelled faintly of lavender. Freddy was a good dresser, although Carson suspected that his clothes used Velcro fasteners instead of buttons and zippers. Freddy could change clothes faster than anyone Carson knew.

The trio met for lunch at a small Italian greasy spoon near the old Midwest Trust tower. Freddy, who had obviously finished his lunch first was trying to construct some sort of building with the small packages of crackers on the table when the waitress brought the bill. After a small game of chance to see who paid for lunch, Freddy was stuck with the bill. "I cannot frickin' believe this," he moaned. "This is three times in a row. You guys are trying to break me."

"Right," said Carson, "three bowls of chili and three Cokes, what were we thinking?" Both Carson and Willie broke into laughter over the look on Freddy's face. Freddy was a notorious tightwad. He still lived with his mother in Evanston, and he never spent a dime when a penny would do. His only weakness was his coin collection. Over the years Freddy had built up quite the collection. He traded coins on the internet, and he scoured the classified ads and had become familiar with all of the small, out-of-the-way coin dealers in the city and surrounding suburbs.

After lunch Freddy suggested they stop by a small coin store he had just learned about. The rain had stopped, so they set out in search of a new find for Freddy. After a short walk, they came to the address but saw no coin store. Finally, Willie figured out that the store was not facing the street, but was facing an alleyway. Sure enough, they found the store entrance halfway down the alley. The entrance was just an old weathered steel door with an aging, faded sign on it declaring that inside was "Moody Coins." They pushed the door open, which caused a small bell to ring, and stepped inside, pausing a moment for their eyes to adjust to the gloom that greeted them. The shop was small and narrow, poorly lit, and not well cared for. Along one wall was a counter with glass sided display cases. The glass was dusty, but even through the covering of dust there was a definite gleam. The gold and silver coins on display against a dark felt background caught what little light there was in the room. A man suddenly appeared from the back of the shop, stepping through a curtain that hung from floor to ceiling in the doorway which apparently separated the showroom from the rest of the shop. He appeared out of place in the shabby store. He was middle-aged, tall, slender, and dressed in what appeared to Carson to be a very expensive and immaculate well-tailored suit.

"What can I do for you gentlemen?" he said in slightly accented English. His words came out as polished and smooth as the stones you would find in the bed of a creek. Freddy explained that he was interested in seeing some coins, and after a discussion of types, quality, and price, the store manager stepped behind the counter and removed several coins from the display cases, set them in a felt lined tray, and placed the tray on the counter for Freddy's inspection.

Carson and Willie peered through the dusty display cases while they waited for Freddy to finish his inspection of the coins. They were getting bored, but Freddy was seemingly enraptured with the coins he was inspecting. Carson was about to step back out in the alley to get some fresh air when the store manager said, "Well, I do have a set of very rare coins in my safe that I think you will find intriguing." With that he motioned for Carson and Willie to accompany him and Freddy behind the curtain and into the back of the store. He led them to a corner of what was obviously a combination storeroom and work area. There was a huge old black steel safe at least seven feet high. On the door of the safe the name "MOSLER" was stamped in gold leaf on the black painted steel. Next to the safe was a tall table with four mismatched chairs. The manager motioned the three young men to sit down and he proceeded to bend over the door of the safe and work the combination. The soft ring of a small bell came from the shop. The manager stood up, looking slightly annoyed, and said, "Excuse me, I'll be just a minute," and he went through the curtain covering the door to the shop. Carson, Willie, and Freddy all looked at each other in puzzlement. Carson was about to make a joke about guarding the vault when they heard loud noises coming from the showroom. It sounded like the store manager was arguing with someone. Curiosity overcame Willie, and he walked to the doorway at the back of the showroom and pulled aside the curtain just enough so he could peek into the store without being seen.

Carson was about to yank Willie away from the doorway and admonish him for being nosy when the sound of gunfire erupted in the shop. Bright flashes from the muzzle of a gun were evident along with the pungent odor of burned gun powder even with the curtain blocking their view. Willie jumped back into Carson, almost knocking him down. In doing so, he jerked on the curtain that he had neglected to release, and the old material ripped from the rings holding it in place at the top of the doorway. The three found themselves face to face with two large and dangerous looking men holding pistols in their hands. On the floor in front of them was the store manager, minus much of his head, bleeding profusely on the old wooden floor of the shop. Quickly overcoming his shock, Willie shouted, "Let's get the hell out of here," and all three of them broke for the back door of the storeroom. Freddy started to fall, tripping over Willie's feet as they both tried to get through the door at the same time. Carson and Willie grabbed him by his coat, jerked him to his feet, and pulled him out into the alley. All three were outside the shop and running at full speed before the two gunmen could react to their unexpected presence. The three ran as fast as they could to get away from the danger that had suddenly erupted in front of them.

They ran with greater speed than they knew they possessed and when they finally came to a stop, completely winded, they were about seven blocks from the coin shop. All three were bent over at the waist, hands on their knees, breathing heavily, unable to talk. Finally, Carson got enough air in his lungs to gasp, "What the hell happened in there?"

Willie was unable to answer until he got his breathing under control. Finally he looked up at Carson and Freddy and said, "I saw two guys shoot the shop manager. They shot him in the head. It was terrible."

Willie was shaking, his red hair waving crazily in the air. Carson grabbed his arm to steady him and said, "We need to get out of here." He led Willie and Freddy to a nearby Starbucks. They took a booth in the back and Freddy sat with a still shaking Willie while Carson brought back cups of hot coffee. Freddy and Carson waited for Willie to calm down and finally, after a few sips of coffee, he described what he had seen in the coin shop.

"I was curious so I pulled the curtain back a little so I could peek through," said Willie. "I could see the guy who waited on us. He had his back to me and he was talking to these two tough-looking guys. They were huge and really nasty looking. They were wearing leather coats and leather gloves. They started arguing with the manager guy and then of one them grabbed him by the tie and pulled his head forward. Then I saw the shorter guy pull out a gun and put it about two inches from the manager's head. Suddenly I heard boom, boom! I was blinded by the flashes from the gun and I fell backwards. The next thing I remember is we were sprinting like crazy down the street.

"You saw those two guys murder the manager?" asked Carson in an incredulous tone. "You mean they just killed him in cold blood?"

"I didn't stay to take pictures," Willie replied sarcastically. "It scared the crap out of me."

"We have to tell the cops what you saw, Willie," said Freddy. "Oh my God, you saw a man get killed."

"Oh right, I just call up the cops and tell them I was nosing around the private area of a store where I had no business being and just happened to see the manager get capped by two goons. I don't think so," answered Willie.

"Freddy's right," said Carson. "We have to tell the cops a man was shot. What if he's not dead. What if he's just badly wounded and needs medical help?"

"That dude is toast," said Willie. "The flash from he gun almost blinded me, but I did see the guy's head jerk back and it like disintegrated. No way he lived through that. Two shots in the head from about two inches away sounds like pretty dang dead to me."

As Carson and Freddy remembered how bloody the manager looked lying on the floor in front of them, they knew Willie was inexorably right.

"Do you remember the address of the shop?" asked Carson. "We need to repot this to the police. We have to. Think of the poor guy's family. They'll want to know what happened to him. Wouldn't you?"

Finally, after much discussion, the three decided to call the police and make a report anonymously. After about ten minutes, and three fruitless tries, they finally found a pay phone that was working and Carson called 911. The police operator took down his information and asked several questions including who Carson was. Being a good citizen and naively honest, Carson gave his name and work phone number. The operator told Carson the police would contact him for more information if needed. Feeling relieved, Carson related the conversation to Willie and Fred who likewise felt somewhat better. All three of them returned to work late, still shaken from their experience. Willie was so upset, he went home after telling his supervisor he was sick with the flu. Carson finished the day but had difficulty concentrating on his work and his mind kept going back to what had happened in the dusty little coin shop.

CHAPTER TWO

The next morning the sun actually peeked out for a few minutes and made the day one that television weathermen in Chicago call "partly cloudy." Carson and Willie did not discuss the shooting, waiting until they were walking to work from the train station. Willie could not really add anything to what he had described before, but he could not get it out of his mind.

About nine o'clock Carson got a call from his supervisor to come to her office. Carson was a little surprised, as this rarely happened. Usually when he got called to the office it was a once a year occasion for a formal performance review. His boss was a woman who worked "flex-hours." In the real world this meant she had learned the system well enough to use it to her advantage. Sandy worked at home three days a week and was at the office in downtown

Chicago only two days a week. During the two days a week she was scheduled to be downtown, she was rarely in her office. Carson always suspected she was more of a professional shopper than a supervisor, but in a large corporate environment she seemed to be doing just fine. As long as Carson got his projects done on time and helped the rest of the staff in his division on their projects, he received good reviews from his seldom seen supervisor.

Carson walked into the office and saw Sandy sitting at her desk talking to two men wearing wrinkled trench coats over their poorly coordinated sports coats and ties. They all stood up as Carson walked in the office. "Please close the door, Carson," said Sandy. "These gentlemen are detectives from the Chicago Police Department and they would like to ask you some questions. Is that O.K. with you?"

After assuring Sandy that he was happy to talk to the police, Sandy excused herself and left them alone in her office. The older of the two detectives, a smallish man with short-cropped grey hair and a soft, almost soothing voice, introduced himself as George Landers and his younger and larger companion as Wilson Hays. Wilson Hays said nothing and watched intently as George questioned Carson. Carson admitted he was the one who had called 911 and related what had happened the previous day. He gave them Willie and Freddy's names and phone numbers. George informed Carson that they would be talking to Willie and Freddy and possibly with him again. George and Wilson each gave Carson a business card and asked him to call them if he thought of anything else. They left Carson alone in the office to then deal with a very curious Sandy when she returned. Carson told Sandy what had happened, and she told him to take the rest of the day off. On his way out of the office, he tried to call Willie and then Freddy on their cell phones, but only got their voice mail. He left a message on each of their phones to call him back.

On the train ride home, Carson called both Willie and Freddy on his cell phone and still got nothing but their voice mail. When he got to his apartment building, the two police detectives, Landers and Hays were waiting for him at the entrance. "Sorry to inconvenience you, son," said Landers, but we need to talk to you and your two friends downtown right away.

An hour and a half later, Carson was sitting in a cramped and grimy conference room furnished with old ugly gray steel furniture that looked like factory rejects. With him were Willie and Freddy, Landers and Hays, and two other uniformed policemen. After three hours of questioning, each of the three young men had signed statements as to what happened and what they saw at Moody's Coins. All of the policemen seemed very pleased with the meeting and when he was alone with detective Landers, Carson asked him what was going on.

"You and your friends have done the Chicago P.D. and the city a very big favor," answered Landers. "What you guys saw was the murder of a guy named Bernard Fleischer, better known as Bernie the Dime. Bernie's coin shop was a front used to launder money for a Chicago mobster named Rico Sabatini, also known on the street as Rico the Rooster. Apparently Bernie was being a little dishonest with his employer Rico, who is a rather large and unpleasant Italian gentleman. Rico and his younger brother Marco were the two men you and your friends identified as the killers in the shop. We had young Mr. Nelson pick out both brothers in a line-up about an hour ago after he had picked their photos out of our book. His eyewitness testimony and the testimony of you and your friend Mr. Conner will guarantee Sabatini and his brother a date with the electric chair for first degree murder. That helps us eliminate a large chunk of the criminal element in Chicago."

Carson was stunned by the cop's explanation of what had happened. "You mean we have to testify in court? In front of these two guys!" he exclaimed.

Landers put is hand on Carson's shoulder and said, "Don't you want to see this guy get punished for what he did? He killed a man. Maybe Bernie was scum, but he was a human being. This is how our systems works. You do the good citizen thing and let us know what happened, and we follow up and collect evidence, build a solid case, and then we arrest the guy. He gets his day in court and you and your friends provide us with rock solid eyewitness testimony that either gets Sabatini fried or put in cold storage for the rest of his life. Either way, society is better off, and believe me, Chicago is a lot better off with Rico Sabatini and his brother Marco out of circulation. You and your friends have nothing to worry about. You are doing the right thing and it's our job to protect citizens like you from scum like Sabatini and his brother."

Carson felt better after his lecture from George but could not get rid of a nagging sense of foreboding about the idea of testifying in court against a couple of violent criminals. That kind of stuff never turned out well in the movies or on television. He waited in the lobby of the Public Safety Building until first Willie and then Freddy came out of their respective meetings with the police. The three of them left the building together, grabbed a cab, and stopped at an old tavern about three blocks from the train station.

Once inside, they ordered burgers and beers and each explained to the others what they had heard and said in their interviews with the police. Over the food and beers, they debated the pros and cons of their current situation. Being a hero was fine, they decided, but having to testify in court against really bad people was something they would just as soon avoid. Carson called his office on his cell phone and confirmed to the others what the police had told them. His boss and Willie and Freddy's bosses were supportive of the need to cooperate with the police, and they had been granted all the time off they needed to assist the authorities. "Why me?" said Freddy. "I didn't see a damn thing. This was just Willie sticking his nose in somebody else's business."

"Hey, I was just curious about the place," replied Willie. "I was getting bored while you had your nose buried in some old coins. I had no idea something bad was gonna happen. You think I like this? I'm the one who has to testify that I saw them kill a guy. You guys are just testifying that you saw those two goons after they shot the coin guy. How tough is that?"

"Calm down, both of you, " said Carson. "I think it's pretty obvious we're stuck with this deal and whether we like it or not, we're going to have to testify in court. I don't like it any more than either of you, but we don't have a choice in the matter. The cops may be talking nice to us, but they are not going to let us avoid testifying. Without our testimony, I don't think they have much of a case other than a very dead body. Frankly, I think we're lucky there aren't four dead bodies instead of just one. If those Sabatini brothers had reacted faster before we got out of that shop, they would have killed us as dead as that schmuck, Bernie what's-his-name."

"That worries me," said Freddy. "If the cops do not have much of a case without our testimony, what keeps the friends of the Sabatini brothers from disposing of us!"

"You have seen way too many movies and television cop shows," responded Carson. "The Sabatini brothers don't have a clue as to what kind of case the cops have, and they have no idea of who we are."

"Easy for you to say," wailed Willie. "I'm the one who stuck his head around the curtain. I'm the one they probably saw."

"Not likely," said Carson. "If the flash from the gun blinded you, it also blinded them or at least affected their vision. Besides, the light in that shop was lousy and if memory serves me right, it was not exactly a sunny day outside. No way anyone in that shop got a good look at any of us."

While it was evident that Carson's explanation made Willie feel better, all three of them were still very uncomfortable with the idea of testifying in court against murderous criminals.

They were wishing that yesterday had never happened, just the way victims of a auto crash feel immediately after the accident occurs. All three of them were silent for a while as though if they didn't talk about it, then the problem might go away. No such luck.

Willie and Carson said good-bye to Freddy and caught a train back to Oak Park. Neither one of them said a word during the entire train trip until they reached their station and then they said good night to each other as they each headed for their respective apartments.

Carlson could not rid himself of the feeling that he and his two friends had gotten in way over their heads and only bad things would come out of their need to testify in court. He managed very little sleep that night and when he reached the coffee shop by the train station the next morning, he was surprised to see Willie already there, sipping a cup of coffee. Willie had the look of someone who had not enjoyed a restful night. His eyes were red and his skin color was paler than usual. He was also holding two steaming hot cups of coffee. This was a first in their three-year working relationship.

Neither spoke on the train ride into the city. Each sat

quietly sipping his coffee, apparently deep in thought until they reached the Ogilvie Center in Chicago. They walked quickly to the ICE building and instead of splitting up to go to their respective work areas on different floors of the office tower, they decided to use a small conference room near Carson's work area. The conference room was empty and after snapping on the overhead lights, Carson shut the door behind them. Willie thought that they should keep the whole thing quiet and not mention a word to anyone. Carson agreed, but said, "Look, if our bosses know what's going on, that means everyone in ICE will know within the next twenty-four hours. There are no secrets in this company when it comes to juicy gossip, and that is just what we've become. I suggest we go to our work areas, report in to our bosses, and try to get some work done on our projects."

"Easy for you to say," replied Willie, "I'm still on assignment to the Midwest Trust project with those two broads."

"I would be very careful about how you describe your co-workers, Willie," said Carson. "Also, I think if you report to your manager, you may find yourself reassigned to some project here in the ICE building where they can keep a close eye on you." Carson's prediction turned out to be true. Both of them were placed on what seemed to be fill-in jobs on existing projects that did not seem to really need any additional help. As Carson had also predicted, their project co-workers were full of questions about what they had heard. The articles in the newspapers and the television news stories initially had very little information other than the basic facts of the untimely demise of the unfortunate Bernard Fleischer, sometime coin dealer.

That was soon to change. A very alert reporter on the police beat managed to squeeze more information out of a source she had in police administration. Very shortly she had put together enough facts to realize that the police were sitting on the very big arrest of a major Chicago crime figure for murder, thanks to some accidental eye-witness accounts. She made some more phone calls and discovered that the Chicago Police had just obtained a warrant issued for the arrest of Rico "the Rooster" Sabatini and his brother Marco Sabatini for the murder of Bernard Fleischer. She decided to wait at police headquarters and get a live shot of the police bringing in the Sabatini brothers. While she camped out at the police headquarters lobby, the reporter began making calls on her cell phone, trying to ferret out the names of the eye-witnesses as they were not revealed in the warrant or the police blotter. Although the first calls were unrewarding, she kept dialing as she knew that someone on her list had the names and sooner or later she would have a huge story.

CHAPTER THREE

Lenny Klein waited at the curb for his driver to bring his car around. His short, pudgy body was elegantly wrapped in an Armani suit. His tie cost more than most people's suits. Lenny was a very successful criminal defense attorney and liked to look the part. He had just left a meeting with one of his biggest clients. Because of the nature of most of his clients, Lenny usually came to a meeting place of the client's choosing rather than his own well-appointed and spacious fortieth floor office on Lakeshore Drive. Although most people would find Lenny's clients distasteful, if not downright frightening, Lenny enjoyed the challenge of dealing with very dangerous people. He also enjoyed the large sums of money they paid him to get out of trouble and then to keep out of trouble. Sometimes the jobs were easy like getting a ticket fixed or arranging for an abortion, or providing a false paper trail. Occasionally, his job was quite challenging, like the time he had to literally create a phony witness, complete with totally bogus documentation, and then have them "disappear" after a successful court verdict.

Lenny's driver brought the car around and jumped out to open the door to the back seat of the stretch Mercedes limo. Lenny climbed in, sat back, and lit a cigarette, while the driver pulled out into the ever-busy Chicago traffic. Lenny sat in the dark, collecting his thoughts about the meeting he had just attended with the rather nervous Sabatini brothers. They knew a warrant for their arrest had been issued, thanks to a snitch in the police station that Lenny kept on his "private" payroll. Lenny had called the brothers with the information, and they had readily agreed to a meeting. Lenny mentally ticked off the items on his current must-do list for the Sabatini brothers. First he had to arrange for orderly surrender to the police and then arrange for bail. It was easier to get bail for your client when they voluntarily surrendered like a good citizen who just found out the police were looking for him. Then Lenny would have to put the brothers in a safe house with some professional baby-sitters. He would need to keep them under wraps and free from any temptations that could lead to more trouble with the police. Finally, he needed to meet with his investigator Tony Picinni. Tony would need to get all the information possible on the case the police had. Things like the names of any witnesses, what physical evidence they were holding, etc. A few minutes on his cell phone put everything in motion and Lenny had his driver take him home as nothing was gong to happen until the next morning. However, when the Sabatini brothers surrendered to the police in the morning, Lenny would be there with them, and he would have most of his information before they were processed into the Cook County lockup.

The female reporter was getting nowhere with her calls with over half of the responses turning out to be voicemail. She would have tried to use her womanly charm on the booking sergeant, but her physical looks leaned more to the mud fence than the movie star. In disgust, she went to the coffee vending machine in the hall for a cup of really bad coffee. Its only redeeming feature was a large shot of caffeine, which was something she needed at the moment.

Just as she was swallowing her first sip of the hot black

swill, her cell phone chirped. Surprised, she grabbed for her phone, shifting her purse to her other hand and managed to spill the coffee on the rather untidy tile floor of the hallway. The call was a return from one of her earlier voice mail messages. What she learned was that the police were thrilled to have nailed the Sabatini brothers for the murder of a small time crook. To them it was a win-win situation, getting rid of more criminal garbage and getting the Sabatini brothers off the street and out of circulation, permanently. She also learned form her source the key to a conviction rested on the backs of three young, white male eye-witnesses. She was unable to get the names, but that was enough to get her a by-line on the morning edition of her paper. She thanked her source, made him a promise she did not intent to keep, and hurriedly dialed the night editor of her paper.

Carson was shaving the next morning when his phone rang. It was Freddy. Freddy sounded like he was on helium gas. He talked so fast the Carson could not understand a word he said. "Slow down, Freddy, I can't understand what you are saying," said Carson.

Before Freddy could repeat his garbled message, Carson heard a tone on his phone alerting him to a second caller. A glance at the caller ID display on his phone let him know that Willie was also trying to reach him. Finally, Freddy was able to verbalize something to the effect that Carson should read the front page of the morning paper and call him back. Carson hung up the phone, which promptly rang with a call from Willie. Willie was excited, but much more understandable than Freddy.

"I thought you said nobody would know about us," screamed Willie. "We're on the frickin' front page of the frickin' paper. We're lucky they didn't ask us to pose for pictures so they could include them, too."

After calming down Willie, Carson told him he would read the paper and see Willie at the train station. Then he went down to the main floor of his apartment building and retrieved the paper from his box. Sure enough, at the bottom of page one was a story on the arrest of the Sabatini brothers for the murder of Bernard Fleischer and the headline was "Eye-witnesses to put the Sabatinis away for life." Carson felt sick to his stomach and had to sit down in a chair to continue reading. However, as he read the entire article, he felt better. The article contained none of their names, only that the eye-witnesses were three young, white males. Still, even that information being published for several million people to digest with their breakfast was disturbing.

The train ride in to the city was one of strained silence. Both Carson and Willie were eyeballing their fellow passengers, hoping they would not somehow make the connection between them and the "three young white males" mentioned in the article. After a while they began to realize how silly that whole idea was. There were no pictures. There were no names. There was nothing except "three young white males." By the time they got to the Ogilvie Center, both were finally breathing normally. Carson had called Freddy back after reading the paper, but he did not get very far in calming Freddy down.

Finally, Carson told Freddy to "cool it" and he would talk to him after he got to work and had a chance to talk to the police about the article.

His subsequent phone conversation with detective Landers was something less than satisfying. Landers basically told Carson that some reporter got lucky with a little information and while that was regrettable, it happens and unless a judge grants a request to seal information, the information about the eye-witnesses would eventually be made public anyway. When Carson pressed him to find out what exactly would be made public, he discovered, to his dismay, that the names of the eye-witnesses would be public information. "What did you think, that we were going to have you testify with hoods over your heads and microphones that distorted your voices?" asked Landers. "This is America. Everyone has rights. The stupid reporter who broke the story, she has rights. The Sabatini brothers, who we arrested this morning, they have rights, and even you three guys have rights. There is very little information that we, the police, collect, that can be kept secret. Obviously, when you testify in court, the world is going to know who you are. The press is going to want to talk to you. Whether you like it or not, the TV guys will have your faces on the ten o'clock news. You may want to change your phone to an unlisted number 'cause you will be getting lots of calls if you're in the book. My guess is you're in the book, right?"

Carson nodded. Of course he was in the book. How else can people call you? Then he realized what the detective meant. Whether he, Freddy, and Willie liked it or not, their lives were about to undergo a drastic metamorphosis.

"What about protection?" asked Carson. "Everything you just said makes it sound like the three of us have just become easy targets for anyone who doesn't want to see the Sabaini brothers go to jail or worse."

"Of course you'll have protection, son," answered detective Landers. "We'll have a policeman watching each of your homes and while the trial is going on, you will have a police escort to and from the courthouse. At the slightest sign of any trouble, we will keep all three of you under 24 hour armed guard in a safe location at the city's expense. You have nothing to worry about. No one messes with the Chicago PD."

"What about after the trial?" retorted Carson. "What kind of protection do we get then?"

"After the trial is too late for the Sabatinis," said Landers. "After they are convicted of first degree murder, you and your two friends will be yesterday's news. Something more exciting will come up and the reporters will forget all about you."

"I'm thinking more of revenge from some the Sabatini brothers' friends," said Carson. "How do you protect us from them?"

"When Sabatini and his brother are convicted, they'll have no friends. Their associates will be fighting among themselves over who takes over the crime operation. With a little luck they'll manage to kill of few of their own in the process. That revenge stuff sounds good in books and movies, but this is not the Mafia we are dealing with. These are your plain old vanilla crooks. They're very dangerous and nasty crooks, but basically, just crooks."

"Somehow that's not very comforting," replied Carson.

"O.K., I'll make sure we have a patrol car check your homes every night for a month after the trail. How about that?" asked Landers.

"I guess it's better than nothing," answered Carson. "Maybe I'm making too much of this. It's just that crooks who think nothing of shooting someone they know at point blank range strike me as something a little stronger than vanilla."

"You have nothing to worry about, I assure you," said Landers. "See you in court."

Carson hung up the phone, but he could not rid himself of a feeling of dread and uneasiness that had seemingly taken over his body during the phone conversation with Landers. Somehow he did not feel reassured by the promises of protection made by Landers.

Carson met with Freddy and Willie that afternoon and he related his conversation with Landers. Although he tried to reassuring to them, Carson could see that either he was not very convincing or they had the same bad feelings he had experienced when he talked with the detective.

"I don't like this, I don't like this at all." moaned Willie. "We stick our necks out and for what? What the hell do we get out of this besides being scared crapless."

"Do we have to testify?" asked Freddy. "What if we decide that we won't testify. They can't make us do it, can they?"

Carson sighed. "Look guys, we have given sworn statements to the police. Our employers know what we said, heck almost everyone seems to know what we said. If we try to change our minds now, we will be lucky to keep our jobs?"

"Being healthy and unemployed might be preferable, based on how I feel," said Willie.

"Well, the cops have promised to protect us and since we are this far in, I don't see how we can do anything else except testify as to what we saw," responded Freddy.

"I don't think we have much of a choice," said Carson, silently wishing for something resembling normalcy to return to his life.

"O.K. O.K. I'll go along and testify, but I still don't like this deal and I'll be much happier when this is all over and forgotten," answered Willie.

After work, Willie and Carson took the train home and they discussed the upcoming trip to Door County. Getting away from the city was starting to look like a great idea. Both of them were actually feeling a little better when they got off the train in Oak Park. As they split up to go to their respective apartments, Carson failed to notice a dark haired man in an ordinary looking tan trench coat following him on foot. The man was careful not to get too close and he blended in well with the commuters who were either getting to their cars in the train station parking lot or were walking to their homes or apartments. He stayed across the street from Carson, walking parallel with him for the six block walk to Carson's apartment. He watched Carson go into the apartment building and waited outside for several minutes before walking up to the front of the apartment building to check the mailboxes for Carson's name and apartment number. He then carefully walked around the building to the rear which faced an alley. He pulled a small notebook out of his trench coat pocket and briefly wrote in it before replacing it in his coat pocket. After glancing around to make sure no one had been observing him, the man then returned the way he had come.

Unknown to the dark haired man, two other associates of Lenny Klein had duplicated his efforts by following both Willie and Freddy.

CHAPTER FOUR

For the next few days things returned to what seemed like a less aberrant routine to all three of the young men. They went to work, they went home, and then they went back to work. Carson even remarked to Willie on their train ride in, "I'm starting to feel like the whole deal never happened and was just a bad dream."

"Hey, I've had bad dreams and this is way out of that league," retorted Willie. "Maybe you think this never happened but try telling that to the cops and the lawyers when it's time to go to court."

Carson smiled. "The court date hasn't even been set yet and probably won't be for several months. We're no longer getting phone calls from reporters or getting hassled at work. Let's face it, we're old news. Thank God."

The two of them decided to meet at Carson's after work to go over the list of things they needed for their upcoming camping trip to Door County. Then Willie asked a question about a problem he was having with his current project and soon he and Carson were discussing the pros and cons of several possible solutions. Pretty soon, the trial and all it represented as an intrusion in their lives was forgotten.

Lenny Klein called his secretary on the phone intercom. "Let me know as soon as Tony is here and bring me in a fresh cup of coffee."

Lenny's secretary was Sarah Milner. Sarah was in her mid-forties and had worked for Lenny for the past twelve years. Sarah could be described in one word, plain. She looked plain, she dressed plain, and she talked plain. Nevertheless she was a good assistant to Lenny and knew him well enough to keep him happy by taking care of all the details in his very interesting law practice. She often marveled at the sometimes infamous people that she saw in his office. People she saw on the television news or the papers were frequent visitors to Lenny's office. Sarah might be plain and she might blend in with the furniture, but she was very aware of what was going on around her.

She was well paid to keep everything she knew to herself and she did.

Lenny's law office was on the fortieth floor of a newer office building on Lakeshore Drive. His office was large and well appointed. He had two associates plus two legal assistants, a law clerk, Sarah, and his investigator Tony. All of Lenny's staff had comfortable offices with the exception of Tony. Tony was rarely in the office and when he was, he was usually on the phone or the computer. His office was very spartan as it had previously been a supply room, and it was crammed with sophisticated computers and state-of-the-art electronic equipment. Tony was a computer genius. He had a doctorate in computer science from M.I.T. He was also a geek. Tony had grown tired of working long hours with mediocre pay for large corporations. He had also grown tired of being dumped on at work by his superiors and his co-workers and by the women he encountered socially. That all changed when he was introduced to Lenny. Within six weeks, Tony was having the time of his life with his work and was almost embarrassed at the amount of money he was being paid. No one dumped on Tony anymore. Even the women he encountered socially were now impressed by his bankroll. Life was good for Tony. It did not bother him in the least that most of his work allowed criminals to go free from the justice system or that it might lessen their court-ordered punishment. Tony had little use for the government and the justice system. He enjoyed beating them at their own game, and beat them he had. In the three years he had been working for Lenny, Tony had come up with information that had allowed Lenny to win over 85% of his cases. Lenny got more clients, Tony made more money, and everyone was happy.

Lenny sat back in his chair, sipping hot coffee and reading e-mails on his computer. He was interrupted by Sarah knocking and then opening the door and letting Tony into the office. Lenny gestured with his hand for Tony to sit down and asked, "What do you have for me?"

Tony pulled out three manila file folders from his briefcase and opened the first one. "Carson M. Andrews, white male, age 26, born Kankakee, Illinois. He's an only child. Mother is Ruth Andrews, age 49. She resides at 1129 River Street in Kankakee. She has lived there for about twenty-two years. She's a teacher at Kankakee High School. Father is Thomas P. Andrews. Parents were divorced when Andrews was only two. I'm unable to find a thing on the father. Inquiries were blocked on almost every level I attempted. I suspect that father is or was involved in some form of covert government work. He could even be dead. No known contact between the son and father. Andrews graduated from Kankakee High School. He had better than average grades and played on the tennis and soccer teams. He was a pretty good athlete. He was the captain of the varsity soccer team both his junior and senior years. It appears his mother kept him out of contact teams. He graduated from Eastern Illinois University in Charleston, Illinois, about four years ago. Majored in

Computer Science. He received good grades and graduated in the top 25% of his class. Belonged to Pi Kappa Alpha social fraternity and was active in student government. He also participated in intramural sports like basketball and flag football. Andrews started work for ICE a little over three years ago when he was hired as a systems analyst. Has done well at ICE and is now a senior systems analyst. He is apparently being considered for a manager's position. Andrews has lived in apartment 225 at 1896 Lloyd Street in Oak Park since he moved to the Chicago area. In short, Mr. Andrews is bright, hard working, relatively underpaid, and has never been in any trouble of any consequence. He has received two speeding tickets in the past ten years. Other than that he is clean."

Tony went on to list all of Andrews' credit cards and charge accounts, complete with balances, what he has been buying, and how much he was paying as well as how much he was earning in the employ of ICE.

"In short, he is boring," sighed Lenny. "So he has no issues or problems we can take advantage of?"

"None that are apparent," responded Tony.

"O.K. Read me the other two," said Lenny.

After another half hour of reading from the files, Lenny held up his hand for Tony to stop. "Good God," moaned Lenny. "Who are these guys, the Waltons? They're all boring and other than the one kid who lives with his mommy, they reek of normal."

"Freddy is the one who lives with his mother," injected Tony.

"Fred, Schmed, whatever," said Lenny. "We need something to hang our hat on. We need some angle that we can use to get these here kids to forget what they saw and refuse to testify against our client. You're the smart guy, the great investigator, how do you suggest we shut them up?"

Tony looked down at his shoes for a few moments before responding to Lenny's question. When he looked back up at Lenny, his face was expressionless and his dark eyes were unusually flat and empty. "The only way to keep these kids quiet is to scare the hell out of them or have them disappear. I personally don't think scaring them will work. It might work initially, but they are young guys and young guys are stupid. Sooner or later they would tell someone what happened, and we would have a brand new problem. I also don't think we can bribe them. Again, they are young and stupid. While one or two might go for it, getting all three to go along is unlikely. Also, being young and stupid, they would likely flash the money and tip the cops off as to what happened. We're very good at covering our tracks, both literally and electronically. These kids would have no idea about how to do that. Any way you look at it, alive they're a liability to our client."

Lenny sat back in his chair and closed his eyes. These were the times he did not enjoy his job. Having to arrange for this kind of unpleasantness did not appeal to Lenny, but considering the nature of his clients, it went with the territory. His client had a problem and Lenny was being well paid to come up with a solution.

Lenny leaned forward in his chair and opened his eyes. "O.K. We have a problem. I agree with you that the only solution to our client's problem is to have these three witnesses disappear. My problem is that how this happens has to appear accidental and cannot have any possible link to us or our clients. Is this understood?"

"I understand. I'll make all the arrangements, and I'll contract with an out-of-state firm so that there will be no possible connection to us or our clients," replied Tony.

"O.K. then," said Lenny. "What else do you have for me?"

Tony then pulled another manila file folder from his briefcase, opened it, and began to read.

CHAPTER FIVE

Three days later, a man got off American Airlines flight 286 from Houston at O'Hare International Airport in Chicago. He was not encumbered with any carry-on luggage, and he proceeded to the baggage area. After an interminable wait, he finally collected his small overnight bag. He then took a taxi to the Ogilvie Center in downtown Chicago. At the train terminal, he proceeded to a row of rental lockers. He searched for the one he had memorized and after locating it, he produced a small key and opened it. He reached in and took out a gym bag, closed the locker with the key in it, and left the building.

Outside he caught a taxi to a nearby auto rental lot. There he picked up a late model Chevrolet that had been reserved for him. He rented the car using a driver's license and credit card that were not his. After placing his two bags in the trunk, he proceeded to an old, run-down motel on the west edge of downtown. He paid for his room in cash and was not asked to produce any identification or a credit card. Once in his room, he checked the contents of the gym bag and was pleased to see that everything he had requested had been provided. He removed a Glock Model 17 semi-automatic 9mm pistol from the bag and placed it in a clip holster he produced from his overnight bag. He preferred the Glock as the high capacity magazines held 17 rounds of hollow point ammunition. In addition, the gun was ready to fire with no clumsy safeties to worry about. He checked the lock on the door, set a portable travel alarm, turned off his cell phone, and then laid back on the bed to get some needed sleep.

The man arose about 5:30A.M. and spent thirty minutes doing a series of exercises in his room. He was of medium height, stocky, with dark bushy hair. Even the eyebrows above his dark brown eyes were extremely bushy, giving him the appearance of a man with two spiders resting above his eyes. He showered, dressed, and drove his rental car to a Perkins Pancake House. He bought a local paper and read it while he finished his breakfast. Then, after the waiter had cleared away the breakfast dishes and brought him a fresh cup of coffee, he pulled a manila folder from his canvas briefcase and began to read and take notes on the margin of the papers he was reading. After he finished, he wrote down a list on a separate pad and tore off the top page and put it in his shirt pocket.

He proceeded to two separate strip shopping centers and made purchases at three different sores, being careful not to buy too much of what he needed at just one store. After checking his list and consulting a phone book, he made two more stops and then drove back to the motel where he took his purchases to his room. He spent the better part of the next two days working in his room and storing everything he had acquired in a cardboard box. When he left the room, he had sealed the box with strapping tape and placed a hair from his bushy hairdo under the tape so he would know if someone had disturbed the box and re-taped it to cover up their snooping. It was rather simple. Hair still there, everything is O.K. Hair missing, time to get out of Dodge. He also studied and marked up a local street map. After completing those tasks, he sealed up the box and locked up his room.

He left the motel in his rented car and then parked outside the target property and carefully took pictures with his digital camera. On the morning of the third day, he placed the completed project in the cardboard box and put the box in the trunk of the rental car and dove to a park about three blocks from his target. There he went to the park restroom and changed into a set of tan coveralls. On he back of the coveralls was the name of a local heating and air-conditioning company and on the front, above the right breast pocket, was the embroidered name "Hal."

He drove to a spot about a half block from the target and transferred his project from the box to a small canvas bag. The bag also carried the name of the same local heating and air conditioning company. He walked up to the house, rang the doorbell, and waited. According to his instructions and his observations, there would be no one home, but sometimes you got surprised and ringing the bell first eliminated that potential problem.

No one answered and he quickly picked the lock, a very cheap model he noted, and stepped into the house. Twenty minutes later he was out of the house and walking back to his rental, carrying his now lighter canvas bag. He got in and drove back to the park where he again used the park restroom to change clothes. He reversed the canvas bag so that no name showed, and placed the coveralls and a few tools he had used in the house in the bag, and walked out to his car.

After checking his surroundings and noting that there were few people around and no one seemed to be paying any attention to him. He walked to his car, got in, and drove straight to the airport. At the airport he placed his canvas bag in a storage locker, placed the key for the locker in a stamped and pre-addressed envelope and then dropped the envelope into the nearest mailbox. He turned and headed to the ticket check-in area and was soon lost in the sea of bodies churning through the various corridors of O'Hare International Airport.

At the same time "Hal" was departing Chicago from O'Hare Airport, a second man was arriving in the windy city by Greyhound Bus. He was short and stocky, wearing well-worn jeans, sneakers, and a black nylon windbreaker. He was middle aged with curly salt and pepper hair and a fairly bushy moustache to match. He had the look of a man who was accustomed to hard work. He exited the bus in the Greyhound Bus Terminal in Chicago and patiently waited for his bag to be removed from the bowels of the bus. He did not mind waiting and while he waited, he studied the crowd around him, his light blue eyes scanning the area for any sign of something out of place. He saw nothing to alarm him. He prided himself on his patience, his attention to detail, and his experience. He considered himself a professional in every sense of the word. He also hated flying and always traveled by bus or train. It took longer, but time was not a problem for him. His experience had taught him that patience consistently kept him out of trouble, that and careful planning and execution.

His brown backpack finally appeared in the driver's hands and the short man stepped forward to claim it. He then proceeded to the street where he waited to hail a taxi. One thing he liked about Chicago was the generous number of taxis on the streets. You could almost always find one. He used taxis exclusively in cities like Chicago. There were so many, you never got the same one twice. Also, like most major cities in America, the drivers were usually foreign and new to the country and had a last name that ended in a vowel. They usually made lousy witnesses. He had the taxi take him to a cheap run-down motel near Midway Airport. The motels around Midway specialized in anonymity. He paid for the room in cash for a week in advance and then carefully inspected the room for any sign of surveillance. Finding none, he proceeded to empty his backpack on the bed. When he was done, he took a quick shower and used the phone to order a pizza. After dressing he walked down to the office and bought a copy of the *Chicago Tribune* and returned to the room to read it while waiting for the pizza to arrive. After he finished the pizza, the *Tribune*, and the local news on the room's small television, he went to bed for some much needed rest.

In the morning he arose early, showered, dressed, and called for a cab. While he waited for the cab, he turned on the television set. The lead story on the local news was about an explosion, presumably from a gas line leak, that had totally destroyed a home in nearby Evanston. Two bodies had been found and identities were being withheld until the next of kin were notified. He heard the taxi pull up in front of his room and after grabbing his backpack off the bed, he checked to make sure the door locked securely behind him and left in the taxi.

He had the taxi take him to the Oglilvie Transportation Center where he caught a commuter train to Oak Park. After arriving at the Oak Park commuter depot, he went inside to the men's room. After selecting a stall, he entered and closed and locked the stall door and sat on the toilet. From inside his jacket he pulled out a thick brown envelope. He carefully read the instructions contained in the envelope and made a few notes on the margins of the papers. Also in the envelope was a local map with a blown-up section of Oak Park. This map was of the neighborhood he would need to become familiar with if he was to get his job done efficiently. After exiting the stall, he paused to wash his hands and checked around him to see that the restroom was vacant. He then took part of his instructions, wadded them up and then flushed them down the toilet he had just used as a reading seat.

After exiting the commuter station, he walked for a few blocks until he found the neighborhood he was looking for. There was a small park located conveniently on the edge of the nine block area he needed to survey, so he paused on a park bench and again reviewed his map. He then walked by every building in the nine block section and made mental notes. After he had completed his walk, he again paused in the park to make notes on his map. The neighborhood was old. Most of the buildings were small to medium sized apartment buildings with a few old homes that had been converted to multi-family dwellings. The trees were large and most of the landscaping consisted of large bushes that had grown way past their original design purpose. There were alleys behind all of the buildings and based on the street signs he saw, parking was probably at a premium. Even in the mid-morning, he noticed that there wee no parking spaces on the streets in front of the buildings. Also the parked cars made the street even narrower than it would normally be. Looking around as he walked, he also noted that because of the overgrown bushes and the parked cars, a person walking on the sidewalk was hardly visible from the street or the buildings. It was almost like walking down a long tunnel.

He left the park and walked past the building he had marked on the map. As he got near the building he slowed his pace, pausing to apparently tie his shoe in front of the building. From his kneeling position he was almost invisible to the street or the building. It was an old three story brick apartment house. Seeing no one around, he walked to the entrance and carefully checked the names over the doorbell buzzers. After finding the name he was looking for, he looked the door over carefully. It was an old wooden door, in need of some paint, with a very cheap lock. He smiled and returned to the sidewalk, being mindful of keeping an even pace and not seeming to be in much of a hurry. In a short time he was back at the commuter station. After checking the train schedule, he bought a paper and a cup of coffee and made himself comfortable until the next train arrived.

After returning to the Ogilvie Transportation Center, he took a taxi to a location that was about a block and a half from the second address he had on his list. A short walk and he was in front of a large modern office building. He went inside and pretended to read the registry for the building.

The lobby was large and brightly lit, with two banks of elevators and a security guard. The guard was wearing a blue blazer and tie and sat at a horseshoe shaped, highly polished wooden desk. Next to the guard were ten small television monitors. Obviously these were the video security cameras. By observing the control panel next to the monitors, he noticed the monitors could be changed to cover other locations in the building. He estimated that there were at least fifty video cameras connected to the monitors. Apparently the guard could call up any of them and would do so if he had a reason. The ten displays were probably of the key areas of the building. Before a few minutes had passed, the guard noticed him and called out to ask if he could be of assistance. The stocky man with the salt and pepper hair paused and said, "No thank you, sir. I must have been given the wrong address."

"Happens all the time," laughed the guard. "No problem."

The man left the building, being careful not to walk too fast or do anything that would call any more attention to him. He hailed a cab and returned to his motel where he spent about two hours going over his notes and maps before picking up the phone and ordering a pizza to be delivered.

CHAPTER SIX

Carson was not really a heavy sleeper nor was he a light sleeper. He was sort of a middle of the road sleeper. Lately he had been having dreams about the killing, the trial, and his job. None of them made any sense when he finally woke up.

It reminded him of the kind of dreams he had experienced when he was a little kid. He had watched horror movies, eaten too much junk food and drank too much pop and "bingo", the dreams from hell were the main feature.

This evening had been a pleasant change as those dreams he did have were more restful and sedate. At least he thought they were when suddenly he was sure he heard alarm bells ringing. Finally it dawned on him that it was the phone in his bedroom, not his mind that was ringing. He flipped on the lamp by his bed and looked at the travel alarm next to it. Unless he was still dreaming it was 4:15 A.M. He reached for the phone, knocking the receiver off the cradle and onto the floor. He finally retrieved the receiver and was able to get a semi-coherent "hello" out of his mouth. What he heard was Willie talking so fast he couldn't understand him. "Whoa, slow down guy, I can't understand a word you're saying," he finally managed to interject when Willie apparently stopped to take a breath of air.

"Carson, you're not going to believe this. It's unbelievable, it's unbelievable," ranted Willie.

"Willie, slow down and tell me what the heck is going on," Carson said firmly. "Take a deep breath and then tell me what happened."

Willie finally paused, and with a strange voice he said, "Turn on your T.V. to Channel nine!"

Carson set the phone on the bed and lunged forward about six feet to the small dresser that supported his television. He turned the set on and after waiting for a few seconds, the picture materialized and he tuned it to

Channel Nine. The early morning news was showing a fire in a residential area. The picture was unclear because of all the smoke, but then the camera changed to a close up and it looked like a house that had blown up and all that was left was a crater surrounded by debris, water, smoke and fire.

Carson went back to his bed and picked up the receiver. "O.K., I am thrilled that you're up on current events and you want to share a story about a house fire at four in the morning. Why are you really calling?"

"Earlier in the newscast they said that the house apparently blew up with two people inside. They think it might have been a gas leak. Both the people are dead and they did not release any names."

"So, what has that got to do with anything?" asked a puzzled Carson.

"They did not give the names, but they did give the address in Evanston. I thought the area looked familiar. That's Freddy's house! You know, where he lives with his mother! My God, if that address is right, Freddy's dead!"

Carson tried to answer, but no words came out of his mouth. He was stunned. Finally, he said, "Look, maybe this is a mistake. We don't know for sure it is Freddy's house. Calm down. I'll get dressed and meet you at the station coffee house in thirty minutes. We'll take an early train in and find out what's really happened. We can check with the cops and see if they know anything. In the meantime, try calling Freddy's home number. This could all just be a mistake."

"God, I hope so," wailed Willie before he hung up the phone.

They took the five A.M. train into the city. Neither of them had much to say. Willie kept trying to call Freddy's phone, and all it did was ring continuously. That was no comfort as Freddy had an answering machine on the phone. Even sips of very hot black coffee failed to jolt Carson from the numb feeling he was experiencing. This was not real. It couldn't be. How could Freddy not be okay? What in the world was happening to them?

They grabbed a taxi at the train station and raced to police headquarters. Once they arrived, Carson asked for Detective Landers. Naturally he was not on duty. Carson then explained to a dubious looking sergeant that he was trying to find out more information about the house fire and explosion in Evanston. The sergeant turned him over to a Detective Dillard. Dillard was a tall slim black man with a pencil thin moustache. He looked very Brooks Brothers with his gray suit and white button down shirt with a red silk tie. His badge hung from his suit jacket pocket. That and the very large revolver occupying a shoulder holster under his left arm somehow did not go with the Brooks Brother's look.

Dillard led Carson and Willie to his desk, a battered old battleship gray steel relic, piled high with papers and a rather new looking desktop computer.

"O.K. Now Mr. Andrews, what's your friend's address in Evanston?" asked Dillard.

Carson gave him the address in Evanston and Dillard

keyed in the information and after a few seconds the screen changed and Dillard hit another key and then a new screen appeared and Dillard began scrolling down the screen. "Bingo!" said Dillard. "This is the address of a suspected gas explosion and fire in Evanston about three A.M. this morning. Apparently two bodies have been recovered. No survivors were found."

Dillard looked at Carson and Willie. Both were speechless. It was obvious to Dillard that they were in a state of shock. "Why don't both of you come over here and sit down. Let me get you some coffee and then we can talk about this," said the detective. He actually took them by the hands and led them over to a wooden bench against the wall by his desk. By the time Dillard returned with cups of coffee for both of them, Carson had regained a little of his composure.

"Thank you," he managed to get out. He and Willie took the cups of coffee and held them awkwardly, like they were unaccustomed to cups. After finally taking a few sips, Carson explained to Dillard that the home that had exploded and burned belonged to his friend's mother and that just the two of them were living there. He then explained the murder by Sabatini, their role as witnesses, and the pending trial. Dillard listened attentively, interrupting Carson occasionally to ask a question. Then he said, "I'll get in touch with detective Landers. This is his case and he needs to know what's happened. I suggest you two go to work today. I'll need your work phone numbers and cell phone numbers just in case we have to call you there."

Carson and Willie each fished their respective business cards out of their wallets and gave them to Dillard. "If I were you guys, I would stay here a while, rest up, and finish that coffee before you leave. You guys don't look so good."

The funeral was set for the following Friday morning at the First Methodist Church in Evanston. Neither Carson nor Willie had known Freddy's mother very well, but they had met her on numerous occasions and they knew that Freddy had a sister who lived somewhere out of state. The church was packed with mourners and Carson and Willie found a spot near the back of the chapel. Freddy had grown up in Evanston and his family had lived there for many years which accounted for the large turn-out. Added to that was the fact that this was such a tragic and unexpected event.

After a long service, the caskets were removed from the chapel by the pallbearers and the mourners filed outside to follow the hearse to the cemetery. Carson and Willie followed the convoy of funeral cars and mourners in Carson's old white Chevrolet Cavalier. The car was not pretty, but it was paid for and Carson had owned it for almost seven years. Carson wished he had taken the time to get the car washed before the funeral as he could almost write his name in the dust on the car's finish. Since Carson rarely drove the car and used the train and public transportation, he kept it stored in an elderly couple's garage near his apartment. Mr. and Mrs. Fahey had only one car and rented the other space in the garage to Carson for a small monthly fee that he always paid to them in cash.

Both Carson and Willie had been tight lipped, but under emotional control at the church. Now during the graveside service, both of them found tears running down their cheeks. The enormity and permanence of Freddy's death was finally hitting home. As they were turning to walk to their car, a well-dressed young woman in a dark trench coat addressed them. "Are you friends of Fred?" she inquired.

"Yes," replied Carson. "We went to college with Freddy and all three of us have been working for the same company since we got out of college."

"Thank you for coming," responded the young woman. "I'm Nancy Hart, Fred's sister."

Carson and Willie introduced themselves and shook hands with Ms. Hart. "I am ten years older than Fred and I moved away as soon as I got out of college, so I was never really a part of Fred's life," said a now tearful Nancy. "I didn't get along well with my mother, and I never took the time to get close to Fred. Now it's too late!" She began to sob and Carson put his arm around her in an attempt to provide some comfort. Nancy quickly regained her composure and thanked both of them for coming to the funeral. Then she turned and walked back towards one of the waiting funeral cars.

Carson and Willie decided to avoid the reception being held after the funeral and they drove to a brewpub located near the campus of Northwestern University in Evanston and took a booth near the rear of the pub. They ordered a pitcher of beer and sat in silence for several minutes. Finally Willie looked up and said, "I cannot believe this has happened. This is something that happens to somebody else, not one of your close friends."

Carson nodded in agreement, but he did not speak. He still could not get over the fact that Freddy was gone. He had read somewhere that death was even harder to comprehend when you were young and he decided that was totally true. They finished their beers and Carson drove back to Oak Park. He dropped Willie off at his apartment building and then started to drive back to the Fahey's garage.

He remembered his displeasure with the condition of the Chevy and found a parking spot near his apartment. He returned to the apartment and changed clothes. He packed up the camping gear and hauled it out to the car and packed it in he trunk. Then he drove to a nearby self-service coin operated car wash and spent half an hour washing and then cleaning and drying the car. Finally satisfied with his efforts, he drove the car to the Fahey's garage and stored it. The three block walk back to his apartment along with the effort expended in washing his car seemed to make him feel better.

CHAPTER SEVEN

When Carson got back to his apartment, he showered, changed clothes and checked his phone for messages. There were three calls from college friends who had heard about Freddy's death as well as a call from Detective Landers. He was about to return the call from Landers when his doorbell rang. Carson hit the intercom switch and asked, "Who is it?" and got a strong response from Detective Landers. He pushed the button to unlock the front door to the apartment building and shortly after Landers knocked on Carson's door.

Landers was quick and to the point. He had missed Carson at the funeral and wanted to talk to him about Freddy's death. Carson offered Landers something to drink and the detective declined. They sat down in the small living room and Carson told the detective everything he knew about what had happened to Fred and his mother. Landers looked up at Carson and asked, "Mind if I smoke?"

Actually, Carson did mind, but decided that this was one time when he could overlook his aversion to tobacco smoke. "No problem," said Carson.

Landers lit a cigarette with a cheap throw-away lighter and sat still for a moment. Finally he spoke. "Do you have any reason to suspect foul play in the death of your friend Fred, or his mother?"

"No" said Carson. "From what I've heard it was an accident, a gas leak that somehow exploded."

"The cause of death was from the explosion that totally leveled the house," replied Landers. It was an older house, probably built in the 1930's and gas leaks are not uncommon in houses that old. I would not be here talking to you if were not for two things. One, Fred was one of three witnesses to a murder committed by Rico Sabatini, a known Chicago mobster.

This is not the first time that a witness to a crime involving Mr. Sabatini has been eliminated due to a convenient accident. Three years ago we thought we had him nailed on an extortion charge when our star witness ending up falling off a station platform in front of a CTA train and landed on the third rail just one week before the trail was to begin.

"You said there were two things?" asked Carson.

"The second thing is that our investigators got a call from Climate Makers Heating and Air Conditioning in Evanston. It seems that they had just finished a seasonal check on the furnace and central air conditioning units in the Hart home two weeks ago and found nothing wrong and no gas leaks of any kind. They were a little shocked to hear the news that the house had exploded." Landers said with a grim smile. "Now, I asked myself, what are the odds that a gas leak would develop within two weeks of having a professional inspection of the system? It seems to me that those are pretty long odds."

"So what are you saying?" Carson managed to squeak out of his suddenly very tight throat.

"What I am saying is that maybe this was not the accident it seems to be and if not, it is likely the person who was behind the explosion is not done with his work," said the detective.

"You mean you think Willie and I are in some danger?" Carson managed to eke out. "How can you be sure it wasn't just an accident that caused the house to blow up?"

"I can't," replied Landers. "I'm just very suspicious. Being suspicious is what I'm paid to do. Having your star witness killed just before a trial is not usually just a happy coincidence. I think Sabatini may have had your friend Hart killed and he may be planning on seeing that you and Mr. Nelson never make it to the witness stand either."

"How can that be?" Carson responded. "Sabatini and his brother are behind bars. You said yourself that they were denied bail. How could they kill someone like Fred when they're in jail."

"Son, you need to broaden your horizons," chuckled the detective. "Guys like Sabatini hire other guys to do the dirty work. Really bad people in jail still manage to manipulate people and make bad things happen. Chances are that Sabatini had one of his people arrange to hire a contract killer from outside Chicago. The killer would show up here, blend into the background, get the data he needed on the proposed target and set up the hit. After the hit, he leaves town with no trace. He knows no one here and no one here knows him. That is why they do it that way. Even if we were to catch the hit man, he couldn't tell us who really hired him. These contracts are usually done through intermediaries and the payment is always cash. Usually they get half the cash up front and the balance after the job is done."

"Really?" said Carson. "How do they deliver the cash?"

"Boy, you are really naïve," said Landers. "They use

a local delivery service or usually they use Fed Ex. And they always pay for the service in cash. In case you hadn't noticed, cash is pretty hard to trace."

Carson was developing a severe headache while listening to the detective and he was pretty sure it was not a coincidence. "So what does this mean to Willie and to me? Are we really in danger? What're we supposed to do?"

"I see a light bulb has gone on in your head," laughed Landers. "I want you both to be aware there could be some danger. I could be wrong about this and about Sabatini. In either case I want you and Nelson to be careful, be aware of your surroundings. I want you to keep to public places and not allow yourselves to be in a position where you are alone. I'm going to add extra manpower to watch both of you until we get through the trial. I'll have a patrolman staking out each of your apartments around the clock. In addition, I'll have a plainclothes cop shadow each of you when you are going to and from work. I'll have a talk with the owners and the supers of each of your apartment buildings to make sure they call us on any repairs or installations being done in your buildings. If someone rings your doorbell with a delivery and you're not sure you ordered it, have them leave it with the super and call this number and tell them who you are and that you have just had an unauthorized delivery to your apartment building. My next stop is a visit with your friend, Mr. Nelson. I will have this same conversation with him to make sure he is on board as well. You also need to keep an eye on each other."

"How long do we need to do this?" asked Carson.

"The trial is scheduled in nine weeks. After we get the two of you in the witness stand and you give your testimony then you should have nothing to fear. Sabatini needs to keep you from testifying. After you have testified, you are of no interest to him and his goons." Landers paused and lit another of his cigarettes with the cheap butane lighter.

"Listen to me, Andrews. I may be wrong. There may be no contract on you or Nelson. The death of your friend Hart may just have been an accident that is an unlucky coincidence. That doesn't matter. We are far better off to be careful and take all of the precautions I've mentioned, and some that I'm not going to tell you about. You're better off not knowing everything I've planned. Just know that you and Nelson will be protected. You can make my job a little easier if you're careful and do what I tell you to do. Understand?"

"Yes, I understand," replied a rather shaky Carson.

Before he left, Landers paused at the door, turned and faced Carson. "You might want to think about replacing this cheap piece of shit lock or at least add a strong deadbolt to this door. Also, check the window locks and the fire exit. Make sure you're locked up tight each night. Got it?"

"Yes, sir."

Landers left and Carson checked the locks on all the windows and the fire escape. Although he was on the second floor, the fire escape allowed access to at least two windows in his apartment. Carson pulled out the yellow pages and called a locksmith, making an appointment for the next morning to have a deadbolt installed on his door.

By Friday, Carson and Willie had gotten used to the routine. They were still following their old pattern of going to work and taking the train in and out of the city. Now, however, they spent their time waiting for the train a little differently. They were constantly scanning the people around them for some indication that something was not quite right.

When you take a train to and from work in Chicago at the same time every day for several years, you get to know your fellow passengers, at least by sight. They kept looking for strangers or anything that was different from what they had become accustomed. After five days of this plus checking their apartments each morning and evening, they were both getting bored.

By now they had figured out who the plainclothes cops were who had been assigned to them. The cops were a man and a woman, neither of whom had ever been on the trains with Carson and Willie before. Being able to spot them in less than three days left both Carson and Willie something less than impressed. The police cars parked by their apartments were also pretty obvious. They were marked cars and due to the shortage of parking spaces in the neighborhoods around the apartments, the cop cars were usually double-parked. Thursday night, Carson had gone for a walk, trying to get a little exercise and enjoy the early spring weather. When he passed the patrol car near his apartment, it was pretty obvious that the cop inside was asleep. Either that or he was watching with his eyes closed, his head back on the seat rest, and was managing to drown out the muted radio calls with his snoring.

Carson decided that this was a little less than reassuring. Or, maybe the cop was as bored with the whole routine as Carson and Willie were. Carson walked home, took a frozen pizza out of the freezer and nuked it in the microwave. Carson downed the pizza with a coke and fell asleep in his chair watching a John Wayne movie *Red River*, which was so old that it was in black and white.

Saturday morning Carson was doing his laundry in the washroom located in the basement of his apartment building when his cell phone vibrated in his shirt pocket. He pulled out the phone and looked at the call ID display. It was Willie. He pushed the button to answer and promptly heard Willie say, "Hey, sleepyhead, let's go into the city and have lunch, do a little chick watching and maybe catch a movie."

"Sorry," Carson replied, "I have an appointment at 11:00A.M. at the dentist to have my teeth cleaned."

"Oh, crap," said Willie. "Just reschedule it and let's have some fun instead. I invited my neighbor Zack Watts, you know, the guy who works as a bartender at Facets in the city. He knows all the cool places. Come on, it'll be a blast. We can use a change of pace."

Carson hesitated. It would be fun and maybe it was time to blow off some steam. However, it had taken him seven weeks to get this appointment at his dentist. "I'm sorry, Willie. I have to keep this appointment or it'll be two months before I can get back in."

"All right," sighed a resigned Willie, "but you're making a mistake. When I get back tonight and tell you about all the fun you missed, you're going to be really sorry!"

Carson hit the off button on his cell phone and muttered, "Don't I know it," to himself. He finished his laundry and showered and changed to make his appointment by eleven. He decided to walk the eight blocks to his dentist. It was a fairly nice spring day for April in Chicago. It wasn't raining and the sun was even trying to poke out through the clouds.

The short man was dressed as an elderly gentleman, complete with a wig and false beard. He sat on a bench in the park across from the Nelson kid's apartment house, feeding pigeons from his sack of breadcrumbs. He watched as Nelson emerged from the front door of the apartment building with another young man. Nelson's companion was a tall, thin guy with a shaved head. They were both laughing as though sharing a common joke.

They left the building together and turned to the short man's left as they headed up the sidewalk. He had not expected the second man and that caused him to re-consider his plans. He was certain they were headed for the train station and he eased out of his comfortable position on the park bench. As he passed the nearest trash container he pulled off his cheap raincoat and threw it in the trash along with the wig and the beard.

The change was startling. Under the raincoat he was wearing a gray and black windbreaker with a small, tan backpack. He pulled a Cubs ball cap out of his pack and placed it on his head. He now looked much younger and more capable of keeping pace with the two young men he was tailing. He followed them to the train station and ducked into the rest room. Taking the first stall, he changed into a dark blue windbreaker and a plain black ball cap, sticking the original jacket and cap in the pack. He purchased a ticket to the city and made his way as close to where Willie and his friend Zack, were standing while they waited for their train. About fifteen people were either standing or sitting on benches waiting for the train. After a short wait the train arrived. Hesitating until he saw Wile and Zack get on the train, the man then stepped on the Chicago bound train.

Once on the train, he began to review his plan. Willie with a friend changed his plan. His backup plan would have to work. He would bide his time and if the chance arose, he would make it look like a random mugging gone bad. If he killed both Willie and the friend, it would look like a random robbery and killing, which was almost as good as an accidental death. The short man smiled to himself. In today's society, a robbery and killing were practically a form of accidental death in a city like Chicago.

Carson returned from the dentist's office feeling a load of guilt from the hygienist who had chastised him for not flossing enough while she was cleaning his teeth. Where do they learn to do that so well, he wondered. It was like they had taken lessons from his mother. He smiled as he thought of his mother. She was the Queen of Guilt. She practiced it every day on him when he was growing up. Heck, she was still using it today. Carson hardly ever got a card or letter or phone call that was not laced with some form of guilt trip.

He never actually knew, but he was pretty sure that her behavior was what drove his father away and probably caused their divorce. He felt a twinge of guilt just thinking about his mother. He had not talked to her since before Freddy had been killed. He should call her, but he dreaded the guilt trip she would invent for him when she got him on the phone. He paused, realizing he had not thought about the father he had never known for quite some time. Even if his mother was the Queen of Guilt, his father should still have kept in touch. As it was, he had just disappeared. Carson suspected his mother had something to do with that, but he could never be sure. Any mention of his father had always caused his mother to change the subject. As a matte of fact, whenever he had brought up anything his mother did not want to discuss, she just changed the subject. The thought of his mother constantly changing the subject brought a smile to his lips. Some things never change.

The locksmith had added the deadbolt and then added a sort of flange around the lock that would make it much harder to force. Carson also had the locksmith check the window locks and replace one that was broken. Now he found himself checking the locks several times a day.

Looking out at the fire escape he decided to see how he could get out of his apartment if the door was not available to him. He opened the window closest to the fire escape and stepped through the window and onto the small landing. The landing, like the rest of the fire escape, was made of rusted steel. The landing was like a grate made with steel rods. On one side of the landing was a narrow stairs going up to the floors above his.

The building was three stories high and there was a corresponding landing and narrow stairs for each story. The exception was his landing to the alley below. On the other side of the landing was a sort of ladder attached to large springs. When he stepped out onto the ladder, his weight caused the ladder to drop down with him on it. As he descended the ladder to the alley, it held in place. When he got to the last rung, he was about eight or nine feet above the alley.

Carson realized that by hanging from the last rung, he would be only about a foot from the alley. Rather than step off the ladder, he climbed back up to his landing and pulled himself back through the window into his apartment.

After rummaging around in his apartment, he came up with some old clothesline. He braided the clothesline together to make a stronger rope and used his Swiss army knife to cut the rope to about a four-foot length. He then took the rope and went back out the window to the landing and descended on the ladder. At the bottom rung of the ladder, he tied the rope to the rung so that about two feet of rope hung below the final rung.

Carson then returned up the ladder to his landing and back into his apartment. He went down to the laundry room and went out the back door of the room to the alley. The back door was locked from the outside, but could be opened by using the panic bar on the inside. The only problem was that after 9:00P.M. the alarm on the door triggered if you opened it and alerted the super who could come to check the door.

He stood below the fire escape and saw the rope was about seven feet above the alley. He used his six foot three inch frame to reach up and catch the rope and pulled on it until the ladder came down. Carson then climbed up the rope to the bottom rung of the ladder and then pulled himself up onto the ladder. Satisfied, he went back up into his apartment. Now he had a back way into his apartment if he needed one. He would leave the window above the fire escape unlocked in case he needed to use his entrance.

Now he had a second way both in and out of his apartment should he need it. Since the fire escape ladder was a little noisy, he made a trip to the hardware store and obtained a spray can of white grease to use on the ladder springs and the connections. He also bought a little can of black spray paint for the rope so that it could not be easily seen. After he had finished his work and cleaned up, he decided he would try out his new exit that night to see if it worked and he could get out of the building without the cop on duty seeing him.

CHAPTER EIGHT

Willie and Zack had thoroughly enjoyed their day in the city. Zack had lived up to his reputation as a very knowledgeable Chicago bartender. He knew all he clubs where there were lots of lovely ladies and where the best bargains on drinks and food were available. He and Willie made the rounds of half a dozen bars and stopped at Uno's for a pizza to have something to soak up all the alcohol in their systems.

They had the restaurant call them a cab and took it to the Ogilvie Center. A check of the published schedule showed that they had a twenty-five minute wait until the next train that would take them back to Oak Park. They sought out a bench in the almost deserted train station and killed time by relating stories of how each of them had failed to pick up any ladies that evening in what had definitely been a target rich environment. "We'll get 'em next time," moaned Zack, who was starting to feel the effects of a full day of bar hopping.

"You forget, this is Chicago," said Willie. "Like all good Cub fans we always say, wait till next year!" Both of them laughed.

When they finally boarded heir train to Oak Park,

they were seated and still talking bout their day when the short man, now dressed in a Chicago bears sweatshirt, sunglasses, his small tan backpack and no cap, boarded the next car just seconds before the train pulled out of the Ogilvie Center.

Saturday night had arrived with a light drizzling rain. The weather made Carson feel even more alone, and he was regretting his decision to keep his dental appointment and not gong with Willie and Zack to the city. By eight o'clock he was bored with television, bored with the internet, and feeling like he had to get out of the apartment and do something or he would go bonkers. Then it dawned on him that it might be a good time to see if he could get out of the apartment without being seen by the cop who was baby-sitting him. The dark night and the drizzling rain would make a perfect cover.

Carson pulled on his new black North Face jacket, one designed for mountain climbing and foul weather. It was made of Gore-Tex and this would be a good test of how it protected him from the elements.

Carson left some lights on, slipped out the window, and carefully closed it behind him. He stepped out on the fire escape ladder, and it quietly dropped down. He carefully descended and after using his arms to move down to the last rung, dropped down to the wet alley below. With the dark night and the rain, there was almost no light. The darkness of the night seemed to swallow the light from the windows of the buildings on either side of the alley. Carson made his way to the end of the alley, which was on the opposite side of the building from where the police patrol car was parked.

He stopped at a convenience store to get out of the rain and gave Willie a call on his cell phone, hoping to get some company to go out for some pizza and beer. All Carson got was the voice mail on Willie's phone. He browsed the magazine section in the store for a while and then headed out into the night.

Two hours later, Carson was eating an early breakfast at a nearby diner and reading the early edition of the *Chicago Tribune.* He tried calling Willie again only to once again wind up on Willie's voice mail. Then he remembered Willie's cell phone number and tried it. There was no answer, and it too took Carson to voice mail.

Carson thought it odd that Willie wouldn't answer his cell phone. He always had it on and was never without it. In fact, about six months earlier, he had broken his phone and he had a fit with the cellular company until he got a loaner phone while his was repaired. Carson paid his check and decided to walk over to Willie's apartment and see if he was home and too drunk to answer the phone. Even if Willie had gotten "lucky" in the city and was not home, it was still something to do, even on a rainy night.

The short man was sweating profusely, even in the cold rain, as he paused to check his work. He knelt below the hedge and carefully checked the ground around him using a small red filtered flashlight. He located the two shell casings that had been ejected from his silenced 9 millimeter automatic pistol and put them, along with the Glock automatic pistol and the silencer, in his small tan backpack under the cheap black rain poncho he was wearing. Mentally he went over every item on his checklist.

After stepping in front of the two young men as they turned off the sidewalk past the hedge at the entrance to Willie's apartment building, he had simply pulled up the pistol he had held at his side and he shot each of them in the heart. They had both died immediately. He slid the pistol into his pants pocket and took out a ten-inch butcher knife that was probably sold in every K-Mart in America and cut both of their throats. The blood from these terrible wounds would make it appear that it had been a knife attack until some coroner found the bullet wounds. The blood from the slit throats always added to the confusion and made the cop's job harder. It also usually scared the crap out of any surviving witnesses. He threw the knife down on the wet grass where it could not be missed. As usual, he wore surgeon's plastic gloves.

He carefully removed the wallets from each of the two victims and took out the cash and credit cards and threw the wallets next to the knife on the ground. His checklist complete, he remained kneeling and he listened carefully. A car drove past and when it was over a block away, he stood up and walked directly across the street and began a leisurely five-block walk to where he had parked his car. With parking in such short supply in this neighborhood, no one would remember him or his car leaving a parking space as they would be focused on getting their car into the space when he vacated it.

While he walked, he removed the gloves and put them in a baggie he had kept in the rain poncho's pocket. As he moved under a streetlight he glanced down at the front of the poncho. There were specs of blood that he could see, but the rain was in the process of washing them off. In the dark, they were very hard to see against his black poncho. When he got to his car, he carefully checked the area around it. There was no traffic on the street and no one was visible on the sidewalks.

He opened his car trunk, took off the rain poncho and put it into a garbage bag along with the baggie containing the gloves and placed it carefully in the trunk. He had been very careful to turn the poncho inside out and to keep it away from his body when he did so. He took a jacket out of the trunk, put it on, and after checking the street and sidewalk again, he got in his car and drove off.

The garbage bag was dropped off at a gas station six miles away when he stopped for gas, which he paid for in cash. He used the rest room to wash up and slipped behind the building to drop the garbage bag in the dumpster located there. The car was stolen. He drove it to O'Hare International Airport and left the car in long term parking, taking a shuttle to the terminal and a flight out to Milwaukee.

Carson was beginning to regret his decision to take a long walk in the rain to Willie's apartment. "All those songs and movies about the joys of walking in the rain are a lot of crap," he thought. "It's cold, my feet are getting wet, and I have to be careful not to get sprayed with water every time a car goes past." In fact he was looking down at where to place his feet when he was walking or he would have seen the blinking red lights sooner.

About three blocks from Willie's apartment he looked up and saw the emergency lights that had to represent four or five vehicles and he could see a small crowd standing on the edge of the vehicles, even in the rain. He started to run, a combination of curiosity and fear trickling down his neck along with the sweat and the rain. As he got closer he could see an ambulance, a fire department emergency services truck, and three Chicago police squad cars, all with the lights flashing making a kind of strobe light oasis in the dark of the wet night.

As Carson got to the edge of the crowd he stopped and tried to work his way to the front to see what had happened. Because of his size and height, he was able to force his way to the front of the crowd where he could see over the squad cars. There were at least a dozen figures in front of the apartment building, some standing, some walking around. A bank of bright yellow police line tape had been strung around the hedge in the front of the apartment building and around to both sides. Carson turned to a heavy-set man to his right and asked him, "What happened?"

"Someone robbed and killed two guys in front of that apartment building. They say someone used a knife and stabbed both of them to death. My God, you'd think we were living next to O.J. Simpson."

A strong sense of fear began to creep up Carson's spine. He could see that the two victims were covered with sheets and the white of the sheets reflected the red flashing lights and contracted starkly with the dark wet grass. He could not bring himself to even imagine that Willie might be one of the two bodies under the sheets. It wasn't possible. It could be anyone. And then Carson saw something that almost made his heart stop.

A short man in a stained tan trench coat was walking away from the bodies and toward the emergency vehicles. He stopped and cupped his hands to light a cigarette. The flash from his lighter lit off his face and danced off his gray, close cropped hair. It was Lt. Landers. Carson tried to call out his name, but all that came out of his fear constricted throat was a dry croak. He tried to push his way forward around the parked police car and was stopped by a very large policeman in a dark blue raincoat. As the policeman began to wrestle Carson back to the line where the rest of the crowd stood, a hand reached out to restrain him.

"Let him go, Jake. It's okay"

Lt. Landers had seen the commotion and then he recognized Carson. He took Carson, who was still speechless, by the arm and led him to a nearby unmarked police car and opened the door for him. "Get in and we can talk?" asked Landers.

Carson tried to speak, but even after setting in the

warm, dry police car, out of the rain and the dark, his voice still failed him. Landers put his hand on Carson's shoulder. "Look, I need to ask you some questions. Can you handle that?"

Carson, still unable to speak, nodded his assent. Landers said, "Why are you here?"

It seemed like such a simple question, but Carson was still having trouble getting his mind to formulate an answer. He found himself starting to shake, not from the cold, but from fear. Landers waited and finally Carson blurted out, "I just decided to walk over to see if Willie was home. He didn't answer his phone, and I couldn't reach him on his cell phone either. Is something wrong?"

Landers lowered his gaze for a moment and then looked into Carson's eyes. Carson's eyes were dark, and they reflected the flashing lights that surrounded them. "Someone murdered your friend Willie and a young man named Zack Watts." He paused, allowing Carson time to absorb the magnitude of his statement. Carson stared at him in disbelief.

"That can't be," said Carson. "Willie and Zack went into the city tonight. Are you sure it's them?"

"We found their wallets next to the bodies. The killer or killers took the cash and credit cards and left everything else, including their driver's licenses. Two of the people in the apartment have positively identified Willie."

"What happened?" Carson managed to croak out. "What happened to them?"

"Apparently they were robbed in front of the building

as they were coming home from the city. The robber or robbers killed both of them with a knife. We found the knife in the grass near the bodies. It looks like a possible case of a robbery gone bad. Maybe Will or Zack tried to resist and the robber or robbers panicked."

"So it was just some dirt bag thief with a knife," cried Carson. "Some piece of crap killed my friend over some lousy cash!"

"That's what it looks like and what my associates in homicide are leaning toward at the moment," Landers answered.

"What does that mean?" said Carson.

"It means I'm not so sure I agree. For one thing, both of them had their throats slit. I could not see any other stab marks, not even defensive wounds on their hands or arms. For another, while there is certainly a lot of blood, getting killed by a knife is usually a lot bloodier and a lot messier. There are no footprints in the blood of the killer or killers. There is a knife, but no fingerprints. There are the wallets removed and again, no fingerprints. For a robbery gone bad resulting in a double homicide with a knife, this is way too neat of a crime scene."

"So what are you saying?" asked a puzzled looking Carson.

"What I'm saying is that of three young men I had as witnesses to a killing by a local mobster, two of them have died suddenly under very strange circumstances before the trial date," answered Landers. He stopped himself, rolled down the window and tossed his cigarette out into the rain. "I think your friend Willie was murdered to keep him from testifying, and it was arranged to look like a robbery gone bad."

"So why Willie and not me?" asked Carson. "I don't get it."

"How long have you been gone from your apartment?"

"I'm not sure. Maybe about three or four hours, why?" responded Carson.

"When I got the call that one of the victims was Willie, I demanded to know where the officer was who was supposed to be on surveillance here. Because Willie had been gone all day, the officer had gone to grab some coffee and take a leak. He was gone about half a hour. I then called the officer staking out your apartment. He did not respond to the radio call. I had a unit dispatched immediately. When they got to your apartment, you were gone and they found the officer dead in his patrol car, slumped over the wheel. He had been shot in the head at close range with a small caliber bullet. Until I saw you here I assumed you were dead also."

"What!" said Carson.

"You hear me correctly, young man," said Landers. "I had your apartment searched. You were gone and someone had been in the apartment."

"How do you know that?" asked Carson incredulously.

"You have a chain on the door that you hook up when you are in the apartment?" asked Landers.

"Yes," said Carson. "I almost always chain the door when I'm home."

"Well, this time the chain had been cut in two and we were pretty sure that was not an accident. It looks like they planned on getting both you and Willie on the same night. You screwed up their plans when you were not in your apartment where they thought you would be."

Carson thought he was going to be sick to his stomach and vomit. About half a cup of bile rose in his throat and he fought it back down. "Oh my God, this can't be happening," he managed to eke out.

Landers put his hand on Carson's shoulder and gently squeezed it. "Look, son, we can't change what has just happen, but we can change what these thugs had planned to happen. We're going to put you in protective custody until the trial."

Carson looked up at Landers, trying to get a read on his facial expression and his eyes. In the dark of the police car, he could still make out enough from Landers to believe that the detective was truly concerned about him.

"What does protective custody mean?" he asked.

"We put you in a safe-house with around the clock police protection. A place these people have no clue exists. You'll be safe and we can protect you."

"Can I have tonight to think it over?" asked Carson.

"Sure," said Landers. "But we'll have two cops outside and one cop in the hall outside your apartment until we get you moved. And I want you moved to a safe place by no later than tomorrow morning."

Carson nodded his agreement and about a hour later

he was delivered back to his apartment. Landers and a uniformed officer named Franks walked him to his door, and Franks remained outside the door. Looking out the window of his apartment, which faced the street in front of his building, he could clearly see the police car parked across the street.

Carson made himself a cup of hot chocolate. When he held the cup up to his lips, he noticed it was shaking. He sat down in his easy chair, and he tried to think. None of what was happening to him seemed real. Death, murder, thugs, killings; these were things you read about or saw on TV, not things you experienced. He forced himself to think. He would have to pack some things for the safe house. The trial was at least a month away, maybe more. That was a lot of underwear days for someone who only owned about half a dozen pairs.

He smiled at the thought of worrying about how much underwear he had on hand. That concern made him think of his mother. That was something she would be worried about. She was always seeing the evil and bad in the world and he had always thought she was extremely paranoid. Now he was not so sure. Maybe she'd been right all along. Maybe everyone in the world was out to get him.

Again, he forced himself to think. His real problem was he knew something he could testify about that would put someone really evil in jail, and if he was dead, there were no witnesses left to testify. If he could stay safe for nine weeks, the trial would be over and no one would be looking for him then. The question was, how did he stay safe for nine weeks?

Carson felt like he had to talk to someone, but now both his closest friends were dead, killed by the same maniac who was trying to kill him. Carson picked up the phone and dialed his mother's number. Maybe he could sneak out and stay with her until this thing was over. Who the heck would look for him in Kankakee! After the second ring, his mother answered. "Mom, it's Carson!" he said into the phone.

Apparently he was talking pretty loudly as his mother answered, "I can hear you, Carson, you don't have to shout in the phone. My hearing isn't gone, yet."

"Look, Mom, a lot of things are happening here in the city and I was thinking about driving down and staying with you for a while until this trial thing is over," said Carson.

"Well, I've been expecting you to call," she answered. "I've had two calls from the police in Chicago asking about you."

"What are you talking about?" asked Carson.

"I just told you that I've already had two calls tonight from some detective with the Chicago Police Department asking if you were here or if I had seen you today."

Carson was suddenly silent. Maybe Landers had called earlier when they could not find him at the apartment. Carson then tried to reassure his mother that things were fine and then she told him that her neighbor Mrs. Palm had called her to tell her there was a dark colored car with two men in it parked in front of Mrs. Palm's house and the men seemed to be watching his mother's house. Carson made his excuses and promised to call his mother back. He quickly found Detective Lander's card and called the cell phone number listed on it.

Landers answered the cell phone on the first ring. "What's wrong?" he asked when Carson identified himself.

"Nothing," said Carson, "but I just wanted to know if you called my mother tonight when you couldn't find me at my apartment?"

"Your mother!" replied Landers. "No, I didn't call you mother. I would've had to check your file to find out where she lived and what the number was and before I got to that point you showed up at Willie's apartment."

"So, no one from your department called my mother," said Carson, surprised at the shakiness in his voice.

"Nope, we were still too busy dealing with Willie's murder," responded Landers. "Is something wrong?"

"No, I think it was just a mistake on my mother's part," said Carson and he hung up the phone.

That was a laugh. Carson's mother had never admitted to making a mistake during Carson's entire lifetime, and he doubted if that was about to change. Someone had called her looking for him and someone was parked across from her house in Kankakee, Illinois, waiting for him to show up. These people were a lot smarter than he had been giving them credit for. It was like they knew all about him and when they could not find him at his apartment, they immediately went to plan B and waited for him to run home to his mother. If he had just taken off for his mother's place, he would have walked right into a trap, just like the one Willie walked into tonight.

Carson could feel the panic rising in his body. He forced himself to stand up and breathe deeply. He stood by the front window looking out at the police car. If these killers were smart enough to know about his mother, they probably were smart enough to know about some safe house the cops had set up.

Having police protection seemed like a good thing twenty-four hours ago, but now it felt like the only good protection was getting out of his apartment and getting as far away as possible and finding the deepest, darkest hiding place he could. Where that was he had no idea, but staying in Chicago did not look like a healthy option to him. He did not want to end up like Willie.

He was sure Landers wanted to help, but he wanted no part of the cops. He didn't feel like they could protect him. Staying in a so called safe house seemed more like waiting in a box until they showed up and killed him.

He pulled out his laptop computer and logged on to the internet. He got on-line with his bank and moved all his money into his checking account. He then pulled up a map service and printed out several maps. He made a short checklist of things and pulled his pack out of the closet. He jammed what he felt were essentials into the pack and slipped his laptop and other items into a small duffel bag. After checking his list again, he turned on his stereo. After adjusting the volume up to a level that was audible, but not too loud, he took out his winter parka, put it on and then pulled on his pack. He carefully opened the fire escape window and peeked out.

The rain had stopped and it was still dark, but with only about two hour until daylight. He slipped out the window and reached back inside and grabbed the small duffel bag and pulled it out on the landing. He carefully closed the window and stepped out on the fire escape. He tied the small duffel bag to his belt and began descending the steps on the escape to the ladder. He looked up and down the alley and saw nothing. He stepped out on the ladder and it dropped down toward the alley, making only a few noisy clicks as it did so until it reached the end of its length. Carson thanked his luck to have greased the ladder to keep it quiet. He lowered himself down to the next to last rung of the ladder with his hands and let himself drop to the alley below. As soon as he hit the alley, he dropped down to his knees and stopped to look and listen. He saw and heard nothing.

He took off at a fairly fast walk down the alley heading for the Fahey's garage. Carson had read somewhere that you should always walk slowly and not draw attention to yourself. He found that hard to do and each step seemed to be faster than the last one as he wanted to put as much distance between himself and his apartment as he could, as quickly as he could.

He got to the Fahey's garage in just a few minutes. He unlocked the garage door and put his pack and duffel bag in the back seat. He took off his heavy parka and tossed it on top of them. He started the Chevy and carefully backed out into the alley. He got out of the car to shut and lock the garage door and then eased he car down the alley with the lights off, trying to keep it as quiet and unseen as possible.

CHAPTER NINE

"Shit!" exclaimed Lenny Klein as he slammed the phone handset down on the receiver. "Jesus Christ, I am surrounded by fucking morons!" He jumped to his feet and began pacing across the expensive walnut hardwood floor in his Lake Shore Drive office. His mind was racing as he tried to think his way through this latest problem. The Sabatini brothers were paying him well to make sure their day in court included no live witnesses to testify against them.

So far Lenny had eliminated two of the three witnesses to the murder committed by the Sabatini brothers. The first job had been done by a talented contractor he had used many times in the past and was made to look like an accident. No problems and the contractor even wiped out the kid's mother for good measure and no extra charge. No muss, no fuss, and no evidence of any kind to point to the Sabaini brothers or to Lenny, himself.

The last two contractors had been hired separately,

but given a specific date to nail the last two witnesses. Lenny had charted out a weekend and had speculated that both of the witnesses, who had been close friends, could have been together at the time of the hits making the job even easier. But, no, the second hit had been changed and messed up enough that the cops were sure it was not a robbery gone bad. At least they had wasted the second witness. But somehow, his contractor had messed up on the third and last witness. They had killed the cop guarding the witness's apartment and had even broken into the apartment only to find the kid gone.

Somehow the kid had given even the cops sent to protect him the slip. All things considered, Lenny would have preferred that the cops tried to baby-sit the kid until the trial. He had plenty of informants in the police department. Cops were underpaid and under-appreciated and easy marks for a wealthy guy like Lenny. He had always looked at his payroll of informants as "insurance." You never knew when you would need them. Now, they were worthless. The cops knew nothing, his contractors knew nothing, and worst of all, Lenny knew nothing about where the kid had run.

As Lenny paced, he mentally went over his options, trying to come up with a plan. Finally he grabbed his phone and yelled for his secretary to get Tony in his office. Tony was his operations guy. There was nothing Tony could not find on a computer. In today's computer age, Tony was worth two million goons on the street. Tony came running into Lenny's office about two minutes later, completely out of breath. Tony was smart, but he had the physical stamina of the Pillsbury Doughboy. Lenny motioned Tony to a chair and began to fill him in on the problem while he continued to pace back and forth, using his hands to emphasize his points.

"So, okay Mr. Computer Genius, how do we find this guy?" asked Lenny finally. "We cannot jut let him wander around out there and hope he doesn't show up for the trial. We need to find him and grease his ass."

Finally able to get his breath back, Tony looked up at his boss and said, "Let me do a complete file work-up on this Andrews kid. I'll get all the updates and then set up a monitoring net on all his known accounts and relationships. If he buys a bus ticket or rents a room and uses a credit card, I can find him. Same thing goes for any credit card phone calls. I can get a monitor on his cell phone account. If he uses any kind of credit card, I'll find it and that will lead us to him."

"I wonder how he got out of town, or if he is actually out of town," mused Lenny. "I don't think he had a car unless he rented one. Otherwise he has to be on a bus, a train, or a plane."

"Don't forget this is a kid, Lenny, he could even be hitchhiking," said Tony.

"If he was hitchhiking, he would be hitching to someone or somewhere that he knows. We have his mother covered and even his job supervisor. I think he'll run to someone he knows and when he does that, we'll nail him," replied Lenny. "Do your magic, Tony and find this kid so I can get rid of him. He is starting to annoy me and I do not like to be annoyed."

Tony nodded, rose and hurried out of the room, his face looking even more pasty than normal.

CHAPTER TEN

After leaving his neighborhood, Carson stopped at a service station and filled his gas tank and checked the oil. Even though the dipstick showed the oil level was fine, he bought two extra quarts of moor oil and put them in the trunk. When he opened the trunk, he saw the camping gear he had stored there and breathed a sigh of relief. He had no idea what he was getting into, but he was trying to be as prepared as he could.

He paid for the gas and oil with his gasoline credit card and was putting the receipt in his glove-box when it hit him. If they know who your family is and where you live, then they know what credit card accounts you have and will likely be able to monitor them. With all the computer hacking that was going on, it wouldn't be hard to get someone to hack into all of Carson's records and keep track of what he was doing. He would need to use cash and while he had taken all the cash he kept at the apartment, that wasn't going to last very long.

He drove to the nearest branch of Midwest Bank and saw that the drive-in opened at 7:00A.M. After glancing at his watch, he had an hour to kill. He drove to a nearby super-market and bought some food and supplies with cash and then took a short nap in the front seat of the Chevy, using his watch to set an alarm for 7:00 A.M. After a quick trip to the bank, he had over a thousand dollars in cash and he headed for the nearest interstate highway and the fastest way out of Chicago.

"What do you mean he's not there!" screamed Detective Landers into his phone. "God damn it, I left you with two patrolmen there all night and you tell me he's gone and you don't know where, when, or how?"

Landers could not believe what he was hearing. Getting two witnesses killed was bad enough, but having some young kid slip out of police protection and surveillance was unacceptable. "You get every available man on this and go over that neighborhood with a fine tooth comb. Check every neighbor, someone had to see something. Nobody just walks out of his apartment in Oak Park and disappears into the night. He had to be on foot, for Christ sakes, and no one saw him? I cannot accept that. Check with the state and see if he owns a car, motorcycle, boat, whatever."

Landers snapped his cell phone closed and cursed under his breath. "Stupid kid. He's going to get himself killed, and I'm going to look like an idiot."

Although the rain had stopped, the skies were still overcast and the air was damp. It was a typical spring day in Chicago. After an hour and a half of driving without any real sense of direction, Carson found himself headed west on Interstate Highway 80. He stopped at a large truck stop and filled the car with gas. He used the restroom and bought himself a road atlas. He paid for the gas and road atlas with cash. He parked the car in the large parking area next to the truck stop and bought a coke from a vending machine.

As he sipped from the can, he studied the road atlas. Carson had been as far west as Iowa on a couple of occasions, but right now it seemed like a good road and a good direction. He tossed the atlas on the passenger seat and exited from the truck stop back onto the interstate. Traffic was heavy and he found himself getting behind a big 18-wheeler semi and just sort of following it like he and his car were being pulled on a fairly long leash.

After three more hours the truck pulled off at the exit for Iowa City, and Carson followed the truck off the interstate into another truck stop. Carson gassed up again, hit the restroom, and bought a six pack of bottled water and some candy bars when he paid for his gas. Again he paid for his purchases in cash. He did not want to leave any kind of trail or clue as to where he was. After a quick check of his atlas, he pulled back onto I-80 and continued west.

The weather was unchanged and the sky continued to feature a gray overcast. Carson adjusted the heater in the car as he felt a little colder. This surprised him as the day had gotten warmer since the chilling cold of his early morning departure.

It was dark out and the lights of the on-coming cars were bothering his eyes. Carson knew he was getting tired. He checked his watch. It was almost midnight and he had been driving since about 7:30A.M. that morning.

He had been thinking while driving and had decided that he could sleep in the car and avoid registering at some motel and spending money he knew he needed to hoard. He decided that the best place to sleep would be at a truck stop. There were plenty of parking spaces and the lots were full of parked tractor trailer rigs equipped with sleeper units, diesel engines idling while their drivers slept inside. After a full day of using truck stops for gas, restroom stops, and junk food, he had learned you could also get a shower there for $5.

After getting gas, Carson parked the Chevy near the eighteen-wheelers, being careful to use parked trucks to screen any view of his car from the station and its entrance. He locked the car and walked to the restaurant in the main building. The area around the gas pumps and restaurant was as bright as daylight with their huge overhead lights, but the area outside the circles of light was pitch black. It was eerie enough to make him uneasy as he made his way to the restaurant.

Once inside he did a quick study of the fairly greasy plastic menu and ordered a cheeseburger and a chocolate shake from a tired looking middle aged waitress wearing too much make-up. While he waited for his meal he studied his surroundings. The restaurant was like most truck stops. A lot of linoleum and vinyl with a little chrome tossed in. He was pretty sure this place never closed. Truck stops seemed to have everything. The shop next to the restaurant sold everything from junky trinkets to underwear and socks. If you were on the road and you needed something, this shop probably had it. Of course you couldn't be too choosy about the style and color, but what the heck.

The waitress brought Carson his food, and he practically wolfed it down. He had not realized how hungry he was. He paid for his meal in cash and walked back to his parked car. He moved his gear from the back seat to the trunk and got out his sleeping bag. He opened it up and placed it in the back seat. He took off his shirt, jeans, and shoes and after locking the car doors, slipped into the sleeping bag and almost immediately fell into an exhausted state of sleep.

Tony kept his gaze on the computer screen in front of him. The light from the computer monitor was the only illumination in the small room. He had been working for the better part of ten hours but barely seemed to notice it. Like many computer "nerds," Tony often lost himself in his projects and time, food, etc. just didn't seem important when he was in the middle of a project.

This was one of those times. He wanted to have a complete report to give to his boss Lenny Stein by the time Lenny got to his office in the morning. That was usually about 9:00 A.M. Tony had not had much of a problem hacking into the systems he needed to get a handle on young Mr. Andrews, but finding relevant data on what Andrews was currently doing was another matter.

He had discovered that Andrews owned a car. It was a ten-year old white Chevrolet four-door Cavalier. The kid had owned it for seven years and only carried liability insurance coverage on the car. "Who the hell owns a crap car like that for seven years," thought Tony. The search had also uncovered Andrew's cell phone account with AT&T Wireless, a Conoco gasoline credit card and a VISA card. He also had a Nordstrom's store credit card. He had a checking and savings account at Midwest Bank and a debit card for his account. He had no balance owed on his VISA and he had made a withdrawal of almost a thousand dollars in cash from the Midwest Bank branch near his apartment on the same morning he had disappeared. He had also used his VISA card for gas at a gas station three blocks from the bank on the same day. Since then there had been no activity of any kind. No gas card usage, no VISA card usage, no cell phone activity, nothing.

Tony learned back in his chair and punched keys on his computer to call up an all night deli that delivered. Tony made his order on line and pre-paid it with his debit card. Tony had spent so much time in his small office when working on a project that he even had a cot set up against the wall. He began to type up his report for Lenny as he estimated he would finish about the time that his breakfast was delivered.

Lenny was not pleased. He sat back in his huge leather chair behind his oversized walnut desk and stared at Tony. "What the hell do you mean that's all you have! You're supposed to be the best. I pay you two hundred large a year for this crap! How can you not know where this punk is hiding. How can he just be gone, vanished, adios?"

Tony sat in his chair looking down at the floor and trying to avoid the wrath he knew was unavoidable. "Holy shit, Tony, this is impossible. This is just a punk kid, a nobody. He can't be that damn smart."

"He isn't," replied Tony. "He's just been lucky. My guess is he's scared shitless and is running as fast and as far as he can. He has no idea where he is going and so neither do we. However, sooner or later he'll make a mistake and then I'll find him. I guarantee it."

"Time is not on our side, Tony," yelled Lenny. "You better find this son-of-a-bitch and do it quickly."

"Look, boss, he will mess up. It will probably be within a few days. We have at least a month until the trial. We'll find him long before that. He'll run out of cash and have to use a credit card or the cell phone and when that happens we've got him," said Tony.

"Okay," said Lenny, but I want a full update every morning and if we get a lead, I want to know about it immediately, no matter what time it is. You understand!"

"Yes, sir, I'll see to it," replied Tony, who was glad to be able to exit the room with his butt intact.

CHAPTER ELEVEN

"Yes sir, absolutely sir, I'll let you know as soon as we have something, sir. Thank you, sir." Landers hung up the phone and rubbed his sore eyes and his aching neck. His boss was hot about the Andrews kid disappearing and so was the chief of police. As in all government bureaucracies, shit runs downhill and right now a whole trainload of it was being dumped on Detective Landers.

Landers reached for what was by now a very chilly cup of coffee, sipped it, and immediately turned and spat it into his wastebasket. "Damn it," yelled the detective, "can't one damn thing go right anymore?" He didn't know if the Andrews kid had been grabbed by the damned mob or was running on his own out of fear of what he had just been through. "If they got him, he's already dead," thought Landers.

In the meantime he had very little to go on. He had figured out that Carson owned a car. The car was long gone and Carson had probably high tailed it out of Chicago, but to where? He had checked with the mother and all the rest of the family he could locate. None of them had any idea of where Carson might be. The mother had talked to him briefly on the phone, but her version of the call from her son was not very helpful. On the one hand, if the kid was running and Landers had no idea of where, then the killers were also in the dark about Carson's whereabouts. That was the good news. The bad news was that he needed Carson as a witness in a murder case and he had less than thirty days to find him, grab him, and bring him in to testify in court.

"Why didn't I listen to my old man and become a fireman," sighed Landers. "So much less complicated." Since finding the kid appeared to be something that was beyond his meager resources, the detective reluctantly flipped through his rolodex file looking for a familiar name of a cop he liked, but did not totally trust.

Carson awoke to the smell of diesel fumes and the sound of metal doors slamming shut. He crawled out of his sleeping bag and pulled on his jeans, shoes, and a shirt. It was cold in the car and he felt unnaturally awkward as he dressed because every joint in his body seemed to be stiff. He grabbed a coat and his pack and headed into the truck stop. After a shower, change of clothes, and a breakfast heavy with calories and grease, he began to feel better. He bought a copy of *USA Today* along with a cup of coffee to go and went out to his car.

He read the paper carefully, but could find no mention of Willie's murder or his disappearance. When he had finished, he tossed the paper and empty coffee cup into a nearby trash can and packed up his sleeping bag and gear and stuffed his dirty clothes into a small canvas bag. Only a few eighteen-wheelers were still parked near his car as he pulled out of the lot and back onto the Interstate. The sky was still cloudy, but not as grey as the day before. Carson could even see a portion of the morning sun peeking out over the eastern horizon. He decided to keep heading west until he could come up with something better.

The next morning Carson awoke from the now familiar back seat bed to the sound of a strong wind that was gently rocking the car. He crawled out of the sleeping bag and looked out the car window. It was early morning and still fairly dark. The sky was completely clouded over and even the air in the car was cold. He rubbed the sleep from his eyes, dressed, and stepped out of the car.

At first he could not remember where he was and then

he remembered he had sought out another large truck stop last night. This one was a lot fancier with a motel, camping area, restaurant, repair shop, etc. He looked up at the sign on the large motel office. "Little America." What a weird name. He remembered from his high school days that there was a Little America in the South Pole, or was it the North Pole. He wasn't sure.

He went into the main building and purchased a shower for $5 and rented a towel for fifty cents. After a shower and a change of underwear and socks, he bought a copy of the *Denver Post* newspaper and read it while he ate his breakfast. It looked like the biggest paper for sale and the closest thing to a regional paper on the sales rack. There was still nothing on Willie's murder or his disappearance. He stopped in the adjacent store and bought half a dozen pair of underwear and socks. He took his purchases to the car and packed them in his bag.

He counted his remaining cash and determined that sooner or later he was going to have to stop and wash some clothes as he had to stretch his cash. He gassed up the car, checking the oil and water and went into the store to pay for his gas. While he waited in line, he kept looking around the store at the people. None of them was paying any attention to him and he decided that he was getting a little paranoid. When he got to the clerk to pay, he inquired about the weather. "Heading east or west?" asked the clerk.

"West," said Carson.

"Got snow tires?" asked the clerk.

"Well no," replied Carson. "Why would I need snow tires? It's April."

"Well mister, replied the clerk. "This here is Wyoming and in southern Wyoming it's high plains desert. I-80 goes straight west. About ninety miles west of here you'll be going up the Continental Divide. The higher you go, the colder and windier it gets. We still get snow up through May and the weather report says a storm is moving south from Montana. Now, when you get about half way between Laramie and Rawlins you'll see a good-sized mountain to the south. That there mountain is Elk Mountain. It attracts bad weather like a magnet. I-80 from Laramie to Rawlins is called the "Snow Chi Min Trail" by the college students at Laramie, and with good reason. If you're headed west, you best be careful."

Carson thanked he clerk and paid him. Once in his car he turned on the radio and fiddled with it until he got a local station. He could tell it was local because all it played was country and western music. He was reminded of the scene in the movie the *"Blues Brothers"* where the lady bartender said, "We got both kinds of music, country and western." During the newscast, he got the local weather and sure enough the temperature was dropping and the weather report indicated a storm warning for a weather front moving down from Montana. The clerk had been very accurate.

Carson looked at the map. He could go north or south on I-25. There was not much north, but Denver was south. Driving south also probably meant warmer or better weather. Still, heading west into bad weather is what anyone looking for him would not expect. When you were trying to hide from someone, you were probably better off doing the unexpected.

Carson went through his gear in the trunk and found his old pair of snow-pac boots and his parka and heavy gloves. He also dug out his only heavy wool shirt, which he put over the t-shirt he was wearing. He put everything on the back seat where it was easy to reach, and he slipped back into the driver's seat. Carson started the car and adjusted the car radio to the least objectionable country and western station he could find. He headed out on I-80 west listening to Johnny Cash sing "I Walked the Line."

CHAPTER TWELVE

The clerk had not lied to Carson. Until he had gotten to Cheyenne, the landscape had been pretty boring. It was so boring that Carson thought that Nebraska and Wyoming were in a dead heat to win the award for worst scenery for a trip. A short distance west of Cheyenne he could tell he was gaining altitude. The car motor sounded differently and he could almost feel the transmission straining harder in shifting gears back and forth depending on the level of his ascent.

"Gas mileage is going to suck on this part of the trip," Carson thought. All around him, he could see jagged rock formations and large gullies. As the car climbed higher in elevation, the sagebrush was replaced by heavier brush and even an occasional tree.

When he passed over the Continental Divide, he saw the Lincoln Memorial in the center of a large median. Now he understood why it was sometimes called the Lincoln Highway. He never knew there was a Lincoln Memorial in Wyoming. When you come from Illinois you think you know everything there is to know about Lincoln. Why was Lincoln in the middle of Wyoming? Once past the Lincoln Monument, the highway began a slight descent, the wind picked up and he could actually see snow flurries. Even though he was warm inside the car, he felt himself shiver involuntarily. He was not sure if it was the snow or his fear. What the hell was he doing driving through Wyoming in a potential snowstorm in the middle of April? He was running as far and as fast as he could from people who meant to kill him. They were not chasing him for money or anger, but because they were afraid he might say something to a jury that would hurt one of them. Whoever "them" was.

So far "them" had been pretty efficient. They had killed four people, two of them his best friends. He knew he could be next. As a result here he was, driving west on I-80 in his ratty old white Chevrolet Cavalier, putting as many miles as he could between him and Chicago.

So far he was safe. No one knew where he was. Actually, all Carson knew was he was somewhere in southern Wyoming, heading west. He had used up a good deal of his cash and he had been afraid to use a credit card, thinking that it could be used to trace where he was, or at least where he had been when he used he card. Carson was pretty sure the people after him were sophisticated enough to find him if he slipped up and gave them any opportunity. Sooner or later he would have to make a decision on where he was actually going and what he was going to do when he got there. Right now, though, he was still concentrating on putting distance between him and Chicago.

He had not used his cell phone, but he kept the battery charged using a charger that plugged into the cigarette light. Carson had thrown the lighter away since he never smoked. He felt the need to talk to someone. He didn't want to call the police in Chicago. They would just press him to tell them where he was and try to get him back for the trial. They might mean well, but he knew now they were not capable of protecting him.

He thought about calling his mother. He had a strange relationship with his mom. They had never been close, even though she had raised him as a single parent. His mother was one of those women who are very insecure and who seek some form of payment for any form of emotion, even something as normal as affection. They had argued often and the result was usually Carson storming out of the house and staying out until quite late. He hated to talk to his mother about normal things. She was always working on a guilt angle to try to get something out of him, even if it was only a compliment. She had used guilt on him as he was growing up, giving Carson the impression that she had sacrificed everything for him and, as a result, she had no life and no man in her life.

Carson had not known his father. His father had left while Carson was very little. But when he was a freshman in college, home for Christmas, he had happened to see his mother's bank statement lying open on the kitchen table. His natural curiosity led to him reading the statement and noticing that there was a deposit of $5,000, which was considerably more than he thought his mother made as a teacher. There was also a deposit for around $3,600 which made him wonder where his mother was getting all the money. When he brought the subject up, his mother used her favorite tactic and changed the subject.

He never did learn the source of the money, but he always suspected that somehow it was coming from his never seen father. His mother insisted that his father was dead, but Carson always wondered if that was a lie. Over the years he had learned that his mother, who was quite self-righteous, was prone to bend the truth whenever it suited her. Whenever he tried to confront her with what he felt was a twist of the truth, she always changed he subject and dodged his question.

Still, she was his mother and right now he was feeling as lonely as he had ever felt. He needed to talk to someone. He needed to make sure he was not going crazy and that his fear was truly real. He also wanted some advice. What should he do and where should he go? Should he find some place and hide? Where and for how long?

He had been very careful, but sooner or later he would have to stop, find a place to live and get some kind of a job. Carson knew if he used his real name and his social security number, there was a good chance it would undoubtedly be picked up by his pursuers. There was no such thing as privacy in the age of technology.

Carson stared at his cell phone, then flipped it open and after checking for a signal, he dialed the familiar numbers. His mother answered. Carson found his mouth dry and he had trouble even saying hello.

"My God, Carson, is that you?" his mother asked. "I haven't heard from you for so long(an obvious guilt job) and now you are the center of attention."

"What do you mean, Mom?" asked Carson.

"Well, I got a call asking for you about two days ago, I think?"

"Who was asking about me?" said Carson.

"Some nice young man called me. He said he was a friend of yours, and he was trying to get in touch with you. I told him I'd not heard from you for at least a month. Then last night, two very large men stopped by the house. They said they were business associates of yours and that you hadn't come in to work for three days, and they were worried about you. I told them the same thing."

Carson had almost stopped breathing. He suddenly felt cold and his mouth was dry all over. "Carson, are you there?" his mother asked.

Carson forced himself to answer her, although it was

like he could not get words to come out of his mouth except with great effort.

"I'm here, Mom. I'm going to be out of touch for a while. Those men you talked to are not friends of mine nor do they work for my company. They are looking for me, and I don't want them to find me. I don't mean to worry you, but the less you know now the better for you. You can't tell them what you don't know. Please, just hang up on them or refuse to talk to them. If they persist, call the police. I'll call you when I can." Carson snapped his cell phone shut, cutting off the connection before his surprised mother could respond.

The less she knew the better, he decided. Once they figured out she didn't know anything, they would leave her alone. He felt an involuntary shudder in his body as he realized how quickly they had located his mother and had begun to dig for information. He put the car in gear and drove back onto the interstate, being careful to keep the car at the speed limit when every nerve in his body was telling him to floor the accelerator and to get as far away as possible.

The overcast sky was now hurling down larger and larger flakes of snow. At first the flakes melted when they hit the highway, but now they were staring to collect and beginning to cover the interstate with a white coating. Carson slowed down as visibility got worse and he had to strain to see the road. Reading the traffic signs along the road became more difficult as they began to cover over with wet snow.

He considered stopping for the night after pulling off the interstate in Rawlins for gasoline. He filled the car up and bought a large cup of coffee and headed back into the untimely spring snowstorm. Although it was late in the afternoon, the overcast sky and the swirling snow made it seem like night. Even with his headlights on, he found he could not drive much over forty miles per hour and still be sure he could keep the car on the road. He considered stopping at the next exit, but fear made him keep on going.

He took some satisfaction in the storm. Nobody would be trying to catch up with him in this weather, even if they knew where he was, which he was pretty sure they did not. Visibility was lousy, but fortunately, there was little traffic.

He stopped for gas in Green River and quickly ate a greasy supper at a fast food outlet. He noticed the lot by the gas station was now full of large trucks, parked side by side with their engines running and their parking lights on. He was temped to park in the shelter of the lot, but fear still made him feel that he needed to keep going and put as much distance between himself and the danger in Chicago.

By now the snow was at least three or four inches deep on the interstate, and he found himself trying to keep in the tracks of a car that was somewhere in front of him. Even then the snow seemed to be coming down harder and gradually filling in the tracks he was trying to follow. After about an hour he knew he needed to find a place to stop for the night and wait for the storm to end.

The snow had covered most of the signs and they were hard to read and the blowing snow made it difficult to see for any distance or to spot any lights. He finally saw a partially covered sign that advertised Little America Truck Stop just a few miles ahead. Apparently there was more than one, as Carson remembered that he had stopped at a Little America Tuck Stop in Cheyenne. Carson slowed the car down to thirty miles an hour and was leaning forward over the steeling wheel, trying to peer through the darkness and the swirling snow that seemed to devour his headlights. "Nothing like spring time in Wyoming," he thought to himself.

Finally he saw a partially covered sign announcing an exit to his right. Carson decided to take the exit and get off the interstate. He would then pull over and check his map and try to figure out where he was. It was difficult trying to make sure he was still on the road as he exited from the interstate. The snow had not let up and his speed was down to fifteen miles per hour. He carefully pulled the car slightly off the road and parked it. He could see a road sign a few yards ahead, but it was covered with snow.

Carson zipped up his coat, put on his stocking cap and gloves and then got out of the car to walk up to the sign. He reached up and wiped off the sign, which proclaimed he was now on Highway 30. Carson retreated to the warmth of the car, switched on the dome light, and pulled out his Wyoming road map. He found his location and discovered he had just gone past Little America and needed to retrace his route back about three miles.

Carson put the car in gear and eased it slowly forward back onto the road. As he attempted to get back on the roadway to make a u-turn, he felt the wheels slip and the rear end of the car began to slide down and away from the road. Carson hit the brakes and got the car stopped. He then tried to slowly move the car forward, but now the tires were just spinning as the car settled deeper into the snow. He tried reverse to no avail. He tried to rock the car by shifting the transmission between drive and reverse and all he did was get stuck more deeply in the snow.

Carson got out of the car with a flashlight and quickly saw that he was not going anywhere without getting help from someone who could pull his car free from its snowy parking place. "Don't panic," he told himself. "Someone will come by. This is only a spring storm, and it can't last. I have almost a full tank of gas, and I have my camping equipment. I'll be fine."

He opened the trunk and took out the sleeping bag and a small emergency kit and got back into his car. The warmth of the car's interior seemed to calm him. He took a thick stubby candle with a holder out of the kit bag. He lit the candle with a match, and set it on the car floor in front of the passenger seat. He then got into the sleeping bag and settled down to wait.

He knew he would have to get up about every hour or so and make sure the exhaust pipe was not covered with snow. He would sleep with the engine off and clear the exhaust pipe before he started it up again. By periodically running the engine he could make the gas supply last until morning and help keep the interior of the car warm. The candle assured him of light without having to use up the batteries of his flashlight, and it also gave off a small amount of heat. Satisfied that he had done all he could, Carson pulled the sleeping bag up to his ears and finally drifted off to sleep.

Carson dreamed he was being chased by a horde of faceless pursuers in large black cloaks that covered their heads. They were shooting at him as he struggled to run in the ever-deepening snow. Suddenly he was awake and the banging noise was not from firearms but from someone out in the snowstorm who was banging on his window. Carson pulled down his sleeping bag and lowered the window. Peering in at him was a giant, bending over from the waist in the swirling snow. The giant was wearing a huge parka topped off with a large gray cowboy hat.

"Are you all right, son?" the giant yelled so he could be heard over the wind of the storm. Carson blurted out something which the giant took for yes. "Let's get out outta here, sonny, before you turn into a popsickle. My truck is right up on the road."

Carson struggled out of the sleeping bag and pulled on his coat and hat and shoes and climbed out of his car. He took the hand the giant offered and found himself being propelled up the slope to the road where a huge pick-up truck stood running with all its lights on. The giant pulled open the passenger door and shoved Carson into the truck. He quickly moved around the truck and jumped into the driver's seat. The inside of the truck was warm and comfortable. Carson could sense that he was sitting much higher over the road than he had with his car. He looked to the side but could not see his car through the dark and the snow, even though he knew it was only a few yards away, down the slope. He wondered how the giant had seen him from the road.

The giant reached behind his seat and pulled out a large silver thermos. He opened it and poured steaming hot coffee into a cup and handed it to Carson. "Saw your taillights stickin' up through the snow. I kinda figured you hadn't been there too long. Storm is only bout three hours old. You sure you're all right?"

Carson sipped the hot coffee and bobbed his head up and down to signify that he was O.K. He looked over at his rescuer. The man was big. He had to be over six foot four inches and weighed about two hundred and fifty pounds. He had curly light colored hair streaked with gray and piercing bright blue eyes. If he had not known better, Carson would have bet he'd been rescued by John Wayne.

The big man stuck out his hand and said, "I'm Dave Carlson, but most people jus call me Big Dave." Carson took the offered handshake and found his hand was engulfed in Carlson's huge hand. Carson could not remember when he had seen such big hands.

He recovered in time to answer, "I'm Carson." He was careful to not offer his full name.

"Carson? Is that your last name?"

"No, Carson is my first name."

"Well, sonny, Carson is a strange first name. I never met no Carson before. I saw your license plates were from back East. Illinois, I think. Maybe they got lotsa guys named Carson back there, but out here in the West, Carson ain't no kind of first name. That kind of first name will get you beat up in every bar in Wyoming. How bout I call you Kit."

"Kit?" questioned Carson. "Why Kit?"

"Ain't you never hard of the greatest scout in the history of the West, Kit Carson?" said Carson.

"Oh, I get it. Kit's a nickname since my name is Carson."

"That be correct, sonny."

"If Kit works for you, it's fine with me."

"Well, Kit, you are one lucky fella. I was in Rock Springs looking for a herder when this storm hit. Didn't have no damn luck atall in finding a herder and didn't want to stay the night in Rock Springs so I headed on home and saw your car's taillights in the snow."

"I'm sure glad you came along," replied Kit. "I guess your truck is better equipped for snow than my old Chevy."

"This here is a ¾ ton four wheel drive pickup with heavy duty snow tires. I also got chains on them snow tires for tracking. I'm headed back home to Kemmerer, which is about thirty four miles north of here. You can stay with me and the missus tonight, and we can come back to get your car out tomorrow if that's O.K. with you?"

Kit quickly agreed to Big Dave's proposal. He was thankful to be safe and out of the storm. He was physically and mentally tired from his long run from Chicago and all of the fear that had gone with it. Before much time had passed, Kit was sound asleep in the warmth of the huge truck's cab.

He barely remembered arriving at Big Dave's home, meeting his wife Carol, and bedding down in a spare bedroom. All Kit knew was that he was exhausted and everything else would have to wait.

CHAPTER THIRTEEN

The next morning Kit sat down to a hearty breakfast of pancakes, sausage, eggs, and coffee. Big Dave was already gone and his wife Carol kept busy making sure Kit's plate was full. Mrs. Carlson was a tall, lean, older woman with gray hair. She had lustrous dark eyes that dominated her wrinkled, but still attractive, face. She moved very gracefully as she attended to several tasks in her very organized kitchen. She explained to Kit that they were sheep ranchers and that their ranch was just outside of Kemmerer, Wyoming, a small town of about 3,000 people located in the high plains desert of southwest Wyoming.

Kemmerer was at an altitude of about 7,000 feet above sea level and like much of southern Wyoming, was windy most of the time. Kemmerer was originally a company town built by the Kemmerer Coal Company to support the coal mines located nearby. The coal mines were still the mainstay of the local economy, but there were other mines operated by other companies, and Kemmerer Coal no longer controlled the entire community. People in Kemmerer went to Salt Lake City for major shopping, which was about 135 miles away. "Just a two and a half hour drive in good weather," was the way Mrs. Carlson described it.

After breakfast, Mrs. Carlson turned down Kit's offer to help with the dishes, and he stepped outside to see where he was. The sun was shining brightly and the snow was quickly melting. He was surprised by how intense the sun's rays seemed to be. He checked a thermometer mounted on the porch and was surprised to see that it only registered about forty degrees, but it felt like it was much warmer.

The ranch was located in a small valley, surrounded by barren rocky hills. He could see little vegetation other than the occasional sagebrush plant. There was a small grove of trees by the ranch house and he could see a small stream about forty yards for where he stood. About a quarter mile down stream, he could see where the stream had been dammed to create a small pond. The ranch had several outbuildings, but they were rather small and not like the farm buildings he was used to seeing in Illinois. Everything here was smaller and seemed weather-beaten and in need of paint.

Kit was startled by Big Dave's arrival. Everything

about Mr. Carlson was big. His size, his voice, his stride, and his manner were all huge. He just seemed to engulf all that was round him. Everything about him seemed to exude confidence. He greeted Kit, asked how well he had slept, and then launched into a description of the ranch. Kit now had a chance to study Big Dave in the daylight and confirmed his original impression. Mr. Carlson was a Swedish Viking version of John Wayne. He was about six feet four inches tall with a stocky build and a huge chest and a rather small waist. He had a light but ruddy complexion with plenty of evidence that he spent his life outdoors, as his skin was rough, furrowed and tanned. His light hair and his bright blue eyes stood out. He was dressed in boots, jeans, denim work shirt with a denim jacket and a well-worn gray cowboy hat.

"Want to see the ranch?" asked Big Dave. Kit quickly agreed and Big Dave led him to the blue Chevrolet Pickup truck that had helped rescue him the night before. Pretty quickly they were bumping along a fairly rough, rutted dirt road, making their way out of the valley and up the side of one of the surrounding hills. The view of the ranch was much more impressive from the top of one of the hills than it had been from the front porch of the ranch house. The valley seemed to stretch to the horizon.

"Is all this yours?" Kit asked and was surprised by Big Dave's burst of laugher.

"Hell, I wish it was all mine, but me and the BLM kinda battle it out," responded the huge rancher.

He went on to explain to Kit that Wyoming was

a state settled in the late1800's and as an inducement to building of the transcontinental railroad, the railroad companies were given every other section of land along the railroad right of way to help finance the railroad's construction. Some sections became towns, supported by the commerce that the railroad helped create. Some were held by the railroad as they could not sell them because they had no water. Many of the sections turned out to be mineral rich with coal, oil, and natural gas.

Exploiting the energy in Wyoming was big business to many of the railroads as well as to other large companies. Settlers took title to land with water under the Homestead Act and what was left still belongs to the government and is managed by the BLM, the Bureau of Land Management. Ranches like Big Dave lease BLM land to add grazing land to the land they actually own.

Big Dave pulled the truck next to the creek bed at a place far upstream from the ranch house. "Let me show you something, son." They got out of the truck and the big rancher knelt down next to a small puddle located adjacent to the creek bed. "Watch this" he said as he lit a match and held it down next to the puddle. The puddle erupted in flame and burned steadily for several minutes.

"How did you do that!" exclaimed Kit.

Big Dave explained that oil seeped into the creek from deposits nearby, but that it was insufficient in quantities to justify commercial extraction by digging an oil well. They jumped back in the truck and soon were at the edge of the ranch road, stopped just at the edge of a concrete highway.

"I think we should drive down and see if we can rescue your car. Is that O.K. with you?"

"Absolutely," said Kit and Big Dave soon had them rolling into Kemmerer. Coming to the ranch the previous night in the snowstorm, Kit had barely seen anything of the little town. Now he was more curious about the place he had stumbled into. They drove slowly through the little town. Kemmerer, unlike every other small town in America built around a square, was built around a triangle. Kit noticed that every other building on the triangle seemed to be a bar.

Kemmerer was not a pretty little town, but it was not what you would call ugly. Kit decided it looked like what it was, a tough little western town. One that had what it took to survive the wind, the weather, and the economic tough times. Big Dave seemed to know everyone he met on the road and he waved to all of them and received waves in return. He kept up a running commentary on everyone they met, and after about half an hour Kit had no idea who was who.

Another half an hour brought them to Kit's car. The car was buried in snow as passing snowplows had unceremoniously dumped about another three feet of dirty snow on the car. Big Dave and Kit got out and after using shovels Carson had brought, they uncovered the car.

After carefully inspecting the old Chevy, Big Dave attached a chain he had taken from the back of the pickup truck and secured one end to the back of the pickup and the other to the frame of Kit's Chevy. He had Kit sit in the car to steer, and he gently pulled the car out of the ditch with his four-wheel drive pickup. Kit was relieved to see it had gone so easily and was surprised to see a frown on Big Dave's face. The rancher slid on his back under the front of Kit's Chevy and slid back out, using the car's bumper to help pull himself up out of the snow. "Not good, Kit," he said. "Looks like you got a busted tie rod, maybe more."

"What does that mean?" asked Kit.

"Well, Kit, I means you can't steer worth a damn, and we need to get this heap towed to Kemmerer. Come on, we'll stop at Andy's and get him to tow you in." Kit found himself nodding his head in agreement and climbing into the truck when in truth he was unsure of exactly what Big Dave was talking about.

About forty-five minutes later, they pulled into a graveled parking lot that was surrounded by chain link fence and the pickup stopped in front of a large metal building. All around them were semi-trailer trucks and trailers, most of them damaged, parked like they were at some truck stop you never left.

There were also two huge tow trucks. Kit had seen tow trucks in Chicago, but these were about three times the size he was used to. Big Dave led the way into a small, cramped and cluttered office. They were immediately greeted by Andy, who exchanged friendly insults with Big Dave and was then introduced to Kit. Andy Bain was about five foot ten inches tall with curly hair and a stocky, muscular build. He had been wrestling with his computer and was glad to have a diversion. "I'll never get the hang of them things," he muttered. "Damn things crash faster than a cheap airplane."

"Don't let him kid you, Kit," snorted Big Dave. "he learned his trade as a diesel mechanic on Navy submarines and he ain't no stranger to computers."

Andy rolled his eyes at Big Dave and turned to Kit. "I got two kids who went to computer school and they can use a Palm Pilot, hook it up to a diesel engine that ain't running, and then figure out what is wrong without taking the engine apart. And I don't have a damn idea of how they do it."

Andy offered them coffee, but Big Dave declined, and explained the problem with Kit's car. They agreed to have Andy tow the car and drop it off at Tang's service station to get an estimate of what needed to be fixed. "Can't you fix it?" Kit asked Andy.

"Son, I only work on diesel trucks and big trucks at that. I've had this shop for thirty years and it ain't never had a car in it." Kit took that for a no, and he followed Andy outside into the yard. Andy led him behind the building where there were two smaller wreckers, more like those Kit had seen in Chicago.

Soon they were headed south on the highway headed for Kit's car. Kit glanced at the speedometer and saw that they were doing over eighty miles an hour. "How do you keep from getting speeding tickets?" he asked Andy.

Andy smiled and explained that he was the only major

wrecker service in western Wyoming. "The Highway Patrol gets a wreck of a semi and it's twenty below zero. I show up and take care of things. Because of that, they allow me a little leeway on the speed limits."

They soon arrived at Kit's car and Andy expertly hooked the car up, and soon they were speeding back to Kemmerer. Andy pulled into a fairly large Phillips 66 station and backed Kit's car into a vacant space and unhooked it. "Big Dave said he would pick you up here in about an hour," said Andy.

"Well, looks like someone had a little car trouble. Who's the new guy, Andy?" Kit was startled by the new voice and turned to find himself face to face with what he first took to be a scrawny, short mechanic in grease stained coveralls. Because his eyes and his ears were not agreeing on what they heard and saw, he just stood there with a stunned look on his face.

Andy came to his rescue. "Hey Tang. This here is Kit. He had a little accident in the storm last night down by Little America, and Big Dave Carlson found him working on becoming a popsickle."

Tang stuck out her hand and said, "Howdy." Kit, finally realizing that he was looking at a woman, not a scrawny guy, came to his senses in time to shake hands. Her grasp was strong, like a man's, and her hand was hard, like a working man's hand, but her hand was small, like a woman's.

"I'm Tang and this is my place. You're pretty tall for a popsickle."

Kit felt his face redden and found himself fumbling for words. "I was lucky Mr. Carlson came by."

"Well then," said Tang, "what seems to be the problem with your car?" Kit explained what happened and what Mr. Carlson had said about the tie rod. Tang said she would look it over and get Kit an estimate. "Should I call Big Dave's place with the estimate?" she asked.

"I guess that will do until I figure out what I'm going to do" answered Kit. He was looking at Tang much closer now and could see she had wisps of red hair sticking out of her dirty ball cap and freckles showed on her pale skin where the grease smudges allowed them to. Her eyes were a soft green. She turned and walked back to inspect Kit's car. Even though she was wearing bulky coveralls and work boots, she moved very gracefully, almost seeming to glide along the ground. Kit followed her to the car and spent the next fifteen minutes answering questions while he was re-packing the gear he had left in the car.

Almost before he was finished, Big Dave's blue pick-up truck pulled into the station, and he stepped out. Big Dave exchanged friendly insults with Tang and then turned to Kit. "You got your stuff out of that car?" he asked. Kit replied he had, but was unsure about what to do next. "Come on, Son, throw it in the truck and we'll git us some lunch and talk a bit," said Big Dave.

They drove into the triangle in downtown Kemmerer and parked. Carlson led the way to Irma's Café, a small store front diner on the triangle. They walked into the diner which was fairly crowded with ranchers and miners.

Big Dave stopped at each table and booth and greeted the occupants. Soon he steered Kit to an empty booth up against the glass window on the front of the diner.

The waitress came and poured them each a cup of strong hot coffee in a large mug and said she'd be back for their order. Pretty soon Kit was digging his way through a chicken fried steak, mashed potatoes with gravy, and corn that obviously had come from a can. When both of them had finished and Big Dave was stirring his coffee after having it refilled, he stopped stirring and looked across the table at Kit. "Just where exactly was you headed when I found you in that ditch?"

Kit looked away and stared down at his empty plate. Finally he looked up at Big Dave and said, "I wasn't really going anywhere. I was just trying to get away from someplace I didn't want to be."

Big Dave paused a moment, and then said, "I suppose that means it ain't none of my business, which it aint. Nevertheless, if you ain't in no hurry to get some place then I got a proposition for you. I'm short one sheepherder. My last herder quit on me and I got one coming in from Mexico, but he won't be here for about a week. I got my youngest boy Thor doing the herdin' for right now but he's got to be back at work at the mine tomorrow morning and I need help for about a week. You interested?"

"I don't know anything about herding sheep," stammered Kit, "I don't really know anything about sheep, period."

"I kind of figgered you and sheep was complete strangers," laughed Big Dave. "What I'm askin' you is do you want a job for a week doing a little hard work. I'll pay you in cash and the job provides meals and shelter. Course the shelter is a tad primitive, but I'll pay you $350 in cash. What you don't know, I'll teach you. You strike me as bright enough to outsmart a sheep. They ain't dumb, but they also ain't the smartest critter God ever created."

The next thing Kit knew, they were back at the ranch packing up some gear and food for Kit. Big Dave handed Kit an old lined denim coat and a baseball type cap with "John Deere" imprinted across the front. He also gave him two pair of gloves. One pair was larger and lined for warmth and the other pair were simple leather work gloves. Kit packed some of his clothes in his duffel bag and soon was standing by the pickup truck in jeans, a long sleeved flannel shirt, the borrowed denim coat, and tennis shoes. Big Dave came out with a box of food, which he placed in the back of the truck. He looked up and down at Kit and stopped at his feet. "My God," said Big Dave, "you look like a damn tenderfoot."

Big Dave was chuckling to himself when they drove off the ranch and onto the highway. In Kemmerer, he pulled the truck into a parking space in front of Sawaya's Dry Goods. He led Kit inside and shortly had him outfitted in wool socks and a pair of heavy work boots that were a cross between a work boot and a cowboy boot. After making sure the boots fit Kit properly, Big Dave paid for the purchases and led the way back to the truck.

"I'll be happy to pay you for the boots and socks, Mr. Carlson," said Kit.

"Consider it part of your first paycheck," said Big Dave as he pulled the truck out into the infrequent stream of cars and pickups that constituted traffic in Kemmerer.

Soon after leaving Kemmerer, the truck crossed the river that ran parallel to the small town of Kemmerer. "What river is that?" asked Kit.

"That there is the Ham's Fork River," said Big Dave. "The river is named after one of the fur trappers who came through here with Sublette back in the early 1800's. The Oregon Trail runs right through the middle of Kemmerer. Right north of town is a shallow spot in the river where the wagon trains crossed the Ham's Fork on their way west to Oregon. Place is called Names Hill. Lots of them scratched their names and dates into the soft rocks on the west side of the river. One of the names is Jim Bridger, although I think that's a joke."

"Why is it a joke?" asked Kit.

"Well, Ole Jim Bridger couldn't read or write and he sure as hell couldn't spell his own name," laughed Big Dave. Kit found himself smiling at Carlson's insight into local history.

CHAPTER FOURTEEN

After about half an hour on the highway, Carlson slowed down and turned off on what looked to Kit more like a trail than a road. It was just two rutted tracks in the dirt winding among the sagebrush. As they drove further down the tracks, the dirt road got more rutted and the ride in the truck grew decidedly rougher. Kit found himself hanging onto the door handle with one hand to keep him from sliding across the seat into Big Dave. Pretty soon he began to get the rhythm of the truck's movement, and it was easier to keep his balance and concentrate on looking out the windshield. The trail meandered through the sagebrush as it continued to climb higher on the side of the ridge to their east. Kit stole a look to the west and he could see the highway they had been on, but now it was more like a small gray ribbon below him.

Finally they were on the top of the ridge and Big Dave stopped the pickup. He pointed down the east side of the ridge to a place about two-thirds of the way to the bottom of the ridge. There was an unusual sight, seemingly right out of the old West.

What appeared to be a small covered wagon was parked next to another small wagon without a top. Next to the wagons were two horses grazing on the sparse buffalo grass. Kit wondered what kept them from wandering off as there were no fences or ropes holding them to the wagons. Beyond the wagons was a large herd of sheep. It almost looked like a cloud of wool slowly scudding over the sagebrush-covered ground. At the far side of the herd, he could see a man wearing a cowboy hat and denim shirt and pants standing next to another horse that was saddled. The man held the horse by some kind of rope. On either side of the man were three dogs, moving in and out around the sheep, keeping them together in a rather loose formation.

Big Dave stopped the pickup by the tiny covered wagon, and he and Kit got out. The man on the far side of the herd mounted his horse, rode over to them, and dismounted. "Meet my son, Thor," said Big Dave. Kit and Thor shook hands and Kit quickly saw that Thor was just a younger version of Big Dave. Both of them were huge. Kit felt his hand disappear in Thor's strong grip.

"You don't look like no Mexican," grinned Thor. Big Dave chuckled and went on to explain to Thor that he had no luck recruiting an experienced herder in Rock Springs, and he was planning to use Kit as a stopgap until the new herder got here from Mexico. "Just how much of a tenderfoot are you?" asked Thor.

After a few questions and answers, it was obvious that while Kit was not a complete greenhorn, he knew very little about sheep and horses. Thor and his father spent an hour and a half taking Kit around and explaining things to him.

Kit learned that sheep are pretty smart, but they can kill themselves by eating the wrong things. Plants like loco weed are bad for them and they can founder and die by eating too much good grass. The idea is to move them slowly across the land, letting them graze and get to water and keeping them from wandering off. The dogs were a big help and did much of the work keeping the herd together.

At night, Kit would erect a chicken wire type of fence and make a large corral by driving in metal fence posts with a fence post driver. Then he and the dogs would drive the sheep into the corral and close it.

The men inspected the two wagons. The wooden wagon without a top was called a "commissary wagon" and it contained hay and oats for the three horses as well as kegs of water and a bag of coal. A large wooden hinged box held staples for the herder. The box contained everything from salt, flour, oatmeal and soap to toilet paper.

The small "covered wagon" was called a "sheep camp". Unlike the covered wagons Kit had seen in movies, this one was smaller and did not have a soft canvas top. The rounded top was metal and both ends of the wagon were closed with wood. At the back end of the wagon was a door with a metal rung below it. Kit noticed that towards the front of the wagon a small metal pipe chimney protruded from the metal roof.

Thor showed him the inside, which was like a small primitive recreational camper. A small potbellied stove was at the far end of the wagon and one side was a bed that doubled as a seating area. A hinged table came down from the other size with a leg that folded down and set into a groove in the floor. Above the bed and table and on both sides of the stove were storage compartments. Thor showed Kit how everything worked and where things were located.

"The stove burns coal and you start it with wood scraps," said Thor. "You'll find a bag of coal and a bag of wood scraps in the commissary wagon." He then showed Kit how to light the stove. "Remember to turn the damper before you light the stove or you will have one smoky sheep camp," he cautioned.

Thor then showed Kit the horses. The two by the wagon did not wander away because they were hobbled. Hobbles were like two leg cuffs tied together to keep the front feet of the horse close together, limiting their ability to walk away. "Why three horses?" asked Kit.

"You rotate using the horses so you don't wear them out. Also, if one is sick or develops a limp or needs new horseshoes, you have backups," answered Thor.

Thor showed Kit how to approach the horses, talking to them while he did so. He showed Kit that each horse wore a rope halter. Another rope could be attached to the halter to tie up the horse or to lead him. Kit learned how to put on the leather bridle and metal bit with reins when you intended to ride the horse. Next Thor demonstrated how to put on a saddle blanket and saddle and how to fasten and tighten the saddle.

"The key thing is to get the cinch tightened properly," said Thor. "These horses know what you're doing, and they'll fill themselves with air and puff out so that when you've finished tightening the cinch, they will then let out the air and the saddle will be loose. You could wind up sitting on the side of the horse, not the top."

"So how do you avoid that?" asked Kit.

"You put your knee into their side and press hard to force the air out before you tighten the cinch" replied Thor. Thor demonstrated by getting on the left side of the horse and putting on a bridle and bit. He then placed the saddle blanket on, smoothing it out, then expertly throwing the saddle on top of the blanket. When the saddle was in the right place, Thor took the stirrup on the left side and hooked it up over the saddle horn to get it out of the way.

He then connected the cinch and brought his right knee forward hard into the left side of the horse. As the horse expelled the air from the force of Thor's knee, Thor tightened up the cinch and fastened it.

Thor went on to explain how to adjust the stirrups to match the length of Kit's legs. He had Kit get on the horse and then he adjusted the stirrups to Kit's long legs. After he was satisfied with his adjustments, Thor removed all the gear and had Kit try to saddle the horse. It took Kit about five tries before he got the hang of it. Thor made him keep trying until he got it right.

Thor whistled for the dogs and they immediately headed for the sheep camp and the two men. While Thor petted the dogs, he had Kit come close so they could smell him and "get acquainted" as Thor put it. He showed Kit some basic signals on how to direct the dogs.

"They know their jobs, but sometimes you want them to go after a particular stray," said Thor. "You whistle once to get their attention, and then you point where you want them to go. They catch on quick. Two short whistles means they are to come to you immediately." He had Kit try to call the dogs and direct them. Kit had a hard time getting the dogs to obey. "You have to command them and show it in you voice and in your hand signals. You have to be firm," said Thor. Kit tried again and had better success.

You need to work on directing the dogs," said Thor. "But the important part is they are well trained and they know what to do most of the time, whether you do or not."

"Are we done?" asked Kit

"One last thing," said Thor. He went to the sheep camp and reached up over the top of the inside of the door and came out with a short rifle. "This is an old Winchester model 94 30-30 saddle carbine. You will notice that your saddle has a scabbard attached to it. The scabbard is to hold the rifle when you are riding. If you need to shoot it, get off the horse first. Shooting a rifle over a horse's ears is a damn sure way to get your butt tossed off into some mess of cactus."

"Why would I shoot it?" asked Kit.

Thor smiled at Kit's obvious greenhorn ignorance. "When you're out here all alone, lots of things can be real unfriendly. Mainly we're talking about coyotes, wild dogs, cougars and the occasional bear."

"Bear!" croaked Kit.

"Well, hardly ever a bear down here," said Thor. "This summer we move the herd up into the mountains, and then you've got bears. Down here it is mostly coyotes and wild dogs. A coyote will kill ten sheep and only eat the lungs. Coyotes are something you are to shoot on sight. Same thing goes for wild dogs."

"Uh, exactly how do I shoot them?" said Kit very softly.

"What do you mean, how?" said Thor with a puzzled look on his face.

"Just what I said," replied Kit. "I've never shot anything before."

Thor was about to respond with something sarcastic when he realized that Kit had probably never used a gun before. "Well," said Thor, "let me show you how this works. You ever see a gun like this before?"

"Yes," replied Kit. "It looks like the ones you see in the cowboy movies."

"That is absolutely correct, Kit", grinned Thor. "This is a newer version of the same rifle made in 1894. It is a Winchester 30-30 caliber and shoots bullets that look like this."

He opened a box of shells into his hand and let Kit pick out one and examine it. Thor showed Kit how to load the rifle by pushing bullets into the magazine and how to use the lever action to push a shell into the chamber. Thorn demonstrated by shooting the rifle at a small cactus about forty yards away and when he pulled down the lever, the empty shell flew out and a new bullet was pushed into the chamber.

Thor then spent some time showing Kit how to hold, aim, fire, and reload the rifle. He explained where the vulnerable parts were in a coyote or dog and showed Kit how to use the sights to aim the rifle and also how to compensate for wind and distance.

The sun was beginning to drift low in the western sky when both Thor and Big Dave helped Kit erect the wire corral and herd the sheep into the pen using the dogs. Then they left in Big Dave's pickup, promising to be back in the morning.

Kit stood and waved until all he could see was a cloud of dust drifting along the top of a small ridge. Then he turned and looked over his new domain. "Good Lord. What the hell have I got myself into," he thought as a crooked grin took over his face.

The sun was going down fast and Kit hurried to check on the sheep, making sure the corral was still tied up tight. Then he checked the hobbles on the horses and tossed a small pile of hay by each of them.

The light was fading when he pulled himself into the small sheep camp. It was dark in the sheep camp and he had to feel around to find the box of matches. He struck a match against the side of the camp and after finding the gas lantern hanging from a hook in the metal roof, he carefully lit it and blew out the match. He decided against a fire in the stove and after undressing he slipped into his sleeping bag and turned out the light. He had trouble adjusting to the cramped space of his bunk, but pretty soon his weariness overrode his anxiety and he fell asleep.

He was awakened by the sound of dogs barking. Carson was confused by his new surroundings and the fact that it was completely dark inside the camp. He struggled to get out of his sleeping bag and spent several minutes trying in vain to find the box of matches. He finally found the door and stumbled out of the sheep camp into the pre-dawn morning clad only in his underwear.

He promptly stepped on a sharp rock in his bare feet and then tripped over something small and furry and sprawled to the ground, managing to put the palm of his left hand right on top of a small cactus in the process.

He was immediately cold, in pain, and humiliated, not necessarily in that order. He picked himself up and was able to pinpoint the sound of the barking. In the soft pre-down light, he could make out two of his dogs chasing something lean and gray over a near-by hill. He looked down and saw what he had tripped over. There was his third dog, looking up at him like he was the stupidest human being he had ever seen.

Carson limped to the camp door and pulled himself in. He left the door open for some light and managed to locate the matches. He lit the lamp and sat down on his bunk to pick the cactus needles out of his hand. Then he realized he was shivering from the cold, and he interrupted his medical experiment to pull on his clothes and his boots.

He then went to light a fire in the stove. He opened the stove door and there was no kindling and no coal. He trudged outside and retrieved coal and kindling from the commissary wagon and placed it in the stove. He then lit a match and held it by the kindling until it caught fire. Then he closed the stove door and returned to trying to remove all the cactus needles from his hand.

Suddenly he was choking and he could no longer see. He realized he forgot to turn the flue on the stove and all the smoke was coming from the stove directly into the sheep camp. He reached up and turned the flue and staggered out of the camp, coughing and rubbing his eyes.

He made it to the commissary wagon and poured some water out of the barrel and cleaned out his eyes. The cold water braced him and made his injured hand sting. The cold morning air made him realize he was a little wet and he was not wearing his coat. He headed back into the now warm camp, ignoring the small amount of smoke that still lingered. The heat from the stove felt much better than the cold air outside. He changed his shirt, put on his coat, and went back outside.

It was much lighter now, as dawn had finally arrived. The horses nickered at the sight of him, and he grabbed feedbags and scooped oats into the bags and tied the bags around the heads of the horses so their noses were in the bags and they could eat. He checked on the sheep, and the pen was sill intact. He fed and watered the dogs and then opened the pen to let the sheep out. He rolled up the wire fence and struggled to pull out he fence posts. He finally got all of them out of the ground and stored the posts and the wire in the commissary wagon.

He checked on the horses and seeing that the oats were all consumed, he took off the feed bags and returned them to the commissary wagon. Suddenly he realized he had not eaten and was aware of a rumbling in his stomach. He went back to the sheep camp and tried to make coffee. Instead of the electric drop coffee-maker he was used to, he found an old coffee pot. There was no internal piece to hold coffee. Cason was stumped on how to use it.

He decided to skip coffee and poured a cup of cold water. He found a large black cast iron skillet. He put four strips of bacon in the skillet and set it on the stove. He then took a box of pancake mix and added water to the mix in a bowl and stirred it up. He took the bacon out of the skillet and put it on a paper towel to drain. Then he began to pour small round pools of the batter into the bacon grease in the skillet. He found a spatula and flipped the pancakes over when they got a little brown. Pretty soon he had a small pile of pancakes about six inches in diameter.

Carson dug around in the storage areas and found a plastic bottle of pancake syrup. He then proceeded to wolf down the bacon and pancakes and chased them down with cold water. At that moment, it was one of the finest meals he had ever eaten. He heated water in a large pot on the stove and washed his meager dishes, hanging the skillet out to air dry on the side of the sheep camp.

As he stepped out of the sheep camp, he was greeted by the morning sun and the smiling face of Big Dave, who was leaning against one of the wheels of he commissary wagon, smoking a small cigar. "Well hells bells, son, you look like you been rode hard and put away wet," said Big Dave.

"I had kind of a rough morning," replied Kit.

"Well, rough or not, you got the sheep out and the animals fed, and that's a good start to any morning," laughed Big Dave. "How come I don't smell no coffee?"

"Coffee?" said Kit, as though Big Dave had just spoken in an alien language.

"Yeah, coffee. You know, the stuff we need to get started in the morning. Don't tell me you don't drink coffee." said Big Dave.

"Sure, I drink coffee," replied Kit. "I just can't figure out how to use the coffee pot."

Carlson snorted with laughter and grabbed Kit by the arm and led him back into the sheep camp. The interior seemed even more crowded with both of them in the camp at the same time. Big Dave grabbed the coffee pot and poured water into it. He then opened up the coffee can and took a handful of coffee and dumped it in the pot. He put the pot on the stove, looked at Kit and said, "Any questions?"

Kit looked perplexed, and he finally blurted out, "How do you keep the grounds out of the coffee?"

Big Dave smiled and grabbed two metal coffee cups. "This here is cowboy coffee, not the lah-te-dah stuff you get in the city. When the water boils, the coffee is done and you take the lid off the coffee pot and pour some cold water in. The cold water takes the grounds to the bottom of the pot and then you pour the coffee into your cup."

"You mean to tell me you get coffee with no grounds in it?" said Kit incredulously.

"No, you get some grounds, but that just adds a little body to the coffee," replied Big Dave. "Now if you were having eggs for breakfast, you could toss the shells in the coffee pot and they help to keep the grounds down at the bottom of the pot as well." Big Dave heard the coffee pot start to boil, and he pulled it off the stove with a gloved hand and poured in a cup of cold water and then poured coffee in both cups. Kit looked at his first, but made no move to drink it. Big Dave looked at him and said, "Now what's wrong?"

"Uh, I usually have cream in my coffee," said Kit with a red face.

"Well, why didn't you say so. We'll just get out the cow." Big Dave then pulled out a can of condensed milk from a storage area and punched a hole in the top of the can with his knife. He reached over and began pouring the contents into Kit's cup. "Just say when."

"When," said Kit, his cheeks red with embarrassment.

They sat on some overturned food boxes just outside of the sheep camp where they could keep an eye on the sheep and sipped their coffee. "This is one of the best parts of the day," said Big Dave. Although Kit had endured a pretty rough morning, he had to admit that he felt pretty good and the coffee tasted just fine, grounds and all.

CHAPTER FIFTEEN

It had been a late night and Tony was badly in need of a hot cup of coffee. He turned on his computer and went into the small break room that Lenny Klein provided for his underlings. He put a filter and coffee in the machine, added water, hit the on button, and headed to the men's room. On his way back through the break room, he stuck a cup over the slowly filling coffee pot and waited as it filled. He took a quick sip and satisfied with his efforts, he continued on back to his small office that was stuffed with electronic and computer gear.

He opened up his computer and set up his standard search programs and sat back to enjoy his coffee. Within minutes, he saw he had a hit in his search and he quickly put down his cup and spent the next half hour focusing on his search. "Bingo," he said out loud. "Gotcha, you little bastard." After completing his search, he printed out a hard copy and headed for Lenny's office.

Lenny had been working since about six A.M. and was irritated to hear the knock at his door. Lenny liked to start work early before the phones, e-mails, and his staff began to disrupt his day. "Come in," Lenny growled, wondering who was interrupting his work at 7:30 A.M. Tony carefully made his way into Lenny's office, making sure to not let the door slam behind him, and came to a stop in front of Lenny's desk.

"Tony, what the hell are you up to this damn early?" said Lenny.

"Well, boss, I finally got a lead on that Andrews kid who flew the coop," replied Tony.

"Great, great," said Lenny, "What did you find out?"

"Well," said Tony, "he made a call on his cell phone two days ago. He called his mother in Kankakee and talked for just over two minutes."

"Where was he calling from?" interrupted Lenny.

"I hacked into the phone company records and

was able to trace it to a cell tower location in southern Wyoming near a place called Green River."

"Where in the hell is Green River, Wyoming? Sounds like some half-assed hole in the road," interrupted Lenny.

"Let me show you," replied Tony. He produced a computer-generated map where he had used a yellow marker to highlight the location of Green River. "Look here," said Tony. "Interstate 80 runs right through this area going from east to west. My guess is our boy is headed west on I-80."

"How do we find him on I-80?" asked Lenny.

"Leave that to me, boss," answered Tony. "I'll use some of our resources and put them west of Green River. I'll have them check out all the truck stops and rest areas. We have a good description of the car and his Illinois license plates. We'll get him now."

"Make sure you let me know as soon as you find him," said Lenny. "I want to be in on how we deal with him. This little bastard has cost me time and money."

"No problem, boss," said Tony as he quickly left Lenny's office holding his print-out and his map, trying to keep the smirk off of his face.

Tony went straight to his office and made several phone calls and then some e-mails as he went about setting a trap for what he was sure was an unwitting Carson Andrews. He then sat back in his chair and drained the remains of his coffee. He looked at the glowing screen in front of him and muttered to himself, "Your ass is mine, sonny."

One day went by, then two and by the third day it was obvious that somehow the Andrews kid had managed to sneak by all the spots they had staked out along Interstate 80 west of Green River, Wyoming. Finally, Tony called in his people from Rock Springs, Evanston, and several small towns along I-80 all the way to Salt Lake City, Utah.

Tony did not enjoy his subsequent meeting with Lenny and having to explain that he was unable to find the kid. Lenny was violently angry. He screamed and cursed at Tony and grabbed a book on his desk and threw it across the room where it bounced off the richly paneled wall. Finally he cooled down enough to talk without swearing every other word. Lenny was not used to failure, and he could not comprehend how they were unable to nail one stupid punk kid.

Tony waited until he was sure he could speak without getting impaled with something on Lenny's desk. After a considerable amount of groveling, something Tony excelled at, Lenny agreed to set up more contacts west of Salt Lake City, and Tony would do a complete new sweep and search of any possible contacts and records. There had been no activity on the credit cards, and Tony was pretty sure that the Andrews kid, who was a computer systems analyst, had figured out that he could be traced by his transactions.

Tony spent several hours going through his search programs. Finally the urge for some caffeine hit him and he went to the break room. The coffee left in the pot had the consistency of sludge so he tossed it out and set about making a fresh pot. While he was waiting for the coffee pot to work its magic, he noticed he had spilled a small amount of the ground coffee when he was loading it into the filter. He pulled a paper towel off the rack to clean it up when it hit him. He was looking at tiny pieces of ground coffee in a haphazard pattern covering about two feet of the white counter top. He quickly cleaned up the coffee, poured himself a freshly brewed cup and raced to his office.

He set the coffee cup down and began working the keyboard of his computer. Soon he had a screen filled with a map of southwest Wyoming with the town of Green River in the center. Seeing the random pattern of the spilled coffee grounds had him realize that maybe the kid had not stayed on I-80. If so, why did he get off the interstate and where might he have gone? He checked for the weather near Green River for the past two days and there was his answer.

A sudden and heavy spring snowstorm had hit a good portion of southwestern Wyoming, including Green River. The storm was bad enough to close I-80 for about six hours. That would have stopped the Andrews kid dead in his tracks. He would have had to get off I-80 and hole up somewhere. The question was where, for how long, and was he now getting back on I-80 or headed in another direction, maybe even back east!

Tony set up a program to list all the motels and hotels in the immediate area of I-80. When he had the list complete, he printed it out and began calling each location. There were more than eighty locations so he knew this would take the rest of the day. Tony used a cover story that he was with the FBI and was looking for a fleeing bank robber. Without exception, he received 100% cooperation with every clerk he talked to. They were all excited and happy to help.

By seven P.M. Tony was exhausted. He had talked to all eighty locations and came up empty. When he found no registrations for Andrews, he followed up with a description of Andrews and his car and still got nothing. Because of the storm, all of the motels had been full for one night and it took time to go through all of the reservations. He even had them cross check on the year, make, and model of the car. Still he came up with nothing. Tony was starting to dread meeting with Lenny the next morning. He looked hard at the blinking computer screen, but saw neither answers nor inspiration.

When Tony awoke, he was still in his office chair. He had spent the night in his office and as he tried to get out of the chair, every joint in his body protested. Apparently sleeping in your office chair was not a good idea. He stumped to the bathroom, did a rudimentary job of cleaning up and found himself lunging toward the break room.

While he was waiting for yet another pot of coffee to brew, he ran several possible scenarios through his mind. The kid could have waited out the storm and then resumed his journey west. The delay of the storm could have been enough to cause him to pass by the checkpoints after they had been abandoned by Tony's people. That seemed unlikely as the checkpoints were in place for three days and the storm stopped traffic for only one day.

Andrews could have decided to go north or south from around Green River. Tony took his coffee back to his office and consulted his map. There were no significant roads going north or south from the Green River area. Either you went north to Montana or Canada or you went south to western Colorado or New Mexico or Arizona. The areas appeared sparsely populated and not likely candidates.

The last idea was that the kid had stayed in the Green River area. Why would he do that? There was nothing in his background that showed any relatives or even any specific connection to the area. According to Tony's extensive file on Andrews, it did not appear that he had ever been west of Iowa. Tony continued to think. Why would the kid stay? Maybe he was sick. Maybe he was in an accident and was hurt. Or maybe he was in an accident and the car was damaged and would not run.

Tony began a new search of the area for hospitals, clinics, auto repair shops, and towing services. Once he had the lists compiled he would check all of them. He would also hack into the Wyoming State Patrol's computers and see if Andrews had been in an accident that had been reported, or maybe he had even gotten a ticket. He would do the same with the hospital computers unless they did not have an online system. Then he would do his work by phone and continue with calling the auto repair shops and towing services.

Tony's plan was a good one, but he made a simple

mistake that is common for people who live in cities. To Tony, fifty miles was an incredible distance, as it is to any city dweller. In a sparsely populated state like Wyoming, fifty miles is nothing. Kemmerer is ninety miles north of Green River. Thus while Tony's search was very thorough, he was unwittingly forty miles short of his goal. All of his reports came back negative. To Tony it was as though Andrews had disappeared into thin air.

Detective Landers was not having a good morning. He had made a major mistake the previous week when he asked his wife what she wanted for her birthday and she had replied that she wanted him to quit smoking. He was trying. Lord how he was trying. He popped another piece of nicotine gum into his mouth where it joined the large wad that had already taken up residence. Earlier that morning his cell phone had died when he was setting up an appointment with a potential witness.

"Why couldn't you have died when the Captain was chewing my butt out for letting the Andrews kid skip out on us?" he said as he looked at his now lifeless cell phone.

He plugged the cell phone into a charger on his battered gray steel desk, and it almost immediately chirped at him.

Startled, Landers picked up his cell and looked at the caller ID screen. It was a number he did not recognize. He snapped open the phone and answered it. He got no further than hello and then he began rummaging around on his desk for a pen and paper. He wrote for several seconds, said, "Thanks," and hung up the cell.

Suddenly he forgot about his need for a cigarette. The call was from an old friend who worked for one of the Federal Agencies whose name was never to be spoken out loud. Like something out of a Harry Potter book. He had asked for help in locating the Andrews kid and now he knew where Carson had been approximately two days ago. His friend had traced a cell phone call from Carson to his mother to the area of origin.

Landers got out a map of the United States and located Green River, Wyoming. "He must be running on I-80 west." Landers picked up his desk phone and began paperwork needed to put out an all points bulletin to every law enforcement office along Interstate Highway 80 from Green River, Wyoming, west to Las Vegas, Nevada.

All of a sudden Lander's day stared looking a little better. He was glad to hear that Carson was alive, but angry that the kid was running and eluding him. He already had been forced to have the trial date postponed and that had been a personal embarrassment. Maybe now he could run the kid down.

CHAPTER SIXTEEN

The thin air was real to Kit. He had gotten used to it and no longer found himself struggling for oxygen when doing hard physical work. His body had adjusted to the altitude. He had also adjusted to the hard physical work.

It was now six weeks since Big Dave had plucked Kit from a snowdrift. His body was now harder, leaner, and more muscular. He had become a good rider and was good with the horses. He had learned to be a better than average sheepherder and found himself enjoying the hard work, living outdoors, and learning how to handle himself in his new role. He took pride in being much more self-sufficient.

Because he had proved to be a quick learner and developed quickly into a good hand, Big Dave had delayed hiring a new herder. Now, Kit was being rewarded with a new and better job. A new herder was due in tomorrow, and Kit would become Big Dave's foreman. He would be in charge of three herds that Big Dave owned and managed.

Each herd consisted of several thousand sheep, a herder, two or three sheep dogs, and the usual sheep camp, commissary wagon, and three horses. The sheep in all three herds had been shorn of their wool by a professional team of wool-shearers from New Zealand. Kit had helped move sheep into temporary pens while the shearing team did their work on his herd and got some basic lessons in using the electric shears.

Big Dave had explained that when you found a sheep dead, which happened more often than he would like, you could at least shear the dead sheep and salvage the wool. The wool was packed into long burlap bags that had to be at least ten feet long. They looked like huge burlap sausages when they were full of wool.

Big Dave had explained the economics of the sheep business to Kit. A sheep herd produced an annual wool crop. It also produced lambs. Some male lambs, known as bucks, were kept for breeding. Other males were neutered and kept to produce mutton. These were called "weathers". The female lambs were called "ewes" and some were kept as replacements for the breeding herd and the rest were sold as lambs for the dinner table. Ewes were kept in the breeding herd until they could no longer produce lambs. This was usually because they became old and lost part of their teeth and could not eat enough. These were called "old biddies" and were sold, generally, to soup companies.

Between the lambs, the wool, the mutton, and the old biddies, a sheep herd could be a very profitable enterprise. The problems lay with losses to the herd due to disease, bad plants(locoweed, etc.), or too much of good plants. Like horses, sheep would eat too much of something like alfalfa, then founder and die of bloating. The main problem in losses was predators, mainly coyotes and wild dogs. It was the herder's job to keep the sheep from eating bad plants, from not eating too much of good plants, to get sufficient water, and to protect them from predators. This he was to do with the help of his sheepdogs, his horse, and his rifle.

It had rained slightly during the night and Kit could smell the pungent odor of damp sage from the sagebrush plants that surrounded his campsite. It gave the air a particularly fresh taste. After saddling his favorite horse, a buckskin mare named Dolly, Kit swung into the saddle and soon was urging Dolly to move the herd, directing her more and more with his knees than with the reins as he had been taught by Big Dave. Kit smiled as he thought about how now he did chores without even thinking about how he was supposed to do them. He no longer had to think, he knew.

His little campsite was now about ten miles from where he had started six weeks ago. He had moved the camp twice and now he was going to be in charge of herders instead of just being one.

Tomorrow he would show the new herder the ropes and then he would move his gear into the old bunkhouse on Big Dave's ranch. Two things he would not miss. One was the rather short bed in the sheep camp that was never designed for someone of his height and the other was "cowboy coffee." He had learned to like coffee fortified by some coffee grounds, but was looking forward to something closer to a Starbuck's breakfast blend from an electric coffee brewing pot.

By mid-afternoon he had made a quick lunch, changed horses, and made sure the herd had moved closer to a small spring where they could get plenty of water. The nights were still pretty cold, but as soon as the sun appeared the temperature went up. Kit found himself becoming an expert at peeling off layers of clothing as the temperature rose and then adding them as the sun began to set. He was pretty sure the temperature variance between the low of the night and the high of the day was between forty and forty-five degrees.

Kit dismounted, tied Dolly to a nearby greasewood stump and sat down on a flat rock. He used this perch to keep an eye on the herd and to enjoy the afternoon sun. Before he knew it, he had started to drift on into sleep when he was brought upright by a sudden commotion highlighted by his sheep dogs barking like crazy. Kit jumped up on the rock and soon saw the source of the noise. About seventy yards away, south of where he was standing, four large dogs were attacking several sheep. The sheep dogs had thrown themselves at the intruders, but were too small to do more than slow the bigger dogs down.

Kit turned to his horse and pulled the Winchester from the scabbard. He pulled the lever down to chamber a round and pulled the rifle up to sight in on the nearest of the big dogs. He made sure his feet were properly set so he was balanced as he sighted in on the dogs. He decided to try to scare the dogs off, so he sighted in on a rock right next to the biggest dog's feet and carefully squeezed the trigger.

The targeted dog jumped sideways, obviously startled by the bullet hitting the rock and the resulting ricochet. The dog looked around for a second and then proceeded to resume his attack on the nearest sheep. Kit swore under his breath and then sighted in the rifle on the dog. He took a deep breath, let half of it out as he had been taught, and then gently squeezed the trigger.

The dog jumped in the air and started to run, then flopped over on his side. The other three dogs were too distracted by their prey and their barking and did not hear the shots as they continued to attack the flock. Kit carefully sighted in on a second dog that was about fifty-five yards away. As soon as the dog paused in his attack, Kit dropped him with one shot. By now the other two dogs had realized what was happening and they immediately ran down an arroyo covered with sagebrush. Unable to get a clear shot, Kit held his fire.

Being careful to release the hammer on his rifle, Kit trotted down to the herd to assess the damage. Both dogs were dead as were five ewes and two lambs. Four more ewes were injured and Kit was unsure of what to do to help them. He ran back to the tree stump where Dolly was tied and slipped the rifle back into its scabbard. He then mounted Dolly and quickly rode back to the sheep camp.

He still had his cell phone, and he thought it was still charged up. He quickly arrived at the sheep camp and retrieved his cell phone. The phone showed power, but no reception. Then he remembered that Big Dave had left a small two-way radio to be used in the case of an emergency. It connected with a base radio at the ranch that Mrs. Carson always kept on.

Kit flipped on the radio, was pleased to see that he had power, and quickly was connected to Carol. He gave Carol the short version of the dog attack and she said she would have Dave at the camp as quickly as she could. Kit replaced the radio, mounted Dolly, and rode back to the herd.

Within twenty minutes, Big Dave was roaring up to the camp in his pickup with a huge dust cloud trailing behind him. He pulled up next to the herd and jumped out carrying a small bag. He quickly knelt next to the first injured ewe and began pouring a white powder on the sheep's wounds. He directed Kit to get the portable electric shears out of the truck and to shear the dead sheep. While Kit was salvaging the wool from the seven dead sheep, Big Dave tended to the rest of the injured sheep.

Finished with the shearing, Kit watched Big Dave expertly use a needle and thread to close up a wound and the asked what the white powder was. "Sulfa," said Big Dave. "It gives them a chance to survive, although they may just die of shock." Big Dave's tone was hard, without a hint of his usually good nature.

As soon as he was finished, Big Dave said, "Come on," and headed for the pickup. Kit jumped into the passenger side, and they were soon headed down the ridge, following the arroyo. "How did you know they went this way?" asked Kit.

"I saw their tracks in the dust, along with some sprinkles of blood from the sheep," answered a grim Big Dave. After about fifteen minutes he brought the truck to a stop and pointed down toward the bottom of the ridge where there was a dirt road. "See them two dogs?" he asked.

It took Kit a minute to finally see the dogs. They blended in with the dirt and the sagebrush. Big Dave exited the truck, expertly lifting a scoped 25-06 rifle from a rack over the rear window of the pickup. He leaned forward and sighted the rifle along the hood of the truck. The dogs had to be 250 yards down from the truck. They were standing by a large sagebrush when the rifle cracked and one of the dogs flopped over like it had been hit with a sledgehammer. The second dog, black with white spots, lunged backwards, almost falling over and then took off running in the direction of Kemmerer.

Without a word, Big Dave got back in the truck, returned the rifle to his holder and began driving expertly down the ridge to the dirt road. Pretty soon they were on the outskirts of Kemmerer. Twice they sighted the dog and when he saw the truck, the dog took off running again. They followed the dog into town and watched it run into the partially fenced back yard of a small bungalow painted a light green. Big Dave got out of the truck, taking the rifle with him. He walked up to the fence, looked over it, and saw the dog standing in front of what was apparently its doghouse. Without hesitating, Big Dave pulled up his rifle, sighted it and killed the dog where he stood. Within seconds the back door of the house burst open and a man dressed in a t-shirt and blue jeans and wearing nothing on his feet ran out into the yard.

He immediately began shouting at Big Dave who promptly began shouting back with authority. Very shortly the man stopped yelling and retreated back into the house.

Big Dave climbed back into the pickup, put the rifle on the rack, and began driving back to the herd. After a few silent minutes went by, he turned to Kit and said, "In Wyoming it's perfectly legal to kill any dog that kills livestock, even in the backyard of the home of the owner of the dog. I told that idiot to take his complaint to the chief of police. If he does complain, he will find out what I just told him is true. He's lucky I don't make him pay for my dead sheep." Then his eyes got hard when he said, "I got no use for sheep killers whether they be two legged or four legged. Once a dog starts to kill sheep they won't stop until you drop them with a bullet."

Kit digested this advice and kept quiet for the trip back to the sheep camp. Big Dave checked on the injured ewes and had Kit put water in a pan near where they were laying. He climbed back into the truck and started the engine. Big Dave paused and looked out the driver's window at Kit. "You done real good today, Kit, real good." And with that he was gone in a cloud of dust.

As Kit was unsaddling Dolly, he realized that he had just killed something for the first time in his life and yet he did not feel remorseful or sorry. The dogs had been killing his herd, sheep that were in his care and it was his job to protect them. He also remembered Big Dave's parting words and again felt the flow of confidence running through his body. He grinned and continued with his chores. That night he sat on the steps of the sheep wagon with a hot cup of coffee in his gloved hand.

He had built a small fire in the dirt and ringed it with

stones. The fire kept the chill of the night at bay and one of his sheep dogs was taking advantage of the warmth and had stretched out next to the fire pit. Kit leaned back and stared up at the clear night sky that was filled with stars. It was amazing. When he lived in the city, he never saw anything like it in the night sky. He smiled as he thought about how things had changed. Less than two months ago, he was alone, afraid, and running for his life. He was no longer afraid, he was no longer running, but except for the Carlson family, he was still alone.

Big Dave had been right. By morning all four of the injured ewes were dead, probably from shock. Kit retrieved the portable electric shears from the sheep camp and he salvaged the wool from the four dead sheep and placed the wool in the commissary wagon. The two dead dogs were left where they lay. Occasionally one of the sheep dogs would wander over and sniff the dead dogs, but the sheep completely ignored them.

By the time Kit had finished his chores and had the sheep grazing on a fresh area of buffalo grass, Big Dave pulled up in his truck with a young Mexican herder. While Kit showed the herder around, Big Dave unloaded boxes of groceries and supplies and stored them in the sheep camp and the commissary wagon. The new herder's name was Odie Lone as near as Kit could understand. He was about Kit's age, but much shorter and more wiry in build. He had brown skin, jet black hair, and dark eyes. Big Dave went over the sheep camp with Odie Lone and used fluent Spanish. Kit had trouble understanding what was being said and could only pick out a few words from his memories of rudimentary high school Spanish.

CHAPTER SEVENTEEN

By mid morning Kit and Big Dave were heading off the ridge in Big Dave's pickup. They pulled into Kemmerer and Big Dave parked the pickup on the triangle that made up the center of town. "I've got to see a couple of people, and I'll meet you at the café at noon for lunch." With that he handed Kit a check for six weeks wages. "The bank is over there," he said as he pointed to the other side of the triangle. Before Kit could answer, Big Dave was gone, heading down he sidewalk.

Kit went to the bank and found he was able to cash Big Dave's check with no questions asked. He thought about opening an account, and then worried that he could be traced so he took he entire amount in cash. His next stop was the barbershop where he got his collar length hair cut to as short a haircut as he had allowed since he was in high school. From there he went to Sawaya's store where he bought a new pair of jeans, leather work gloves, a denim jacket, and a gray Stetson cowboy hat. He stood looking in the mirror, trying to look like a cowboy in his new hat when he heard a female voice say, "My, don't you look different."

He turned, saw Tang standing behind him with a grin

on her face, and he found himself blushing, despite his best efforts to avoid doing so. She was dressed in stained work coveralls, but this time she had no hat on and he could clearly see her lovely red hair pulled back into a pony tail. She was smiling and her green eyes seemed as bright as emeralds. He found himself tongue tied and stumped for what to say when she rescued him by laughing and saying, "How about buying a girl a cup of coffee?"

Minutes later they were in the café drinking pretty strong coffee out of large mugs. She looked up at him and said, "You've come a long way from getting pulled out of a snow drift." He looked puzzled and again she laughed. It was not an insulting laugh. Rather it was like a pleasant tinkle of chimes.

"I heard about what you've been doing working for Big Dave Carlson, including shooting those dogs. You don't look like a tenderfoot anymore. Big Dave likes you and around here that is a pretty big deal."

Kit felt embarrassed by the praise and he found himself looking down at his mug of coffee and unable to look her in he eye. "Well, I just tried my best, and Mr. Carlson is a good teacher."

"Big Dave is one very tough son-of-a-bitch," she said without flinching. "His family homesteaded this area, and during the Great Depression his family killed deer to feed the railroad workers as a way of surviving. Dave Carlson is tough, honest, and a good friend or a bad enemy."

"Which is he to you?" asked Kit.

"He was a good friend of my dad's and to all of my

family. My dad died five years ago and I moved back here to run the business and take care of my mom. He helped me when I came back and made sure I got some business I probably would not have gotten otherwise."

"Where did you come back from?" asked Kit.

Tang paused for a minute, stirring her coffee as though she was stalling while she considered her answer. "What you really want to know is why do I have a name like Tang and what am I doing running a gas station and auto repair business in a backwater town like Kemmerer."

Kit found himself blushing again and somehow he stammered out that he was sorry if he was being too personal.

Tang looked up at him with those brilliant green eyes and smiled. "No, that isn't too personal. In a small town like Kemmerer whatever you do is everybody's business. See all these people in the cafe. They are all dying with curiosity about why we are sitting here and what we are talking about and what are the details about who and what you are., Someone farts in Kemmerer and everybody in town knows about it by sunset. My story is pretty simple. I was born and raised here. My daddy wanted a boy, but he got me. He named me Mustang Kelly. That was a mouthful and quickly got shortened to Tang. I graduated from the University of Wyoming with a degree in anthropology and received a fellowship to do graduate work at the University of Chicago where I received my Masters Degree. I worked for the Field's Museum in Chicago as an assistant curator until Daddy died and

Mom needed help. She couldn't run the business and she was not willing to move, so I came back and have been here ever since."

She paused to drink from her mug and then looked up at Kit. "Well, that's my tale of woe. What brings you to Kemmerer other than a spring snowstorm and a bad tie rod?"

Kit had never been good at lying, but he had decided when he took Big Dave's offer of a job that he was not going to tell anyone the real truth. He had concocted a cover story that he felt was close enough to the truth to remember and still sounded believable.

"I grew up in Illinois. My dad disappeared shortly after I was born so I was raised by my mother. I graduated from Eastern Illinois University with a degree in history and a minor in computer science. I worked for a large consulting firm in Chicago and got laid off. I was sick of the Midwest and decided to try to find work in the West. Getting to Kemmerer was an accident of nature."

"You worked in Chicago!" exclaimed Tang. A look of shocked surprise came over her face. "Did you ever go to the museum? Did you ever eat at Sweetwater or Mike Ditkas? Did you spend time hanging out in Old Town?" Tang and Kit spent the next half hour comparing their experiences at various Chicago restaurants, galleries, museums, theatres, and bars. It was amazing that they had been to so many of the same places and had similar opinions of the experiences.

"So, how does it feel going from a systems analyst to a sheepherder?" asked Tang with a smile.

"To tell you the truth, it feels good," said Kit. "I enjoy working outdoors and I really have come to like the physical part of the job. I feel stronger, healthier, and more in control. I've learned a lot, and I find I get a great deal of satisfaction from being a much more self-reliant person. I can't believe how much I've changed. Two months ago I went to work in a suit and now I'm shopping for jeans and leather work gloves."

"Don't forget the hat," said Tang.

"You think the hat is a bad idea?" asked Kit.

"Oh, no, I think it looks good on you. Besides, if anyone has earned the right to wear a cowboy hat, you have. According to Big Dave you're the best hand he's had in years."

Kit took the compliment in stride and then he asked Tang what had been on his mind. "I understand that you came back to run your dad's business because your mom wouldn't move. Are you planning to stay here?"

Tang smiled, her green eyes sparkling. "We're back to what's a nice girl like me doing in a place like this. The business does okay and my mom is happy with staying here where she has all her friends. I miss the city and the museum, and the restaurants, but this is my home and as critical as I can be about it, Kemmerer has been good to me. Sometimes the slow pace of a place like Kemmerer is a welcome relief from all the pressure of living in the city. Things go slowly, but they don't change much. I take comfort in that."

Kit smiled at her answer, but found himself, very uncharacteristically, wanting to know more about her. "So what do you do for entertainment in Kemmerer?" he asked.

"Boy you have been stuck out with the sheep for a while," laughed Tang. "Here in Kemmerer almost everyone has satellite television dishes and big screen television sets. We have a small local movie house, a tiny library, and an even smaller museum. We have J.C. Penny's actual home in the park next to the senior citizens center, which seems quite appropriate. Most social things happen in the bars and the school and church functions. Then there's the outdoors. If you like hunting, fishing, or just being outdoors, you're less than ten minutes away from any of that. We also have our share of fossils, as this part of Wyoming used to be a large lake and thus we have Fossil Butte National Monument just outside of town."

"So, which of those things do you take part in?" asked Kit.

"I watch television, I read books, I poke around in the mountains for signs of Indian tribes. Mostly I stay out of the bars and churches. Either one can get you in trouble. I do occasionally go to some of the high school games, concerts, and plays. What do you do to keep busy?"

"Well, said Kit, "I haven't been here long enough to do anything but work. I was wondering if I might buy you dinner sometime." Kit was stunned to realize he had just asked Tang out. He had thought about it, but wasn't sure how it would go over. Usually when he felt that way, he avoided all problems by saying nothing.

Tang looked down at her now almost empty coffee cup, stirred the remains with her spoon and then looked up at Kit and said, "Sounds like fun. Just call me a day before so I can make sure I can get away."

Before Kit could say anything else a huge shadow loomed over them and Big Dave's voice was booming out, "My, my, what have we here. Shame on you Tang for taking this poor boy's mind offa his work."

Tang laughed and said, "No problem, Big Dave. I have to get back to work anyway. Good to see both of you." She turned to Kit and said, "You might want to call me or stop by the shop and I'll give you the details on your car." With that, she gracefully exited her seat and was gone out the front door of the café.

After lunch with Carlson, Kit rushed to finish the rest of his errands including getting his laundry done and buying some personal supplies. He met Big Dave at the Stock Exchange Bar and joined him for a beer. Big Dave introduced him around to several sheepmen, cowboys, and miners. As they were preparing to leave to go back to the ranch, Kit asked if they could stop by Tang's to check on his car. Big Dave grinned at Kit's eagerness and they drove several blocks to Tang's auto repair shop.

They stood outside the shop while Tang finished with a customer. When she came outside, Kit mentioned her request to talk about his car. Tang seemed different than she had earlier in the day. She was friendly, but all business. She showed Kit what she had fixed and showed him the itemized costs. It was a little more than he had available and even then would clean him out of cash.

She seemed to notice the effect the bill had on him and she paused and then said, "I have a deal for you if you're interested. I have an old 1949 ¾ ton GMC pickup in the back. A local rancher died three years ago and his wife came in and asked me to buy it. The truck is in pretty good shape, but needs some wiring, a battery and tires. I could add those things to the truck and trade you even up for your car. I'd fix your car and take it down to Salt Lake City and sell it to one of the used car lots. Are you interested?"

Kit quickly found himself going over the old pickup with Big Dave. He looked to Big Dave for his opinion. Big Dave said, "This is a solid truck. It belonged to old Ernie Granger. He had the motor and transmission replaced about six years ago. It can't have 5,000 miles on the motor." The old truck was quaint, almost cool. It had a badly faded green paint job and the unique rounded side windows on the cab. Big Dave noticed Carson's attention to the windows. "This is what they call a five window truck," he said. The truck still had a removable stock rack on it. The rack was included and Kit and Tang shook hands on the deal. Kit promised to bring the signed title to Tang to finalize the transaction.

"How about you buy me dinner Saturday night and we'll swap titles?" said a grinning Tang.

Kit blushed and Big Dave roared with laughter.

"Sounds like a hell of a good deal to me," said Big Dave. Kit agreed to stop by the shop about 7:00P.M. and pick up his new truck and Tang and take her to dinner at Bon Rico's steak house.

CHAPTER EIGHTEEN

Kit unloaded his purchases from Big Dave's pickup when they got back to the ranch. He was the sole occupant of a small, but comfortable bunkhouse. There was room for four bunks and a bathroom with a shower and a small kitchen. The bunkhouse had baseboard electric heat, but also had a small wood-burning potbelly stove in the middle of the sleeping area. The stove was similar to the one in the sheep camp, but larger.

The bunkhouse was dusty from lack of use and after moving his gear from the ranch house, Carson spent the rest of the day cleaning. He worked hard on getting the bunkhouse clean, especially the bathroom. Mrs. Carlson interrupted him twice to bring him some towels from the bathroom and kitchen along with some cleaning supplies and soap. The second time she brought in three large cardboard boxes. "These belonged to our oldest son Mike," explained Mrs. Carlson. "He was killed in the Gulf War and I just never got 'round to getting rid of his clothes. Please look them over and see what might fit and take what you like. I'll come back tomorrow to take back what you don't want."

Kit started to say he was sorry and Mrs. Carlson hushed him. "I appreciate the words, but that was a long time ago, and Dave and I have come to terms with his death. He was a good boy, but a wild one. We kind of thought the Marines would calm him down. He was proud of being a Marine. We're still proud of him." With that she was gone, the door banging shut behind her.

Kit joined the Carlsons for breakfast at 5:30A.M. the next morning. Big Dave laid out his plans for the day. "We buy groceries for the three camps, divide them up into boxes and then deliver them. I want you to learn how we do that. You need to learn where the camps are and what the herders should be doing. I also want you to get a good count of the herd and make sure they are where they're supposed to be." Big Dave grinned at the stunned expression on Kit's face. "What, you mean you can't figure all that out in your head? I thought you was a college boy!"

Big Dave went on to explain that he had topographical maps for all the areas they ran herds on, and he then went to his den and returned with a small plastic piece of equipment that looked like a small TV set. "This here is a GPS unit. It runs on batteries and uses satellites to allow you to get a fix on where you are. It gives you a location in longitude and latitude and you can then find it on the maps."

Big Dave spent the next hour getting Kit familiar with the maps and the GPS. He also gave him a compass, a military flashlight with a red filter, and a fire starter kit consisting of flint, steel, and a magnesium bar. Big Dave explained how you could shave off slivers from the bar using a knife, then light the shavings and start a hot fire right away. "Do you have a knife, son?" asked Big Dave.

Kit shook his head to indicate no and Big Dave again made a trip to the den, returning with a six-inch knife in a leather sheath. "You got any coins, son?" asked Big Dave. Kit reached in his pocket and came out with a quarter. "That'll do," said Big Dave and he exchanged the knife for the quarter. "It's bad luck to give a knife without getting something in return," explained a grinning Big Dave.

Within a short time they were headed out of town in Big Dave's pickup, the back end of it filled with cardboard boxes of food and supplies for the sheep camps. All three of the camps were within about ten miles of Kemmerer. Kit took notes on a tiny notebook Big Dave had given him. After using the GPS, he had good locations for all three camps.

The herders were Mexicans, like Odie Lone. Each of them had a small list of things they wished to have at their camps. Big Dave explained that they would pick up the new lists when they arrived at the camps and include the items in their next trip. Tortillas, beans, red chilies, batteries for their radios, and some sweets appeared on all three lists.

As they drove back from the last camp, Big Dave explained that they would be moving the herds to the mountain pastures above LaBarge Creek in the Bridger Wilderness. This was pasture that Big Dave leased from the federal government to feed his sheep herds on during the summer from about June through the end of August. The terrain made it much tougher to get around and supplying the camps would have to be done by pack mule.

"Pack mule?" said Kit in amazement.

"You bet, son. Why we'll make a first rate muleskinner out of you in no time" said Big Dave with a grin. Somehow, Kit did not think it was going to be all that easy. For once, he was right.

The next day was Saturday and Kit and Big Dave spent the morning repairing fence on the ranch. Kit marveled at Big Dave's obvious strength and skill in repairing barbed wire fence. Big Dave explained how it was done and what tools were used. As far as Kit could see, nothing had changed in fence repair in over a hundred years. They came in for lunch and Dave told Kit to take the afternoon off. Kit showered, shaved, and put on a pair of khakis and a dark blue golf shirt with a pair of loafers.

Big Dave and Carol were going out for dinner with some friends, and they gave Kit a ride into town. Kit was surprised to see that instead of the big pickup, Big Dave was driving a late model white Lincoln Town Car. Big Dave looked Kit over and said "Ain't you dressed like a city dude." Carol told Big Dave to shut up and told Kit he looked very nice.

They dropped Kit off at the auto shop and he walked up to the shop and tried the front door. It was locked. Kit looked around and could see no one. The place looked deserted. In the window on the front door was a "Closed" sign. Confused, Kit started to walk to the side of the building when he heard a car pull up behind him. He turned and there was Tang in a bright yellow Wrangler Jeep. She got out of the Jeep and apologized for being late. She was wearing jeans, boots, and a white blouse. Her hair was pulled back into a long, full ponytail. Kit noticed she was actually wearing some make-up, something he had not seen on her before.

"Let me show you the truck," she said. They went to the rear of the shop, and there the truck sat on top of brand new tires. The truck and been washed and looked pretty good, even with its faded green paint job. Tang slid in behind the wheel of the truck and fired up the engine. "I adjusted the clutch and threw in some new brake shoes. I think it'll be just fine."

Kit said "You've got a deal." He walked over to the Chevy and took the title out of the glove box, signed it, and handed Tang the signed title to the Chevy. She gave him the title to the truck along with a bill of sale.

"Now," said Tang, "how about the dinner you promised. I'm hungry enough to eat a horse."

They took her Jeep and drove south out of Kemmerer, down through what Tang explained were called the "flats." "They're called that because they are just a flat area with bluffs on each side about ten miles apart," Tang explained.

"How far is this Bon Rico?' asked Kit.

"Oh, it's about ten miles," replied Tang.

Shortly Bon Rico's steak house came into view. "How

did they get this out in the middle of nowhere?" asked Kit. He couldn't see anything else around except sagebrush and there was a lot of that.

"Originally there was a town and a mine near here called Cumberland and Bon Rico's is all that's left. J.C. Penney actually opened his second store there, and like the town, it just disappeared," explained Tang.

They parked in the gravel lot and went inside. The building was an old wooden one story structure with a high false front that gave the impression that it was two stories, not one. Kit noted that the building, like a lot of Kemmerer, looked like it could use a little maintenance.

As they stepped inside, Kit was pleasantly surprised. The bar was to their right and the dining room to their left. The bar was straight out of an old western movie with an authentic looking back bar complete with mirrors. The bar stools looked well worn, but they seemed to fit in with the bar. An older well dressed lady greeted them and quickly had them seated in a wood paneled dining room that was dimly lit with old fashioned lamps that looked like they were fueled with gas. On closer inspection kit determined they were just very good reproductions. A young man dressed in a white shirt, black slacks, and matching black vest brought them menus, large glasses of ice water, a basket of fresh bread, and a small relish tray. They each ordered a steak and a beer and the young waiter left with their order.

"So what else is Kemmerer famous for?" asked a curious Kit.

"Well," replied Tang, "Kemmerer was founded as a town by the Kemmerer family who owned the Kemmerer Coal Company. The Oregon Trail ran through here, and there are several places north of town where wagon trains crossed the Ham's Fork River."

"So why is it called the Hamm's Fork River?" asked Kit.

"Originally, the first white men here were fur trappers who came here individually or in groups where they were sponsored by companies. Hamm was one of those original fur trappers and the river was named after him. You can find some graves north of town where settlers are buried who died on the trail heading to Oregon. The Union Pacific Railroad ran a line through Kemmerer to provide direct links to Oregon, thus it was named the Oregon Short Line. We've had our share of excitement as you would expect in the Old West," smiled Tang.

"Like what?" asked Kit.

"Well, you've probably heard of Butch Cassidy and the Sundance Kid, have you not?" asked Tang.

"Of course," said Kit, "who hasn't seen the movie several times."

"Well, Butch and his gang robbed the bank in Montpelier, Idaho, and then headed west to their hideout in Wyoming. They had a small hideout near Kaycee, Wyoming. You can only get to it through a hidden cleft in the rocks at the top of a ridge. They call it the Hole in the Wall and Cassidy's gang was called the Hole in the Wall gang."

"They came all the way from Idaho?"

"Montpelier, Idaho, is only about seventy-five miles from Kemmerer. Legend has it that they ran into trouble near LaBarge, Wyoming, which is only about thirty miles north of Kemmerer. No one knows if it was Indians, other outlaws, a posse of lawmen, or what, but they supposedly holed up in some small canyon for three days and then managed to sneak out of the canyon in the middle of the night and make their way to the Hole in the Wall. According to the legend, they left one of the gang, who was wounded, with his share of the loot."

"Did anyone ever find out what happened to the wounded guy or where this canyon was located?"

"No." Tang answered. "Legend still has it that the outlaw died in the canyon with his loot and neither he nor the money has ever been found."

"Sounds like a pretty tall tale to me," snorted Kit.

"I would agree with you except for one thing," replied Tang. "The gang robbed the State Bank of Montpelier of $20,000 in newly minted $50 gold pieces. 100 of those gold pieces have never reappeared and are on many coin collectors list of most wanted coins."

"Really?" said Kit.

"Well, that's what I've been told by a lot of old timers around here, and I did check up on the coins and that part of the story is true. They have never turned up. Of course, they could be buried someplace else entirely."

Tang's story was interrupted by the arrival of their meal. During the meal Tang talked about the Indian tribes that had lived around Kemmerer. The Arapahoe and Shoshone were the most prevalent and they had occasional visits by the Cheyenne and the Sioux. She mentioned that when the FMC coal mines and the Kemmerer Coal Company mines were expanded, they had to file environmental statements with the U.S. government. While digging, they uncovered several Indian campsites and burial grounds, some of them hundreds of years old.

"What happened?" asked Kit.

"They had to preserve the campsites and burial grounds and allow museums and universities to send teams to excavate the sites. I worked with a few of them at first, but I really didn't have the time, although it was exciting work," replied Tang.

"It must have made you wish for the old days at the Chicago Museum of Science and Industry," said Kit.

"No, those days are over. I have my life here and taking care of my mom is my number one priority," responded Tang.

Kit asked her other questions about people and buildings he had seen in town, and she warmed up to the topic and gave him a pretty vivid picture of who was who and who did what to whom in Kemmerer.

Before Kit knew it, Tang was dropping him off at her shop and thanking him for the dinner. As Kit stepped out of the Jeep, Tang gave him a smile and drove off. He found his '49 GMC pickup with the keys in the ignition and was surprised to see that it started immediately. He found the headlight switch and put the pickup in gear and was soon heading down the highway to the Carlson ranch.

CHAPTER NINETEEN

Tony sat back in his chair with his hands behind his head. He had just finished a series of reports to Lenny updating him on several projects they were working on. One report was extremely short. The Andrews file had nothing new in it. Every lead had turned out to be a dead end. Several careful searches of every database Tony knew existed had turned up nothing. The trial date had been extended for several more months. In the meantime, Lenny was becoming more and more difficult to face. Lenny did not take failure easily, and Tony was very uncomfortable about taking this report to him.

Still, Tony mused, if the kid has disappeared, then he had also disappeared from the cops as well. His informants in the police department had told him that even the FBI had failed to find a trace of the Andrews kid. He was just plain gone. Well, if he was gone where Tony couldn't find him, then neither could the cops. The kid had made no effort to contact the cops or anyone else, for that matter. Tony was pretty sure that he would never show up to testify against Lenny's clients.

Still, orders were orders and his orders were to find the kid and take whatever measures necessary to eliminate him permanently. Tony decided he would stick to his plan to do a thorough search every two weeks until something turned up. Sooner or later it would. Nobody could hide from the databases forever, not in the Twenty-First Century.

Kit felt kind of overwhelmed by the silence. He was riding Dolly and leading a pack mule with a packsaddle loaded with supplies. Every ten or fifteen minutes he would stop and get a reading on his GPS and alter his course slightly, using his pocket compass. It was impossible to travel in a straight line when you are riding on horseback and going uphill in the heavily wooded mountains.

Kit used what trails he could find, and made sure he was on course by periodically checking his compass. Twice the pack mule had decided to stop and almost jerked Kit off his horse. On flat ground Kit would have simply tied the lead rope off on his saddle horn, but with the rough terrain and constant changing of direction, that method could get him knocked off his horse.

He paused in a small clearing and took a drink of water from his canteen. When they first set up the sheep camps in the mountains, it had seemed easy as Carlson went from place to place like he was on a well marked street in town. Also, they had taken longer routes so they could get the wagons up the grades. Now Kit was going to the camps by the most direct route and that was not always the easiest route nor was it one that was simple to follow.

He pulled out his small topographical map and checked the compass. He had come up from the south fork of LaBarge Creek and this was the third and last of the sheep camps he had to supply this week. He put the map and the compass away and sat there listening. He could hear the wind in the pines, and he could smell the strong pine scent. Other than a couple of magpies, he had seen nothing else on the ride up. He untied the lead rope from the saddle horn and urged Dolly up a small draw in the same direction as his last compass heading.

Kit smelled the camp before he found it. He could smell smoke from the small stove in the sheep camp. Soon he was out of the timber and into a meadow where the sheep camp and commissary wagon were parked. He and the herder unloaded the supplies quickly and Kit departed with a new list from the young Mexican and a pack mule happy to have gotten rid of his load.

Kit decided to go more with the terrain on the trip back and periodically adjusted his route after checking his compass. Kit discovered what was obviously a game trail, and stayed on it for over an hour. He had just stopped to check his compass when he heard a gunshot somewhere below him. The shot seemed to echo in the trees. Kit eased Dolly forward, being careful not to let her move too quickly down the trail. He saw a small clearing below him on the trail and as he got closer Dolly began to act strangely. He had to pull hard on the reins to bring her under control as she seemed to suddenly want to go back where they had jut come from instead of moving forward toward the clearing.

Kit slipped off Dolly and tied her and the pack mule

securely to a small tree. He pulled the Winchester out of the scabbard and moved carefully down the trail. As he neared the clearing, he could hear what sounded like a wild animal noise and he was sure he could heard someone swearing.

As he carefully looked around a large pine tree at the edge of the clearing, Kit saw an amazing sight. In the middle of the clearing was a solitary Juniper tree. Up in the Juniper tree was a fairly short, stocky man who was bellowing out curse words in a very loud and deep voice. Below the tree was a good-sized black bear who was standing on her hind legs and trying to shake the tree with her front paws. A short distance from the bear were two small bear cubs who were watching their mother in action.

Kit checked his rifle and then stepped out from behind the tree, taking care that he was not between the bear and her cubs and holding his arms and the rifle over his head he began advancing toward the bear, shouting as loudly as he could. The bear stopped shaking the tree, dropped to all fours and turned to face Kit. Kit stopped and fired his rifle, careful to hit the ground right next to the bear.

The bear, obviously surprised at this new threat, ran back to her cubs and quickly exited the clearing, taking the cubs with her. Kit walked over to the tree as the short man began climbing down. He was perspiring freely when he reached the ground. Kit thought he looked familiar. He had a mustache, wore round wire rimmed glasses and looked amazingly like Teddy Roosevelt. Kit half expected him to say "Bully".

The man extended his hand. "Harrison Woodly at your service, sir. My friends call me Woody. And I might add, my most sincere appreciation at your timely appearance."

Kit introduced himself and asked, "What happened here?"

"Well sir, I was coming back from a small fly fishing expedition, and I came around a bend in the trail and ran into this sow and her cubs. My horse panicked and threw me. I landed in a bad place, between the sow and the cubs. The sow charged me and I drew my pocket pistol and shot at her and missed. That only made her madder. Then the gun jammed, and I ran for the nearest tree. The bear was trying to shake me like an apple from the tree when you showed up. Thank heavens."

Are you from around her, Mr. Woodly?" asked Kit.

"Of course, my boy. I was born in Kemmerer and have spent almost all of my life there. You said your name was Kit? Are you the new hand David Carlson hired?"

Yes, I am," replied Kit. "How did you know?"

"Well, I heard you were a tall lanky lad, and I know David has a sheep camp on his grazing rights north of here," replied Woodly. "I'm surprised I've not seen you in town or with David."

"You know Mr. Carlson?" asked Kit.

"My goodness sakes alive, I should say so. We grew up together. My father was a judge and David's father was a rancher. David and I went to the University of Wyoming together, and I stayed on for law school."

"Law school?" said Kit.

"Yes. I'm a lawyer and have been one most of my life. I have two passions in life, the law and fly fishing. Do you fly fish?"

"No, I've never done much fishing."

"Oh my, it's one of the great passions in life. A true gentlemen's sport. It is, in fact, an art form, not like all those stupid wormers."

"Wormers?"

"You know, all those idiots who put worms on a hook and think that is a sport. What dolts!"

"So what happened to your horse?"

"She was last seen fleeing back to the south fork of LaBarge Creek. The ungrateful wench."

After checking to see that the bear and her cubs had truly left, Kit led Mr. Woodly back to his horse and the pack mule. Kit adjusted the packsaddle and helped Mr. Woodly up on the mule's back. Then they headed back down the trail that Mr. Woodly's mare had taken in her flight from the bear. Along the way they found several pieces of Mr. Woodly's fishing gear that had fallen off the fleeing horse. When they reached the creek, they crossed it and there was Mr. Woodly's mare, standing next to his pickup truck and horse trailer. Soon they had the mare unsaddled and loaded into the trailer.

"Where's your transportation, Kit?" asked Woodly.

"According to my GPS I'm parked about two miles further down the creek," said Kit.

"Well, there's a small tavern in LaBarge called the Red

Dog. Meet me there, and I'll be happy to buy you a drink for saving my butt from that bear."

Kit agreed to meet Mr. Woodly and he headed down the creek, leading the pack mule.

Kit pulled his pickup to a stop in front of a small ramshackle building with a faded sign proclaiming it to be the Red Dog. Sure enough, next to the sign was a picture of a dog painted red.

Mr. Woodly was sanding by the front door with a cold mug of beer in his hand. He welcomed Kit and led him into the dim confines of the Red Dog Saloon. It was cool inside the bar and dark enough to hide the inevitable dirt and dust that one normally found in such an establishment. They found a table and chairs at the back of the bar. The bartender, an older lady with gray hair tied back in a pony tail, quickly appeared at their table with two more mugs of cold beer.

"Thank you, Dot!" exclaimed Mr. Woodly as he plunked down his now empty beer mug and hoisted the new one. He paused after taking a large swallow. "Dot, this here is young Mr. Kit, Big Dave's new hand."

Dot smiled and revealed a couple of missing teeth. "Glad to meetcha," said Dot. "You must be pretty tough to be working for Big Dave."

Kit acknowledged her with a grin and a nod of his head.

"Most folks around here think Big Dave Carlson is the second coming of John Wayne," said Mr. Woodly. "They aren't that far off the mark. He is the toughest man

I ever met. I was with him once when we were in a bar in Rock Springs. Some fella came in who owed David money and Big Dave went up to him at the bar and asked him when he was gonna pay up. The fella didn't care for David's question and the next thing I knew a fight had erupted, and within minutes it was like one of bar room brawls you see in the movies."

"You were in a bar room brawl with Mr. Carlson?" said Kit.

"Actually I spent most of the fight huddled under a table where it was reasonably safe. I had an excellent view of the proceedings and it was pretty obvious that David did not need any help, certainly not mine. David came over and pulled me from under the table, and we exited the bar through the back door, making sure to get out of the parking lot before the local police showed up."

"What happened to the fellow who started the fight with Big Dave?"

"Well, last I heard of him he was eating through a straw because of his busted jaw. I never did hear if he finally paid David what he owned him."

By now both men had grown accustomed to the dim light of the bar and could see things around them more clearly. Kit noticed that Mr. Woodly's clothes, although somewhat worn, looked like they were expensive. He also noticed that Mr. Woodly was looking at him rather intently with a somewhat surprised expression on his face.

"Mr. Woodly," began Kit.

"Just call me Woody, son. Everyone else around here

does," said Mr. Woodly before Kit could continue. "You know, son, you look very familiar to me. Are you sure we haven't met somewhere before today?"

"No sir," answered Kit. "I'm sure I would have remembered meeting you."

Woody roared with laughter at that remark. "Well, I have never been one to be considered a shrinking violet. I tend to make my presence known. Still, you definitely remind me of someone, but I cannot quite place it. Oh well, how about another beer?"

It was about an hour later before they parted, with Kit agreeing to accept Woody's invitation to stop by his office for lunch the next Friday.

It was suppertime when Kit returned to the ranch and unloaded Dolly and the mule. He fed them and was on his way to the bunkhouse when he was intercepted by Mrs. Carlson. "Why don't you come up to the house and join us for supper," she said. Kit wasn't foolish enough to pass up one of her fine home cooked meals and excused himself to get cleaned up.

At the supper table Kit filled in Dave on what had happened on his trip up to the LaBarge sheep camp. When he got the part about the bear he got an unexpected response from Big Dave. "You didn't shoot the bear?" he asked incredulously.

"No sir. I just scared her off so she could take her cubs and leave."

"Son, never pass up a chance to kill one of them damned sheep-killing bears," roared Big Dave.

Kit thought he was joking until he looked into those bright blue eyes and found them as cold as ice. He knew then Big Dave was not joking.

"Still it was a good thing you rescued old Woody. He's the only lawyer worth a crap in western Wyoming. Besides, it will be a long time before old Woody lives this down. Treed by a bear and saved by a tenderfoot. Ha, Ha, Ha."

"Tenderfoot?" said Kit.

"Well, son, actually you ain't no tenderfoot any more and maybe it's time we got you a proper rifle just in case you was to run into some more bears."

"What's wrong with the Winchester?" asked Kit.

"Oh, the Winchester is fine as a brush gun and for scaring off coyotes and wild dogs, but when you run into a cougar or a bear, it's about as useful as a jack handle."

"What do you mean, a jack handle?"

"Just this. Out here in the west, you need the right tool for each job. If you was up against a cougar, the Winchester is almost worthless. You could use it to stick in a jack and use it as a jack handle, but that's about it. Anything less than what you really need to get the job done right is about as useful as a jack handle."

Kit fell asleep in his bunk with Big Dave's words ringing in his ears. Tomorrow Big Dave promised to take him to town to get a "proper rifle."

Detective Landers slammed down the handset on his desk phone and cursed loudly. He followed that up by kicking his already battered old steel desk. All that got him was a sore big toe. He swore again and fell back into his well worn desk chair. After removing the offending shoe and while carefully rubbing his sore toes he considered the facts. Neither the FBI nor any of the law enforcement agencies along Interstate 80 had come up with anything on Carson Andrews or his old white Chevrolet Cavalier.

After gingerly putting his foot down on the floor, Landers pulled out his road atlas and opened it to the map of the state of Wyoming. His finger traced down the line that represented I-80 and saw nothing of substance. Based on what he saw, Wyoming had very few people. The cows probably outnumbered the people.

Landers looked for significant road junctions where Andrew might have gone south or north and he found none. Was he in Utah, Nevada, Arizona, or California? He knew that each passing day was a problem. The longer Andrews remained missing, the less likely he would be on the radar screen of most cops. Out of sight and out of mind.

His boss and his bosses boss and everyone on up to the Mayor of Chicago was not happy that the key eyewitness to a murder by a known Chicago gangster was still missing. The longer they had to wait to finally get to court meant the defense attorneys would have that much more time to build a case for their clients. That assumed there would be a trial. Without a witness, there might not be a trial.

Landers gently slipped his still aching toes back into his shoe. He had work to do. He had to find Andrews.

CHAPTER TWENTY

The next day found Kit and Carlson on a deserted portion of the ranch where a flat parcel of land led up to a sheer canyon wall. Big Dave placed half a dozen empty tin cans on various rocks on the face of the canyon wall.

He and Kit then took up a position about one hundred yards away. Big Dave produced a long rifle with a bolt action. He demonstrated how to shoot prone, sitting, kneeling, and then standing. After a thorough explanation of the rifle and how it operated, he had Kit take a prone position with the rifle and sight in one of the cans. He instructed Kit to take a deep breath and let half of it out, and then gently squeeze the trigger when he had the can in his sights. Big Dave had Kit dry fire the weapon, which meant there were no bullets in the rifle.

Finally he handed Kit a large bullet and told him to insert it in the chamber of the rifle. Kit did and then pushed the bolt forward until it stopped, and then he brought the bolt down against the right side of the rifle to lock it in place. Kit sighted in the tin can and released the safety. He took in a deep breath and let half of it out and then gently squeezed the trigger. Kit was surprised by the recoil and the noise the shot generated. This was a lot more weapon than his Winchester carbine. He looked up to see the tin can bouncing among the rocks. When he and Big Dave retrieved the can, it had a large hole through the middle of the top end of the can.

"Good shootin'," said Big Dave. "Let's see if you kin do that again." They practiced for about an hour with Kit shooting from all four positions.

"This here is a very good all-around rifle. It's a Remington rifle in 30-06 caliber. It's big enough for black bear and cougar and fast enough for a coyote. It's a bolt action and the magazine holds three rounds. Course, you don't need lots of rounds if you hit what you're aiming at. One round should be enough. One shot and one kill. You did pretty well with iron sights. We'll get you a good scope for this gun that'll make you even more accurate."

"What do I owe you for the rifle," asked Kit.

"This here was my son's rifle. It's been gathering dust for years, and Carol and I think it would be better off in your hands."

Kit thanked Big Dave profusely as he examined the rifle. They returned to the ranch where Big Dave brought the rifle and a cleaning kit to the bunkhouse and taught Kit how to clean and care for the weapon.

Four days later, Kit was coming down from bringing supplies to the sheep camp above the Hamm's Fork drainage. He had gotten a late start and the pack mule had decided to stage his own personal rodeo and had dumped many of the supplies from his pack. Kit got the mule settled down and then repacked everything. By the time he was headed back home, it was getting dark. There was a full moon and there was plenty of moonlight, but it still made the trip back a lot slower. Kit had stopped by a small stream to let Dolly and the mule drink when he heard a strange noise.

Kit knew sound traveled a lot farther in the mountains and especially at night. Still he could swear he could hear what sounded like several lawnmowers running at full throttle. The sound seemed to be coming from the west, and he rode at a westerly angle as he descended from the mountain. Periodically he stopped to listen and each time the noise seemed to be louder. He rode out of the trees to an open rocky area where he stopped and dismounted.

He could see that he had an arroyo to his right and as he stood to look down the slope to the west, he could see lights. Some of the lights were moving and one set had stopped. As he watched, all the lights came together and then they went out. The lawnmower like noise also stopped. Kit got out his GPS and got a reading on where he was and then did an estimate for the location of the lights. He then rechecked his position and where the truck was at the bottom of the slope.

It was too dark and dangerous to go wandering around when you could not see clearly. He decided to head back to the truck and to come back in the morning and check out the location where he had seen the lights. Kit remounted Dolly and used his compass and a small flashlight to find his way back to the main trail. Within half an hour he was back to his truck and had Dolly loaded in the back of the old pickup.

The next morning he told Big Dave he was going back to the Hamm's Fork drainage to check out something he thought he might have seen the night before. Big Dave told Kit to be back by noon so they could take a sick horse to the vet in Montpelier.

It took Kit about an hour and a half to drive to where he had parked his truck the night before. He got out of the pickup and took a reading with his GPS. After he determined his position, he spread a map over the hood of the pickup and marked where he had been last night when he saw the lights and where he was today.

He made an estimate of where he thought the lights were and took a compass heading from his current location. Soon he was slowly driving across the prairie at the base of the mountain, keeping one eye out for holes and arroyos and one eye on the compass. After about half an hour he came to a point where a stone outcropping from the mountain came down like a leg and sprawled into the valley, effectively blocking off the other side from Kit's sight.

He detoured around the rock line and came back to the other side from where he had started. There were small caves in the rock line and in the base of the mountain. Between the caves on the prairie were several large holes with piles of dirt next to them. It looked like giant prairie dogs had been at work. Kit walked over to the nearest hole and judged it to be about six feet in diameter and about two feet deep.

The hole was fresh and he saw recently dislodged plants in the dirt piles. The plants were sill alive. He found plenty of tracks around the holes. Most of them appeared to be boot tracks. Some were smooth and some looked like the soles of hiking boots with lugs. Kit slowly went from hole to hole trying to figure out why they were being dug. At the third hole he found his answer. Around the edge of the hole and in the bottom of the hole were shards of what appeared to be some kind of pottery.

He found shards at some of the other holes and took a handful back to the pickup. There he used water from his canteen to clean them off and was able to discern small markings on the shards. He walked back to the holes and past them to one of the small caves. Here he found more remnants of pottery and also what appeared to be arrowheads, spear heads, and pieces of animal bones that were crudely made to be used as knives or some kind of cutting tools.

Walking away from the caves and the holes and following the boot tracks in the dust, he came to where there had been several vehicles parked. He could see the tire tracks and in two cases, areas where oil had leaked from the vehicles' crankcases. He checked his watch and realized he would have to hurry to get back to the ranch by noon as he had promised Big Dave. Kit wrapped the shards and arrowheads in an old burlap bag which he placed in the bed of the old pickup and headed back to the ranch.

After lunch he showed Big Dave the shards and the arrowheads. "Where did you find these?" asked Big Dave?

Kit explained about seeing the lights the night before

and using the GPS to track the location. He showed Big Dave on his map where he had found the caves and the newly dug holes.

"Pot thieves," said Big Dave.

"Pot thieves?" responded Kit.

Big Dave explained that he was pretty sure the area Kit had shown him on the map was the site of an old Indian encampment. Big Dave related how he had once ridden through there and seen several examples of pottery and stone tools coming out of the ground. He had never gone in to any of the caves but was pretty sure that for many years Indians had used the site as a camp while they hunted and fished in the Hamm's Fork drainage.

"Someone has found the site and is illegally excavating it and is stealing the pottery and artifacts to sell to private collectors around the world. The ground is BLM and belongs to the government. Taking artifacts from any Federal land is a crime. They may have someone working the digs during the day time, and they come up at night to collect the artifacts and take them to some location where they clean and sort the stuff and then sell it."

"How can they sell illegal artifacts?" asked Kit.

"They sell them on the internet or they contact key brokers or individuals they know who've got a lot of cash. We'll stop by the sheriff's office on the way back from Montpelier and you can tell him what you found. Meantime we need to get this horse to the vet's."

They loaded up the horse in a horse trailer and headed for Montpelier. During the trip Big Dave told Kit about the Indians, mostly Arapahoe, Shoshone, Cheyenne, and Sioux who had previously lived in this part of Wyoming. He explained that the campsite Kit had found might be from Indians who predated any tribes that Big Dave knew about. He knew that some of the campsites found in Wyoming were hundreds of years old. "The older the campsite, the more valuable the artifacts are. Even though taking them is illegal, most of the sites are very isolated and their best protection is no one knows where they are except maybe the BLM."

The vet was at his office when they got to Montpelier and after examining the horse, he recommended they leave it with him for a week. Soon they were on the road back to Kemmerer and within an hour they were in the sheriff's office in the county courthouse in Kemmerer. Kemmerer was the county seat for Lincoln County.

The sheriff was not in, and they talked to a deputy about what Kit had seen and found. The deputy was a short, wiry man who looked like he was born to ride a horse. He wore cowboy boots, Levis, and a tan sheriff's department shirt with a badge. The deputy introduced himself as Sam Kent. He listed carefully to Kit's story and then had him locate the site on a huge map that covered most of one wall in the outer office. Sam told Kit he would make a report to the sheriff and drive out and check out the site. He thanked Kit for his help. As Big Dave and Kit exited the courthouse, Big Dave declared that all this talking had made his throat dry and they headed for his favorite bar The Stock Exchange.

Kemmerer was different than most small towns in that the downtown was built around a triangle, not a square. The only thing in the triangle was a tiny museum full of dusty artifacts including a two-headed calf. Situated around the triangle were various storefronts including the bank. Almost every other building was a bar and each had a particular place on the social pecking order of the town. The bar at the bottom of the list was the Star Bar. It consisted of most of the lowlifes in the town and the patrons had such little self-esteem that their softball team wore t-shirts proclaiming them to be "Star Bar Trash." Big Dave's destination, the Stock Exchange was one of the better bars on the triangle and its clientele were mostly stockmen and their help.

As they entered the bar, their eyes attempted to adjust to the gloom after being subjected to the bright sunlight just moments before. Big Dave immediately headed to a large table at the back of the bar that was occupied by two men. As they drew closer, Kit recognized one of the men as Woody, the attorney he had rescued from the black bear. The other man was a stranger. Big Dave and Kit were quickly greeted by Woody who then introduced Kit to the stranger. "Carson, may I introduce you to Chris Conner, a good friend of mine. Chris, this is Kit, the young man who rescued me from the clutches of a very angry black bear sow."

Conner shook hands with Kit, his handshake firm and strong. They all sat down and the bartender was instantly at the table taking their order. Kit noticed that Conner wore denim pants and shirt like the others, but they were clean and looked pressed. Conner wore his hair short and had a very military bearing about him. Instead of cowboy boots he wore boots that looked to Kit like what a paratrooper would wear. His black boots sparkled with a brilliant shine, even in the gloom of the bar. Conner's eyes were grey and they looked hard. Kit was pretty sure Conner was in excellent physical shape. His posture, even sitting at the table, was ramrod straight.

Soon Woody and Big Dave were regaling them with stories of high jinks they had survived in their youth in Kemmerer. Each story told received more laughter than the previous one. One thing that Kit had noticed was he heard Big Dave tell a couple of stories that he previously told Kit and that each detail was exactly the same as in the previous telling. Usually stories Kit heard repeated had changes in them. The bartender returned with fresh bottles of beer and Kit failed to notice that the first bottle of beer he had finished had disappeared from the table before the bartender arrived to retrieve the empties.

Kit tried to engage Conner in conversation, but Connor was very careful in his answers to Kit's questions and kept the verbal exchanges very short. Kit did learn that he was correct and Conner was ex-military. He was a retired Lt. Colonel in the Army and had moved to Kemmerer where he could hunt and fish to his heart's content. He was vague about where he lived and Kit could only conclude that he did not live in town, but probably in a more isolated location.

Before long the bar was filled up with locals and smoke, western music from the jukebox and colorful swearing filled the air. Finally Big Dave indicated to Kit that they needed to head home for supper. They shook hands with Woody and Conner and made their way toward the front door of the smoky and dimly lit bar. As they were walking past the pool table, one of the players stepped backwards from taking his shot and ended up right in front of Kit who could not stop in time and bumped into him.

"What the hell. Watch where your goin', you clumsy bastard," he shouted at Kit as he caught his balance.

"I'm sorry. It was an accident," said Kit.

"Accident is right, you stupid shit. You look like an accident lookin' for a place to happen," snarled the pool player.

Kit stopped and looked straight at the pool player. He was dressed in worn and dirty denim topped off with a dirty baseball cap. The man stood about six foot tall with a fairly husky build. It was obvious that he was fairly drunk.

"Like I said before, I'm sorry," said Kit.

The pool player looked like he was about to continue the argument when he noticed Big Dave standing behind Kit. He sort of swallowed hard and turned around and went back to the pool table without uttering another word.

When they were outdoors and back in Big Dave's pickup, Dave said, "Never pick a fight, especially with someone you don't know, but never back down from a fight or an argument. You did a good job of handling that drunk, but you need to understand that occasionally you're going to have to knock someone silly before they get the message. You showed him you weren't afraid or intimidated and that was good."

CHAPTER TWENTY-ONE

The next morning at breakfast, Big Dave asked Kit if he wanted to go back to the spot on the Hamm's Fork where he found the diggings. Kit was delighted with the idea and soon they were headed up the Hamm's Fork drainage, pulling two horses in their horse trailer. When they were about a mile from the site, Big Dave pulled the pickup and trailer over and parked them in a grove of pine trees. As they unloaded the horses, Big Dave explained that he thought it best to keep the pickup out of sight and not give anyone the idea that they were here to specifically look at the diggings.

They rode around the rock formation to the digging site. Nothing had changed since Kit's last visit. He showed Big Dave the holes, the shards of pottery and the small caves at the foot of the mountain. Big Dave carefully looked over three or four of the caves and came back to where Kit was standing. "This is not good," said Dave. His normally friendly face was grim.

"This appears to be an Indian burial ground, not

a campsite. These holes are graves as are the caves, and they've been looted," said Big Dave.

"Graves!" exclaimed Kit. "I don't see any bones. How can they be graves?"

"These graves are so old the bones have fossilized. The grave robbers take the entire fossil and detach the artifacts they want at a later time. Besides, any bones they were not careful with just became dust again."

"How old do you think they are?" asked Kit.

"I dunno" answered Big Dave, "but I would bet that they are several hundred years old, if not older. And if I'm right, that explains the looting."

After searching all of the remaining caves they could locate, Big Dave pulled out a small digital camera and took some pictures of the holes and the caves. Then they quickly mounted and headed back to the pickup. While they were loading the horses back into the horse trailer, Big Dave explained that he planned to talk to the BLM about the digging and felt the pictures would help him get their attention. As they drove away from the digging site, Kit felt a tingling sense of danger that he had not felt since the night he slipped down the fire escape from his apartment in Chicago. He did not enjoy the sensation.

That afternoon Kit drove into Kemmerer to cash his paycheck at the bank and run a few errands. He stopped at the grocery store to pick up some toiletry articles and found himself at the small magazine and bookrack at the back of the store. He found a couple of interesting looking novels and a locally published paperback *History of Lincoln County, Wyoming.*

Kit went to the nearest register to pay for his purchases and was surprised to see none other than Tang Kelly standing in line. She was wearing her standard grease monkey outfit with her hair carefully pulled in around her cap. "Hi there stranger," said Kit. Tang was startled and when she turned around, she had a surprised look on her face.

"Well hi there yourself, Kit" she said. "Doing a little shopping I see. How domestic!"

"For me, this is a lot of shopping, not a little," replied Kit. "I hate to shop."

"A typical male response," she smiled. "How's the truck running?"

"The truck is doing fine. I really like it and thanks again for coming up with the idea of a trade. By the way, how did you make out on my old Chevy, if you don't mind me asking?"

"You're welcome. I just about have the old Chevy all fixed up and plan on taking her down to Salt Lake City in a couple of weeks."

"You think it will sell better in Salt Lake City than around here?" Kit asked.

"Actually, it will probably sell to some Mexican migrant who works in the Salt Lake City area who will drive it to Mexico and it will never see the USA again. At least in one piece," replied Tang.

"You have time for a cup of coffee?" said Kit with a smile.

"Actually, I'm in kind of a hurry, but maybe next time," relied Tang. She quickly paid for her groceries and left without saying another word to Kit.

Kit felt the smile drain off his face. He was disappointed and a little surprised. She seemed fairly friendly, but not as friendly as he had expected her to be. She also seemed surprised to see him and not necessarily in a good way. Kit felt kind of awkward, and then realized hat he was reading an awful lot into something that was probably nothing.

By the time Kit had finished all his errands, it was dark out. Kit drove back to the ranch and loaded up Dolly, his 30-06 rifle, GPS, compass, a thermos of coffee, and a small flashlight. He drove to the same grove of pine trees where Big Dave had parked his truck before, and Kit was careful to hide his pickup in the grove. Then he rode Dolly about a half a mile up the mountain and moved horizontally to position himself above the diggings. He tied Dolly behind some sagebrush and small trees and carefully made his way down the slope, keeping himself behind as much cover as possible.

He found a good position behind a fallen tree on the edge of a small knoll and sat down to wait. He had a cup of coffee and watched as the clouds scudded across the sky, covering and then uncovering the moon and the galaxy of stars hat had taken up residence in the clear night sky.

After about an hour he could hear the sound of engines. Soon he could see lights coming from the west, just as he had before.

He pulled out his binoculars and waited for the cloud cover to free itself from the full moon. After about fifteen minutes he could see the outlines of four vehicles, all of which appeared to be pickup trucks. The trucks pulled into a flat area about thirty yards from the diggings. As Kit continued to watch them through his binoculars he saw something that made him gasp in surprise. In the bright moonlight he could clearly see that one of the vehicles was a bright yellow Jeep Wrangler.

Kit was tempted to get closer, but it would only expose him to possible discovery, and he really did not know what the grave-robbers might do if they discovered him. As he watched heir flashlights move around the old holes towards the caves, he began to hatch an idea of how he might scare them off without risking injury to himself or to any of them. He used his vantage point to make some distance estimates of how far he was from the holes and caves and the parked vehicles. He smiled to himself as he began to make his way back up the slope to where he had tied off Dolly.

The next day Kit found time to stop into Chappy's Sporting Goods Store in Kemmerer. Chappy's was located in an old frame building surrounded by about twenty mobile home spaces on the edge of town. Chappy was a colorful old coot who had actually represented the USA in the Olympics in Japan as a hammer thrower. He had played football at the University of Wyoming and managed to play golf about 200 days a year in a town where it was winter for about eight months a year.

Although he was only about five foot ten inches tall, Chappy still had the broad shoulders and stocky build of an athlete. He also had a booming voice and an amazing ability to know just about everything that went on in Kemmerer, legal and illegal.

"Well now, don't tell me I'm finally gonna meet the mysterious tenderfoot from the east who got dumped in Kemmerer by some spring snowstorm," he thundered.

Kit grinned sheepishly and shook hands with Chappy. "Son I'm glad to see you've got a firm grip. Nothing I hate worse than a flabby handshake. So, what can I do for you today?"

Kit pulled out a list and after asking some questions he made several selections making good use of Chalppy's advice. When he explained to Chappy the purpose of his selections, Chappy roared with laughter and gave Kit a discount on them. "Anyone with this good of an imagination deserves a break on the price. You be sure to let me know how this works out, young fella," he admonished.

Kit promised Chappy a report and took his purchases out to his pickup and drove back to the ranch. He assembled all his new gear and packed it into an old duffel bag and put the bag in the bed of his truck. After stocking up with supplies for the sheep camp on the Hamm's Fork drainage, Kit loaded up Dolly and the mule in the horse trailer and headed for the Hamm's Fork trailhead.

By the time he was finished unpacking the supplies for the herder, it was mid-afternoon. Kit broke out his purchases from Chappy and practiced in the open meadow next to the sheep camp, to the amazement and amusement of the herder.

By late afternoon he headed down the mountain, moving much faster than he had when he originally made this trip because now he knew the trail and was much better at riding and leading the mule. It was dusk when he rode into the trailhead. He loaded up the mule and ate a lunch he had packed and drank semi-warm coffee from his thermos. Normally he would have made a fire and warmed up the coffee, but tonight he didn't dare risk the smoke or the smell of a fire.

Kit had pulled the duffel bag off the mule and slung it over his saddle horn. After mounting Dolly, he rode her up the mountain to the grove of trees where he had tied her off on the previous visit. He carefully made his way down to his vantage point behind the fallen tree. He laid out his new gear and checked them for tightness. He drank some water from a water bottle attached to his hip and he waited.

He was about to give up after fighting off the growing cold and his own drowsiness when he heard a high revving engine in the distance. In the mountains and even on the high plains, sound seemed to carry further and more clearly.

Soon Kit could see the lights of what appeared to be three vehicles making their way slowly toward the Indian burial ground. He checked his watch. It was almost ten o'clock. There was quite a bit of cloud cover so the moonlight had trouble penetrating the clouds, making it a much darker night. Darker was better for what Kit had in mind.

He had estimated the distance from his hiding place to the caves and to the vehicles and was sure they were well within his range. He waited almost half an hour until the vehicles were parked and he could hear the voices of the group as they made their way to the caves.

Satisfied that they were close enough, he notched a fire arrow to the long bow he had brought with him. Using a small lighter he ignited the fire package near the tip of the arrow and let it fly. The first arrow hit about fifteen yards in front of the group of diggers. Kit had notched and lit a second arrow before he heard their yells. Very quickly he had launched six fire arrows in front of the caves.

In the dim light he could see the men turning and running back to their vehicles. One of them tripped and fell in the dark, screaming as he did so, and that just seemed to add to the confusion and fear that the arrows had created.

Now Kit took aim and began to drop fire arrows amongst the vehicles, actually hitting the hood of one. He saw the arrow strike and bounce off the vehicle, sending sparks flying off the arrow as it did so. In five minutes it was over and all Kit could see was the taillights of the three vehicles as they bounced up and down as they drove too fast for the terrain. Soon clouds of dust obscured even the retreating taillights.

Satisfied they were gone, Kit returned to the tree grove

and rode Dolly down to the burial ground. A couple of small fires had started in the dry buffalo grass and Kit put them out with handfuls of dirt and water from his bottle. Finally he urinated on the last embers.

Kit found and retrieved all his arrows, mounted Dolly and returned to his old pickup. After loading Dolly, Kit headed back to the ranch. He drove slowly for the first couple of miles with no lights on and kept the truck in first gear. Finally satisfied he was truly alone he flipped on the lights and shifted gears as he sped toward home.

It was late in the afternoon when Kit stopped in town and walked into the Stock Exchange Bar. He was immediately greeted by Woody, who insisted on buying him a beer and bringing him up to date on all the excitement.

"If I live to be a hundred, I don't think I'll hear of anything funnier," he exclaimed. "Somebody reported a wildfire to the BLM people last night up by the end of the Hamm's Fork drainage. When they got out there they found a couple of small burned areas and an old Indian burial ground that someone had discovered and was looting. Around the burned areas they found small holes in the ground that looked like sticks had been plunged into the dirt. Either the Indians had spooks visit them or we had some of them space invaders. Ha, ha, ha. Poor government boys don't know what to think."

Kit laughed along with Woody and enjoyed his beer. He was not sure how well his trick had worked, but he had a feeling it scared the crap out of the grave robbers and after all, they were in a graveyard a night. Aliens from space was an angle he hadn't thought about. Leave it to Woody to make it more interesting.

CHAPTER TWENTY-TWO

Kit kept up his work of re-supplying the sheep camps and each time he came down by the Hamm's Fork drainage trailhead, he checked the burial ground. There was no new sign of any digging, and once he was pretty sure he saw a BLM truck partially hidden in some rocks about a mile south of the burial ground.

About a week later, Big Dave asked Kit to ride with him on a trip to Salt Lake for some supplies. They drove down the flat to Interstate 80 and stayed on it all the way into Salt Lake City. They stopped at a number of stores that catered to the ranchers in Utah and western Wyoming and picked up supplies. They had lunch in a Mexican restaurant where the food was excellent. Kit mentioned to Big Dave that while the place looked like a junior high school cafeteria, the food was the best he had ever eaten. Big Dave smiled and pointed to the kitchen at the back of the room. "You go in there and yell Green Card and over half this place and all of the help will be headed for an exit."

Kit frowned at that, and Big Dave went on to explain

that most of the customers and probably all of the help were illegal aliens from Mexico. A more careful examination of their fellow diners confirmed what Big Dave had said. Kit wanted to know how they got away with that. Big Dave explained that unless someone files a complaint no one was going to bother the illegal immigrants. Sometimes a government agent would get all self-righteous and clean out the help. Two days later the restaurant would have new help from the same source and be back in business.

The two made one final stop at a wool brokerage. Big Dave wanted to pick up a few of the large burlap sacks Kit had seen used for packing wool. It was dark when they left the wool broker's parking lot and they began heading back toward Interstate 80, their route back to Wyoming. Traffic was fairly heavy and they moved slowly from stoplight to stoplight. Suddenly Kit noticed that Big Dave was very agitated and cursing under his breath.

"What's wrong?" asked Kit.

"Sumbitch in the car behind us has his brights on. I've blinked my lights and so have several cars coming toward us in the other lane." After passing through two more stoplights, Big Dave stopped at a red light, reached under the seat for a large wrench, then opened his door and got out heading back toward the car stopped behind them. Upon seeing the huge cowboy heading toward him with a big wrench in his hand, the driver, a mousy young man with a hippie type of hairdo, began to frantically roll up his window.

Instead Big Dave headed for the front of the car and

in two quick swings, he smashed out both headlights. Big Dave returned to the pickup, put the wrench behind the seat, and drove forward as the light turned to green. "That'll slow that dumb bastard down," said Big Dave. Kit wisely remained silent until they reached the interstate and were well on their way home. Kit now had a good idea of what a truly angry Big Dave was capable of and why he had such a fearsome reputation in Wyoming.

Kit had been dreading getting a notice in the mail from the State of Wyoming, but it had arrived in the mail and now he needed to talk to Big Dave. Kit had managed to get temporary tags for his pickup when he bought it from Tang, but now he needed to record the registration and get real license plates. The State of Wyoming took this very seriously as they collected personal property tax on every vehicle when they sold them license plates. In Wyoming this was done in each county and each county issued license plates with a designation that identified them with the county they belonged to. Kemmerer was in Lincoln County and was identified on the license plates by the number 12.

Kit walked over to the ranch gas tank where Big Dave was filling up his pickup and asked if he could talk to him for a moment. Kit explained that he needed to file the registration for his pickup and that he had a personal and a legal problem in doing so. He wanted Big Dave's advice. Big Dave's expression became stern and he asked Kit for an explanation of his personal and legal problem.

Kit explained that he was not using his legal last name.

Big Dave kind of grinned and said, "Son, there is a lot of fellers in this county who ain't using their real name. What's the problem?" Kit explained that the registration required his social security number and if he used a fake one to go along with his fake name, he was sure the computer would recognize a fake and bounce it out.

Big Dave thought for a minute and then he said, "Kit, I could register the pickup in my name, but while I ain't fond of the government, I don't lie on my taxes or anything else. As screwed up as our state government is, your name is more likely than not to get lost or get misspelled by some damn clerk. I wouldn't worry about it. I'd use my real name to register the pickup. Kit thought about it and decided Big Dave was probably right. Then Big Dave said, "Just what is your name, son?"

"I'd rather not say Mr. Carlson. Knowing who I really am could get you in trouble, and the last thing I want is to get you and your family in any trouble."

"What kind of trouble? Are you in trouble with the law?"

"No sir, not the law. I got some people mad at me and it would be best for everyone, especially me, if I just kind of disappeared for a while. Which is what I've been doing since I came to work for you."

Carlson brushed some imaginary dust away from his pants and then looked up at Kit. "Kit you've done a good job for me and I want to keep you on as a foreman. You've learned a great deal in a very short time and me and my wife are fond of you. I won't intrude on your secrets, but understand this. I trust you and I don't want you telling me no lies. Do you understand?"

Kit gulped and said, "Does this mean I have to tell you who I really am?"

"No, son, to me you're Kit Smith and that's fine. However, anything else you tell me had better be the truth and nothing else."

"I promise, Mr. Carson. I won't tell you any lies," replied Kit.

Kit went back to his pickup and began loading Dolly and the mule into the horse trailer. He had worried that he had to tell Big Dave about using a phony name. He was a little ashamed about explaining his deception, but it seemed like Big Dave was not surprised at all. Kit wondered if Big Dave had known all along that Smith was not his name. It was a pretty stupid choice, but Kit had not thought about needing some kind of cover story and Smith had been the first name that had popped into his head when he had been rescued by Big Dave.

He wanted to tell Big Dave about the murder he had witnessed and the death of his two best friends. He wanted to tell him why he had fled to Wyoming, but he knew that telling Big Dave might only get him in trouble as well. It was hard to explain why you had both the cops and the killers looking for you at the same time. He had not thought about Detective Landers or the Sabatini brothers in quite a while. He had managed to lose himself in his new surroundings and the hard physical work that went with it. He was proud of what he had learned and how capable he was at his job. Kit had a sense of confidence and physical well being that he had never experienced before. He was pretty sure he could remain in hiding in Wyoming for several years. He was also sure that eventually he would be old news and of little interest to either the Sabatini brothers or the Chicago Police Department.

CHAPTER TWENY-THREE

Several hours later Kit reined in Dolly on a bald knoll about three-fourths of the way up the mountain to the LaBarge sheep camp. He turned Dolly back facing the way they had come and reached down for his canteen. Kit took a long swig of water and sat quietly in the saddle looking down the mountain to the small valley where he had left his truck and horse trailer. He could see for miles, but the truck and trailer were hidden from his view.

As he watched, he saw a golden eagle soar just off the knoll he was resting on. The eagle had caught an updraft and was soaring higher and higher, climbing in tight circles until finally Kit lost sight of it. He took another swig of water and sat quietly, just listening. He could hear the wind in the trees and also the songs of several birds, but nothing else. In his mind he thought that this must have been what it looked like two hundred years ago when the only white men around here were trappers.

Thousands of immigrants had come through here on their way to Oregon and there was hardly a thing to mark their passing.

Kit replaced the canteen, turned Dolly back up the mountain, and they headed for the sheep camp. Once again, Kit could smell the camp before he could actually see it. He smelled the smoke of the campfire, and thought he could actually smell the sheep as well. He found Odie Loan making burritos for lunch. Kit unloaded the supplies from the mule and set them on the ground by the sheep camp. Then he hobbled Dolly and the mule and tied a burlap bag containing some oats over each of their mouths.

Soon he and Odie were wolfing down the tasty burritos that consisted mostly of beans , onions, and spices. They cleaned up the cooking pots and moved the supplies into the sheep camp and the commissary wagon. Kit had taken off the burlap feeder bags and was letting the horse and mule graze when he heard the dogs barking frantically and some kind of roar that could not be good. Kit grabbed his rifle from the scabbard and ran to catch up with Odie who was heading for the herd about 75 yards away in a small meadow.

As Kit rounded a small thicket of aspen trees, he caught up with Odie and both of them immediately came to a stop. There in front of them, about forty yards away, was a large black bear, standing on its hind legs, roaring at the two sheep dogs that were barking and making short vicious rushes at the bear. Kit could see at least three or four dead sheep behind the bear and one of the sheep dogs lay motionless about ten yards in front of the bear.

Kit could see that Odie was scared and almost frozen in fear. Odie had stopped, but seemed physically incapable of raising his arms and aiming his rifle. Kit stepped to his right and stood next to a tall Aspen tree. He pulled back the bolt and chambered a round. Then he used the tree trunk to steady his aim with his rifle and sighted in on the bear. He remembered that Big Dave had told him how hard the skull of a bear was and he aimed for the base of the bear's throat.

He flicked off the safety and took in a deep breath and let half of it out and then slowly squeezed the trigger. The recoil from the high-powered rifle took his sight off the bear and he had to re-sight the rifle to see what had happened. The bear had what looked like a surprised expression on his face and let out what sounded almost like a scream. Still standing upright, he began to wobble and then dropped down to all fours. As soon as he hit the ground, Kit fired again, this time aiming to a spot just behind the bear's front shoulder. The bear started to run and took about a dozen steps before he toppled over.

Kit and Odie, who had quickly become unfrozen when he saw the bear drop over, ran toward the bear, who was now surrounded by the remaining two sheep dogs who were barking ferociously. Odie went to pull one of the dogs back and Kit stopped him. "Don't get too close. He might not be dead. Point the end of your rifle barrel close to his eye. If he doesn't blink, he's dead."

Odie complied and sure enough the bear was dead. Odie was rapidly jabbering away in Spanish that Kit could not possibly understand, and Kit felt a sudden need to empty his bladder.

After checking around the meadow, they determined that the bear had killed three sheep and injured two more. One sheep dog was so badly hurt that Odie had to use his rifle to put the dog out of her misery. It also appeared as if at least two dozen or more sheep were missing, and Kit assumed they had run off when the bear had attacked. After doctoring the two injured ewes, Kit set off with Dolly to look for the missing sheep while Odie happily began to butcher the bear.

Odie's Spanish had slowed down sufficiently for Kit to understand that Odie wanted to butcher the bear for the meat and to skin the hide and then tan and preserve the bearskin. Kit told Odie that was fine with him and headed to the other side of the meadow and began looking for signs of the missing sheep.

Just past the edge of the meadow Kit found the signs he was looking for. The sheep were obviously in a panic and running hard and as a result their hooves had dug into the soil and made a clear trail as to their passing. Kit turned Dolly's head toward the sheep's trail and urged her on. He moved slowly, being careful not to lose sight of the trail. He also did not want to suddenly come up on the sheep and scare them into running off in all directions again.

After a little more than an hour, Kit came out of a stand of timber into a small meadow and saw sheep grazing about one hundred yards off. He pulled Dolly to a stop and got out his binoculars. After scanning the meadow carefully, he could make out what he thought were about fifteen head of sheep. He dismounted and began walking across the meadow, leading Dolly. As he got closer the sheep gave him some nervous looks, but continued grazing.

Kit slowly moved to the right flank of the small herd and once he had made his way to the other side of the sheep, he mounted Dolly and began to slowly move the herd back the way he had come. He counted the sheep and came up with sixteen head. As he was sure that at least twenty head had run off, he stopped Dolly and pulled his GPS out of his saddlebag and waited until the tiny system got the satellites locked in. Then he took a position report on his current location and saved it into the GPS. He knew he needed to take the sheep he had found back to the sheep camp, but he needed to know where to start looking for the remaining sheep when he came back.

Satisfied, Kit began herding the sheep back on his previous trail. After about half an hour, he saw Odie Lone riding toward him. Odie rode up and explained in Spanish and a little broken English that he had finished dressing out the bear and had built a night corral for the sheep. He had then left the dogs to watch the sheep and come looking to help Kit. Kit turned his small band of escapees over to Odie and headed back to the meadow where he had found them.

It took Kit about fifteen minutes searching the far side

of the meadow to find the tracks of the remaining sheep. Once again he moved slowly to keep sight of the smaller trail and to make sure he did not surprise the sheep and spook them into running off again. The sun was moving lower in the sky as the afternoon light began to fade. Kit knew he might have to make camp and spend the night thanks to his stupid livestock.

The trail was moving down the mountain. The trees began to thin and Kit could see more open country, much of it rocky. Finally he found himself at the edge of a small stream. He pulled out his GPS and his topographical map and pinpointed his location. He was on the edge of the south fork of LaBarge Creek. According to the map he had come about ten miles from the sheep camp. Kit dismounted and let Dolly drink her fill from the creek. He pulled out a piece of beef jerky from his saddlebag and drank from his canteen as he chewed on the dried meat.

Dolly's head came up from drinking at the creek as though she had heard or smelled something. Kit stopped eating and tried to listen. He heard the wind in the trees overhead and the sound of the water in the stream running over the smooth rocks in the stream bed, but nothing else. Then he heard it. A buzzing sound like a small motor makes. It sounded like several of them, and they were getting closer. Pretty soon he could see the source of the noise slowly making their way toward him, driving on the side of the creek, coming from downstream.

There were four of them. Four bright red ATV's, each with a driver wearing a red helmet. Kit pulled Dolly over to a small tree and tied her off while he waited for the small caravan to make it to his location. As soon as they reached Kit's position, all four drivers pulled off the trail and turned off their engines. As they dismounted, each driver pulled off their helmets. Kit could see that three of the drivers were men, and one was a woman with short blonde hair.

The first driver to reach Kit was a short, stocky balding man with thick glasses and a friendly smile. He introduced himself as Seth Chambers, a geologist with the Star Oil Company as he shook hands with Kit. Then Seth introduced his companions. Slim Wilkins was a tall, thin scholarly looking fellow with long dark hair. Blair Masters was a tall, black haired man with the kind of good looks you only see in magazines. Kit instinctively did not like Blair. Finally, Sheila Register, a tall slim blonde with bright blue eyes. Sheila was, even in her current hot and sweaty condition, one of the best looking women Kit had ever seen.

Seth inquired as to what Kit was doing by the creek and Kit explained the search for the missing sheep. Seth said he had seen at least two head of sheep at the mouth of a small box canyon about three miles back.

"I thought I smelled something bad," said Blair, "it was the stink of sheep." Kit now knew why he had instantly disliked Blair. He purposely ignored Blair's insult and asked Seth what he and his team were doing driving up the south fork of LaBarge Creek.

Seth explained that they were conducting a geological

survey for their company and were having a tough time finding their targeted locations.

"Well, Mr. Chambers," said Kit, "I think you're pretty seriously off track."

"What the hell do you mean by that?" snarled Blair.

Kit ignored Blair and kept his attention to Seth. "This is part of the Bridger Wilderness. Geological surveys are allowed, but only with written permission from the BLM and no motorized vehicles can be used in the wilderness.

Seth looked confused and again Blair challenged Kit. "How the hell would some two bit sheep tramp like you even know where we are!"

Kit turned and looked Blair straight in the eye. Although Blair was tall, Kit was a good two inches taller and broader at the shoulders. "According to my GPS and topographical map you're at lest five miles into the Bridger Wilderness."

Before Blair could make a retort, Seth intervened and asked if Kit would show him the GPS reading and the map. Kit pulled both from his saddlebag and after the GPS had logged on with the satellites, he showed Seth were they were.

"Oh, crap," said Seth. "We should have turned north when we got to that little box canyon about thee miles east." Seth ushered Blair back to his ATV to check on their maps, leaving Kit standing by himself.

"Don't mind Blair," said Sheila softly. She had somehow quietly materialized next to Kit. She was even more striking close up than she had been when Kit first saw her.

"I don't think Blair likes me much," muttered Kit.

Sheila laughed and smiled and said, "Blair is a legend in his own mind. He doesn't like competition. Especially tall, good looking competition."

Kit felt confused. "What?" was all he managed to stammer out of his mouth.

"Come on, cowboy. That can't be the first time a woman has told you that you were good looking," she said with a smile.

Kit managed to recapture his sense of humor and responded by saying, "Lady, I think you have been out in the sun a little too long and your judgment has been impaired."

Sheila laughed and said "Maybe, but I think not. We're staying at the Antler Motel in Kemmerer. I'm Sheila Register. Give me a call when you have some free time."

Before Kit could respond, Seth had yelled for everyone to head out the way they had come, and Sheila was quickly mounting her ATV and firing up the engine. They turned their machines around and were out of sight within seconds, with only the buzzing of the engines giving testimony to their presence.

Kit mounted Dolly and began to follow their trail downstream. If Seth was right, the sheep might be in the small box canyon where Seth had seen them. Kit kept Dolly at a solid walk, but soon he could no longer hear the buzz of the ATV motors. Their trail was a different matter. It was easy to see where their tires chewed up the soil along the riverbank. As Kit rode further downstream, the country became more open with less trees and more sagebrush and rock. The creek had created small canyons with the canyon walls soaring up on both sides of the stream. Sometimes the trail beside the creek was narrow and sometimes it broadened out for several hundred yards.

Finally Kit saw what appeared to be a cleft in the canyon wall to his left. As he got closer, he saw one of his missing sheep grazing by the edge of the small opening. When Kit was about fifty yards away, he could see that there were not one but three sheep grazing by the cleft in the canyon wall. The narrow opening in the rocks was not easily noticeable. Only when Kit was exactly opposite the cleft could he see that it was actually an almost hidden entrance to a small box canyon. As he approached the grazing sheep, they took notice and ran into the canyon. "Crap," said Kit as he spurred Dolly forward. He knew he should have been more careful in approaching the sheep, who were probably still pretty spooked by their encounter with the bear.

As soon as Dolly trotted though the narrow entrance to the canyon, Kit reined her in to a stop. The canyon was small, maybe two hundred yards deep and sixty yards wide. The canyon floor was fairly flat and covered with sagebrush and rocks. There were no trees. The late afternoon sun had sunk below the canyon walls and the canyon floor was covered in shadows.

As Kit scanned the canyon, it dawned on him that

there was no sign of the three sheep he had seen run into the canyon only minutes before. Sheep did not just vanish. He could not see any kind of other entrance to the canyon and he was pretty sure the three of them did not fly out. The canyon walls appeared to be too steep and too high for the sheep to climb out, so they had to be in the canyon somewhere. Kit carefully rode around the perimeter of the canyon, looking for another entrance, a cave, or even a depression the sheep could be hiding in. Pretty soon he was close to the entrance where he had started his search. He could see nothing that could conceal three full sized ewes.

Then he noticed something that was different. About forty yards from the entrance, up against the canyon wall was a large sagebrush. As he looked around the canyon, nowhere else was there such a large brush up against the canyon wall. Kit rode up close to the sagebrush and tied Dolly off. He walked up to the sagebrush and looked down in the dirt around the bush. Sure enough, there were several footprints from his sheep. The bush was taller than Kit and thick enough he could not see through it. As he moved to the right of the bush, he could see a space of about two feet between the back of the bush and the wall of the canyon.

Kit carefully made his way behind the bush and used his hand against the canyon wall to steady himself. Suddenly as he went to place his hand on the wall to take another step, there was no wall and Kit fell off balance and landed awkwardly, banging his shoulder against the wall which had reappeared about three feet from where it had been.

The next thing he knew, Kit was being trampled over by three sheep who were desperately trying to get back into the canyon. Kit pulled himself to his feet, dusted himself off, and saw the source of the magical disappearance of his sheep. An eight foot high rock wall came out from the canyon wall and ran almost parallel for about fifteen feet. Behind the rock wall was the entrance to a cave. The entrance was about five feet high and almost six feet wide. Kit stepped up to the entrance and felt cold air. He also felt the hair on the back of his neck stand up. He was pretty sure that was not a good sign.

Kit walked back to where he had tied Dolly. He could see the three sheep grazing about twenty yards away. He saw nothing else in the canyon. He took a small flashlight from his saddlebags and took his rifle out of the scabbard. Kit was not sure what might be in the cave, but he wanted to see for himself, and he wanted to be prepared if he found the cave occupied by something unfriendly. He was pretty sure the cave was safe or the sheep wouldn't have run in there. Still you can't be too careful, he thought.

Kit switched on the flashlight, chambered a round in the rifle, and stooped down to enter the cave. He immediately hit his head on the low rock outcropping and knocked his cowboy hat to the ground. Kit cursed his fate as a tall person in a short cave. He retrieved his had and carefully entered the cave in a low crouch. He stopped just inside the entrance and slowly shone his light around the cave. The cave was only about five feet high and about six feet wide. Water dripped down the side of one wall and there was a small pool of water in a depression where it met the rocky cave floor. The cave continued further back into the canyon wall.

Kit slowly made his way toward the back of the cave. He felt the floor seem to rise as he made his way along one wall. He used the flashlight to illuminate the walls, but he saw nothing. As Kit went to take another step his boot hit something light that moved with the impact. He lowered the beam of his flashlight and almost fell backwards in shock and surprise. His feet had come in contact with what appeared to be a human skull. After regaining his composure, Kit dropped to his knees and used his flashlight to determine what he had found.

After a careful inventory, Kit found most of a human skeleton, some remnants of what appeared to be a belt or a gun belt, corroded ammunition, and the rotten remains of a saddle and saddlebags. He also found a slightly rusted revolver and a rifle. The rifle appeared to be in better shape than the revolver. The receiver of the rifle seemed to be a brighter color than the rest of the metal. Kit decided to move the items out of the cave into the sunlight. Trying to move the items turned out to be not such a good idea. As he went to pick up the saddle, it almost came apart in his hands. He quickly set it back down.

He carefully made his way back out of the cave and over to where he had Dolly tied off. Kit removed his bedroll ground sheet and took it back into the cave. There he spread the ground sheet out on the floor of the cave and gently slid everything he could fit onto the ground cloth. The saddlebags were surprisingly heavy and were more difficult to move than the saddle, itself. Kit carefully took one end of the ground cloth and pulled on it, using the ground cloth like a sled. Soon he had the entire collection pulled out of the cave into the open canyon and the fading sunlight.

It was almost dusk and Kit realized he would need to camp in the canyon for the night. He unsaddled and hobbled Dolly and set up his bedroll, saddle, and gear next to the cave entrance. Kit made a fire pit and lit a small fire. Soon he was stretched out on his bedroll next to the fire chewing on a supper of jerky and water. He lay back on his bedroll using the saddle for a pillow and looked up into the night sky. It was a clear night and Kit could see the sky was filled with thousands of stars. In the distance he heard the howl of one and then several coyotes. Making sure his rifle was within close reach, Kit pulled his bedroll around him and rolled over with his back to the fire.

The next morning was crisp and cold. Kit shook some frost off his bedroll and rolled up his gear. He made sure Dolly was fine and pulled on his boots. Kit squatted down on the sandy floor of the box canyon to look over his discoveries from the cave. The pistol was an old Army Colt 44. The rifle was an actual Henry carbine. The saddle was falling apart. There was an old canteen and what appeared to be a coil of rotten rope.

When he opened the saddlebags, the covers almost

came apart in his hands. Almost nothing was recognizable in the bags except for an old tin cup, a rusty knife, and twenty shiny fifty-dollar gold coins. The coins looked like they were brand new. The gold coins caught the morning sunlight and reflected it back in Kit's eyes. He held one of the coins up closely, and he could see that the coin had no wear as though it was fresh from a mint.

Kit remembered the story that Tang had told him about Butch Cassidy and the Wild Bunch and how they'd robbed a bank over in Montpelier and then escaped back through this part of Wyoming. As he remembered the story, one of the gang had been badly wounded or hurt and had been left behind. Kit also remembered that the loot was newly minted gold coins some of which had never turned up. Kit speculated that this skeleton was the gang member who was wounded. He must have found the cave and used it to hide and heal up. Instead he'd died from his wounds. The gang must have split up the money right after the robbery and the dead man still had his share on him when he died.

Kit dragged the ground cloth back inside the cave and wrapped it around the dead man's possessions. Then he broke off some sagebrush and used it to brush away all the tracks around the entrance of the cave. When he was finished, he took a GPS reading on the cave's location. Then Kit mounted up on Dolly, rounded up the three wayward sheep, who were still grazing in the canyon, and began herding them back up the mountain to the sheep camp.

About the time Kit was halfway back to the sheep

camp, a middle aged widow named Sarah Wilson was writing out a check to Karl's Kleen Kars in Salt Lake City. She had given up on her old Volkswagen Bug. The old Bug had died something of a natural engine death in the alley behind her apartment. She had been looking for a new car for two days and she was tired of the process. She had decided the Chevrolet Cavalier was worn, but had been well cared for and was easy for her to drive. The automatic transmission was easier on her joints than the standard transmission of the old Volkswagen Bug. She didn't believe a word that "Karl" had said about the car, but after test driving it and having her nephew look at it, she knew it was what she needed and could afford. Late that afternoon, "Karl", who was delighted with the price he got for the Chevy, sent the properly signed Illinois automobile title along with the proper paperwork to the Secretary of State for the State of Utah.

Because of this piece of mail, two things would happen, one good and one bad. The good thing was that Sarah Wilson would get a new Utah vehicle title in her name for the Chevrolet. The bad thing was that the record of the transfer of the title from Carson Andrews to Sarah Wilson would now be on the computer of the State of Utah.

It took Kit until midday to get the three pesky ewes back to the sheep camp. Kit ate a hot lunch of fresh bear meat stew with Odie Loan and then he, Dolly, and the mule headed back down the mountain to where his truck and horse trailer waited for them. He pushed the pace as he was in a hurry. Fortunately Dolly and the mule seemed to sense his need to move more quickly and they responded. It was late afternoon when Kit arrived back at the ranch and unloaded Dolly and the mule and fed and watered them.

Big Dave came out of the ranch house and walked over to the corral while Kit was putting oats in the feed trough. He had been concerned when Kit was not back at the ranch last night and had been prepared to ride up to the camp first thing that morning, but his wife had convinced him that Kit could take care of himself. In any case he was glad to see Kit back in one piece.

Kit led Big Dave into the bunkhouse and set a pot of coffee on the small cook stove. Armed with a fresh cup of hot coffee, he related his experiences of the past two days, carefully omitting his encounter with the lovely Sheila Register.

Big Dave was alternately furious about the bear attack and overjoyed with the killing of the bear and the recovery of the sheep. He looked a little puzzled when Kit explained his encounter with the geological survey team. "Them damn fools have no business in the Bridge Wilderness," he exclaimed. "They must be making them even stupider if all they can do is get lost."

Kit smiled and then carefully told Big Dave every detail he could remember of his tracking down the sheep into the small box canyon and his discovery of the cave and its grisly, but historic, contents. When Kit had finished with his story, including his tying it in with the story he'd heard from Tang about Butch Cassidy and the

Montpelier bank robbery, Big Dave sat there speechless, his mouth hanging open.

Big Dave quickly recovered and he had Kit get out his topographical map and his GPS reading and determined exactly where the cave was located on the map. They decided that since the cave was on BLM land in the Bridger Wilderness, they would return to the cave the next morning and bring along Ted Newton, the BLM manager for the Bridger Wilderness.

When Newton heard about what Kit had discovered, he added three more people from the BLM to the group, including an anthropologist from the University of Wyoming who happened to be working in Kemmerer. By noon they had finished measuring and photographing the interior of the cave and all of the artifacts Kit had found. The skeleton was carefully photographed, measured and packed in a padded box. The anthropologist and one other BLM staff member stayed to do a professional search of the site and sift through the sand in the cave to try to find more artifacts and clues.

Kit, Big Dave, Mr. Newton, and the other BLM staff member left on horse back with two pack mules carrying padded boxes containing the skeleton and the artifacts. "What happens to the gold and the guns?" asked Big Dave. "Does the kid get to keep them if they ain't claimed by a relative?"

"Jesus Christ, Dave," replied an exasperated Ted Newton. "We don't even know who this dead jasper was, let along who his relatives might be. I'll have to check with our office in Salt Lake to find out what the procedure on recovery is and then I'll let you know."

"You sure as hell better," replied Big Dave. "You tell them jaybirds in Salt Lake that I took pictures of everything that came out of that cave and I don't want no government puke stealing the kid's stuff. That goddamned Henry cleaned up is worth fifty thousand dollars!"

"Nothing is going to happen to this stuff, Dave, but remember it was found on U.S. government land."

"Exactly what scares the holy crap out of me about it getting stolen," retorted Big Dave.

Big Dave and Newton kept bickering at each other to the point they began to sound like some old married couple. Kit was pretty sure this was standard practice when they got together. He knew from Big Dave that Newton was a stand-up guy. Big Dave took Newton with him on his elk hunting party every October and that was a privilege extended to very few. Kit was also sure the twenty fifty dollar gold coins in mint condition had to be worth a lot more than $1,000 in today's money.

The other BLM staff member, a young fellow named Ike Toller brought his horse even with Kit. "Boy, are you gonna be famous!"

"What the hell are you talking about?" asked Kit.

"You are gonna be on every newspaper and television news program in the country. This is part of a big mystery about Butch Cassidy, and it's going to be news all over this country."

Kit was suddenly silent. This was just the kind of

publicity he did not need and could not afford to have. He had to figure out a way to keep his face and name out of the news. When they stopped at a small stream to water the horses and the mules, Kit pulled Big Dave aside and told him his problem about no publicity. Big Dave told him not to worry and that he would take care of it. Feeling relieved, Kit mounted Dolly and tried hard to enjoy the rest of the ride down to where they had left their trucks.

Sure enough, by the time they drove back to the BLM office in Kemmerer, Newton and Carlson had agreed that it was Big Dave who had found the cave. Kit was not mentioned. They had not been back in the BLM office for half an hour when Stumpy Dean, the editor and only reporter for the *Kemmerer Gazette*, was running in the door, pad and pencil in one hand and camera in the other. Stumpy was an okay newspaperman who had two loves, running the paper and hunting mushrooms. Stumpy got his name from a limp he acquired as a young man, the result of an early and short-lived attempt to be a rodeo bronc rider. Hunting mushrooms was a good deal less risky.

After some discussion, Newton let Stumpy take pictures of the artifacts, and he got the basic story from Newton and Big Dave. He took a picture of Newton and Big Dave standing behind a table with the artifacts displayed. He took a separate picture of the skeleton. "Who do you think this was?" he asked Big Dave. Big Dave explained that he thought the dead guy was one of the Wild Bunch who was wounded in the Montpelier Bank robbery and was left behind when the gang escaped to the Hole in the Wall. You could almost see the light go on in Stumpy's head. "Wild Bunch, Butch Cassidy, Holy Cow," and like a shot he was out of the office heading for the newspaper computer to do some research for the story.

As Kit and Big Dave were driving back to the ranch in Big Dave's pickup, Kit thanked him again for keeping him out of the story. "Don't be thanking me just yet, son," replied Big Dave. "I think we need to get some legal advice on the gold. I don't want those government twits to end up with it. I called Woody and made an appointment for you and me to talk to him about the gold at ten A.M. tomorrow. We'll see what he has to say about it."

Kit took a shower, made a quick supper, and was fast asleep before his head hit the pillow. His dreams were not about gold, skeletons, or Butch Cassidy. They were about a blond beauty named Sheila.

CHAPTER TWENTY-FOUR

At nine o'clock the next morning Kit and Big Dave walked into Woody's law office on Opal Street in Kemmerer. Woody owned a small one story brick office building that had two other offices he rented out. Alice Cleary, Woody's secretary, led them back to Woody's private office and closed the door behind them.

Woody's office was large and contained an old scarred roll top desk with an oversize leather chair at one end. A long conference table with eight chairs at the other end of the room completed the furnishings. Seated at the table were Woody and Chris Connor. Kit was puzzled by the presence of Mr. Connor, but he assumed that Connor and Woody were just finishing up some business and Connor would be on his way.

Kit was wrong.

As David closed the door to the office behind them, Woody and Mr. Connor stood up to shake hands with Kit and congratulated him on shooting the sheep killing bear and finding the remains of one of the Wild Bunch. As all four men sat down around the conference table, both Big Dave and Connor looked at Woody as though the next move was up to him.

Woody cleared his throat and looked Kit directly in the eye. "Years ago, both David and I were in the military. Both of us excelled in marksmanship and field crafts which was probably the result of growing up in Wyoming. We were recruited for a special unit. It was a military unit unlike any that had ever existed before in the U.S. military. Unlike what you might think of today with some of the anti-terrorist units and special forces, we were actually a terrorist unit. Our job was to terrify individuals, groups, government, or whomever our superiors wanted us to terrify. We were extremely successful in the terrorist business. We did things like sneaking into a dictator's highly defended compound, where we disemboweled his favorite pet and left the carcass on the foot of his bed while he was sleeping in it. Our terror was based on what we could have done if we wished to, and letting our intended target know that without any possible doubt. We were so secret we had no official unit designation. We were actually listed as part of a motor pool unit in Alabama that none of us ever actually saw.

We did have an unofficial name. We were called "The Comanches." It was an appropriate choice. Very few Indian tribes were as vicious and bloodthirsty as the Comanche. Just ask most of the poor unfortunate settlers on the West Texas plains. We operated all over the world in countries both friendly and unfriendly to the U.S. All of our missions were successful and none of us was ever captured. Usually our targets were unaware of our presence until we were long gone."

"The leader of our unit was a man who was better than any of us at anything you could choose. He could use a gun, a knife, a club, his hands, his mind, or anything else you could name better than any of us. Yet all of us were considered the best the U.S. military had to offer in what we did. David and I served under this man for four years. When we finished our final hitch, both of us returned to Kemmerer and our current lives.

Six years later we had a surprise visit from our former unit leader. He spent a thirty-day leave in Kemmerer and fell in love with Wyoming. He told us he had been doing special missions for the CIA and had been offered a very lucrative deal by the CIA to work exclusively for them on a contract basis. He had resigned his commission and had become a contract worker for the CIA. His job had changed from being one who inspired terror to that of a professional assassin. Five years later he retired and settled here in Kemmerer. He built a rather unique home on a five hundred acre tract on this side of Nugget Canyon."

"Four years ago he accepted some kind of special assignment and he met with David, Connor, and me. Connor had served under him after David and I had left the military and Connor also came here to live when he retired. Our former leader told us that he was concerned about what might happen on this assignment and he waned to put his affairs in order. He'd made a great deal of money working for the CIA and he'd invested it very wisely."

"The money and the real estate he owned were put into a special trust with me as the trustee. David is the successor trustee if something would happen to me. If our former leader did not return from this assignment, I was to continue to manage the trust and Connor was to take care of his ranch as a caretaker. Connor was reimbursed for all expenses from the trust and was to live on the property for free. Connor has since purchased his own place, but still takes care of the property. As you might suspect from this conversation, our former leader has not returned from that assignment and is presumed lost."

"The trust has a very special provision. Our former unit leader had been married and divorced long ago. He had a son whom he had not seen for many years. He believed that the son would eventually come here looking for him and if he did, and if we were able to legally verify his identity, 50% of the trust was to be diverted to the son, including the use but not the title to the Nugget Canyon ranch. The trust currently holds assets with a present value of approximately twelve million dollars. That is exclusive of the five hundred acre ranch."

"David and I became suspicious of you when you first arrived. We were pretty sure that you were not who you said you were and we didn't know why. It is not uncommon for people to come to a place like Kemmerer to hide. Also, much of your physical appearance and even some of your mannerisms seemed familiar to us. For example, even your walk is familiar to us. To confirm our suspicions of who you were, we took your fingerprints off a beer bottle you used and tried to get them identified. You have no fingerprints in the FBI or military database, so that was a strikeout. Then we got a sample of your DNA from several hair follicles that David retrieved from your hairbrush on his ranch. We had a specialist in Salt Lake run the DNA at his lab. He called us yesterday and bingo we had a match."

Our unit leader Thomas P. Andrews had a son named Carson M. Andrews. Your real name is Carson M. Andrews and your father was our leader and our best friend."

The silence in the room was overwhelming. Kit was speechless. The other three men remained motionless, patiently waiting for Kit to break the silence and speak.

"How can this be true?" said Kit.

"Science says it's true, son," said Woody. "You are our

best friend's son and you are entitled to the benefits of his trust and our friendship and loyalty. We all owe our lives to your father."

I don't know what to say," stammered Kit."

"Well I sure as hell do," said Big Dave. "Welcome home, Kit."

"Absolutely," chimed in Connor, "welcome home."

With that all three men rose and took turns hugging Kit and shaking his hand. Woody showed Kit copies of the trust, the financial statements, and the test results and gave him a legal envelope containing an additional set of copies.

"This calls for a drink," said Woody.

"Hell, everything calls for a drink with you," growled Big Dave.

A few minutes later, all four had managed to drink several toasts and the initial excitement and surprise had somewhat drained away.

"I have a question for the lad," said Woody. "Did you come here looking for your father?

"Actually, no," replied Kit. "I think you do need to know how I got to Kemmerer and why."

All three of the men smiled as one and leaned back in their chairs as Kit began to relate what had happened to him in Chicago on a rainy spring day such a short time ago and yet so long ago.

CHAPTER TWENTY-FIVE

When Kit was finished with his story, the questions began. Connor, in particular asked him about every possible incident where Kit might have left a clue to his identify and his whereabouts. He was obviously trying to determine if such a leak might have occurred and what the consequences might be. Both Big Dave and Woody were concerned about Kit's safety, and they had a heated discussion about what to do next. Woody saw nothing wrong with Kit using his real name, and Big Dave felt they should wait until after the trial back in Chicago was over and the real threat posed to Kit was gone with it. Woody was not comfortable with Kit avoiding testifying in court, although he was unsure of how to accomplish that without endangering Kit.

Finally Connor, who had said very little, came up with his suggestion. "Kit's dad made me promise that if his kid ever showed up in Kemmerer, I was to teach him everything about protecting himself that his dad would have done if he'd been afforded the opportunity. I propose we move Kit to his dad's ranch. Almost no one around here even knows about it. I'll stay there with him and use the time to teach him the things his dad would have taught him While I'm doing that, Woody can use his connections to find out what is going on back in Chicago and try to get some idea of what we might be up against."

After more discussion, they all agreed to Connor's

idea. Woody had some forms for Kit to sign, including a bank account with a private bank in New York City. He gave Kit a set of codes, a credit card that would access his account, a check book, and a business card with the name of his private banker on it. "I've set up everything so you can access the bank account directly by phone, computer, using the card, or writing a check. If you need anything done with the money in the trust, all you need to do is call me," and he gave Kit his card with his cell phone number written on the back. Finally Woody reached in the drawer in his desk and extracted a small cell phone. "Here, Kit, this is yours. Considering what you told us today, I'm pretty sure you might need it."

Kit took the cell phone from Woody and thanked him. Then he turned to the three men who had been a part of his father's life and now were a part of his. "I have a question," Kit said.

"Of course, Kit. What is it you want to know," replied Woody.

"Just who was my father? I know he was Thomas P. Andrews, but what kind of man was he? What kind of a friend was he to all of you?"

"Well, son," said Woody, "the answer is a pretty long story and with my throat being so parched I will be in need of some liquid refreshment before I can begin." Big Dave roared with laughter and passed the bottle over to Woody.

Two hours later they broke up the meeting and decided to meet the following Friday at the Andrews ranch by Nugget Canyon to plan what they should do next. Connor drove Kit back to Carlson's ranch to get his things and his truck so he could follow Connor back to the Nugget Canyon ranch.

Kit noticed that the plain gray Jeep Grand Cherokee was inconspicuous, but the rumble of a large V-8 engine under the hood meant otherwise. It took them about thirty minutes to drive to the ranch. They drove northwest toward Cokeville and just before entering Nugget Canyon, they left the highway on a dirt road that headed in a southwesterly direction.

They began to climb up out of the valley towards the face of a tall butte. The open meadows of sagebrush gave way to an increasing amount of timber, most of it lodge pole pine and quaking aspen. The road became rougher and more rutted and they went through a series of switchbacks. As they came out of the switchbacks, the trees ended and Kit saw a large, rambling one-story log cabin up against the sheer wall of the butte. Next to the cabin was a large metal barn that looked like an old airplane hanger. Attached to the barn and running down the slope from the butte was a sizeable empty corral.

Kit slowed his old truck and looked back towards the highway in the valley that he had just come from. He could see nothing because of the trees below him. Obviously, the cabin and the barn could not be seen from the valley. He followed Connor on the road which had suddenly become well graded with a solid stone base.

When Connor pulled up in front of the barn and

parked, Kit followed suit. He got out and looked back toward the valley. They were on a small plateau that seemed to come out from the butte like a shelf. The plateau sloped slightly down toward the valley and was all meadow before ending in pine trees at what seemed to be the end of the plateau. The meadow was surrounded on three sides by heavy timber and ended on the fourth side by the steep butte that seemed to rise about five hundred feet above the cabin. Connor was standing by the Jeep, smiling at Kit. It was the first time Kit remembered seeing Connor smile.

Connor pulled a small remote control device out of his jacket pocket, and the next thing Kit saw was the large door in front of the barn began to rise and seemingly disappear. After the barn door opened, Connor got back into the Jeep and with Kit following, they drove inside the barn. As they entered the barn, lights automatically came on illuminating the inside of the large structure.

Kit found himself in what looked like a sizeable steel garage that could hold about twelve vehicles. The area was well lit, and he saw at least two more vehicles that Connor had parked his Jeep next to. Kit parked the truck and stepped out into the garage.

"Surprising, isn't it?" said Connor. Kit just nodded his head in agreement. "The Barn door is reinforced steel, made to look like wood. The barn is actually a reinforced steel Quonset building and will hold twelve vehicles easily, more if you squeeze them in a little. On the west side of the barn there are stalls, supply room, tack room, and shop. You get to them through that door." Connor pointed to a dutch-door painted red. "The stalls open to the corral." They walked to the edge of the well-lit garage to a large steel door.

"This end of the barn is against the rock wall of the butte." There was a small panel with pushbuttons on the right side of the door. Connor entered a code and pulled down on the steel handle and the door opened easily. They entered a small hallway and found themselves in a small shooting range that had been carved out of the stone butte. The range ran twenty-five yards back into the butte. There were three separate firing position, each with power controls that allowed targets to be loaded and run to the end of the twenty-five foot range and then returned. There was also a shop with repair and reloading equipment and a walk-in vault. The vault had an old style bank vault door with slightly faded letters that still spelled out their heritage as DIEBOLD.

"What's in the vault?" asked Kit.

Connor spun the two separate dials on the face of he vault door and turned the large steel wheel on the front of the vault door to the left and pulled the door open. Inside along the back wall were several heavy gauge steel lockers with padlocks, and on both sides were racks holding rifles, shotguns, and pistols. Below the racks were shelves of ammunition boxes. "This all belongs to your father, but I'm sure he won't mind you using them and starting tomorrow, you'll learn how to use all of them."

Connor closed up the vault and led Kit back into the barn. They exited from the barn through a side door on the east side, which was also controlled by a combination locking system.

The cabin faced slightly northeast and had a large front porch that wrapped around the cabin's front and sides. The cabin appeared to be built flush against the sheer rock wall of the butte.

They entered the front door after Connor used a combination lock system. The front door was heavy gauge steel, made to look like wood and to fit in with the log siding. They found themselves in a narrow foyer that appeared to be some sort of mudroom. A bench with storage bins under it ran along one wall. Above the bench was a long board with wooden pegs to hang coats and gear from. On the opposite wall were floor to ceiling cabinets with a small sink at one end and a cabinet above it. The floor was slate.

They walked through the door at the end of the hallway and were standing next to a sizeable kitchen. The kitchen was done in southwestern tiles with a slate floor. The countertops appeared to be black granite and the woodwork and cabinets were cherry wood. All the appliances were done in stainless steel. The kitchen appeared to be well lit, but Kit had not seen Connor turn on any light switches.

Connor gave Kit a tour of the "Cabin". The total square footage was about three thousand square feet, all on one level. Although the building seemed to be a log cabin, it was actually a concrete and steel structure with log walls on three sides. Light came from many skylights that were camouflaged to look like the rest of the shingles on the roof and strong enough for a man to walk on and not damage. The south end of the building was the sheer rock wall of the butte.

The cabin was decorated like a southwestern ranch house. The furniture was mostly wood and leather and very comfortable. One wall of the great room was solid bookshelves filled with books and pictures. The ten-foot high walls were stucco, and the floors were slate with throw rugs. There were exposed oak beams and western art on the walls. Each room had a good deal of indirect lighting, and all the lighting seemed to be tied to a motion sensor.

The great room or combination living and family room was up against the south end of the house with large glass windows and tremendous views of the valley and Nugget Canyon. Connor explained that there were four bedrooms, but one was Kit's father's and it was to remain locked. Kit could have his pick of the other three bedrooms. There was a huge stone fireplace in the great room and Kit noted that there were small fireplaces in each of the three bedrooms. "Where do the chimneys go?" Kit asked Connor.

"The chimneys are designed to diffuse the amount of smoke they let out, and they and the exhaust pipes are disguised as rocks on the face of the butte.

"Where does the electricity come from?" asked Kit.

"Down by the entrance to the property is a power company riser set up as though to serve a home site that has not been built on and never will be. We buried the power and phones from there to up here. We also have a large standby generator that runs on propane. There are three buried propane tanks at the edge of the meadow. The propane is used to heat the house and to heat the water. There are two water wells, both hidden from view. There is also a pond inside one of the corrals. At the top of the butte is a spring fed pond. The pond drains down by a hidden pipe to the pond in the corral. We get television and internet service by satellite. There is also a buried gasoline tank that holds five hundred gallons. The complex is set up to be very self sufficient and very private. We have cameras by the entrance and there is a system of sensors surrounding the entire meadow and the road."

"Wow," was all Kit could manage to get out. He was overwhelmed by the cabin. This was to be his home? He brought his duffel bag and pack in from his truck and put them in the largest of the three remaining bedrooms. It was about four hundred square feet and had a fireplace, a walk-in closet, and a huge bathroom with a large stand-alone tub, a huge tiled shower with dual water sprays and a bench, and a large double sink vanity. There was even a heat lamp with a timer over the space just outside the shower door. The entire bathroom including the floor was done in tile. A skylight above the bathroom provided natural light. There were two large reading chairs next to the fireplace and a large flat panel television set located above the fireplace, recessed into the wall.

Kit went back into the great room where Connor was waiting. Connor showed him where the electrical panel was and explained the heating and cooling system, the well, the generator, and the security system. Connor gave

Kit a key to a key box mounted in a hidden compartment in the wall behind a small picture. Each key had a tag attached explaining its purpose.

"You'll want to stock up with food as the only thing in the refrigerator is beer. I built my own place over a year ago and haven't had any meals here since."

Kit nodded and turned to go back to the bedroom. "Wait. I have a few questions," said Connor. "You ever do any reloading?"

"No," replied Kit.

"How about shooting?"

"I've done a little with a rifle."

"Well, we'll start on that tomorrow when I come back," said Connor. "I've got a lot of training to do with you and judging from your current circumstances, the sooner we get to it, the better. I'll be here at eight sharp tomorrow morning. Have some coffee ready."

With that Connor led Kit back to the barn and almost before Kit knew it, Connor was in his Jeep and the heavy garage door was opening. Connor waved and roared out of the garage, the door slowly closing behind him.

CHAPTER TWENTY-SIX

Since it was still mid-afternoon, Kit made up a list of groceries and went out to the garage. He flipped on all the lights and discovered a late model Ford F-250 4x4 pickup with a snowplow attachment. The plow was sitting on a wooden pallet next to the truck. Next to the plow was a John Deere tractor with several attachments, a John Deere Gator 4x4, and a Polaris snowmobile sitting on a flat utility trailer.

Kit started up his old '49 GMC pickup and hit the remote for the garage door. The garage door opened straight up and Kit pulled outside into the sunlight and hit the remote again and the door closed behind him. He drove down the lane to the dirt road and headed toward Nugget Canyon and the valley floor. Kit reached the highway and headed into Kemmerer. He'd gone about three miles when he saw an older pickup truck on the side of the road. Next to the pickup was a tall, broad shouldered man with a rangy build wearing worn denims and a battered cowboy hat. As Kit slowed down and got closer, he could see the truck had a flat tire and the left front wheel was jacked up and the tire was off and laying on the ground. Kit pulled to a stop next to the disabled pickup.

"Howdy," said the driver with a smile.

Kit jumped out of his truck and introduced himself. "Kit Andrews," he heard himself say.

"Chance Jackson," replied the driver. "I've got myself a bit of a problem. A flat tire and the spare is flat as well. Could you give me a lift into Kemmerer?"

"You bet," said Kit. They put both tires in the back of Kit's truck and headed for Kemmerer.

"Hell, this truck is older than I am, and I thought my

truck was old," laughed Chance. "It sure is in dang good shape, though."

"It gets me around," said Kit. "What were you doing up in this neck of the woods?"

"I was delivering a part I made to the Nelson Ranch."

"You make parts?"

"I'm a blacksmith and I can make or fix just about any kind of part you can name if it's made out of metal. If it's broke, I can fix it," said Chance.

"I wouldn't think there would be enough work for a blacksmith in Kemmerer," said Kit.

"Well, blacksmith work is what I love, but to pay the bills, I also have a welding service. I have a portable welding unit and I service a lot of the oil and gas wells we have here in Lincoln County and I do a lot of work in Sweetwater County and even some in Jackson County. How about you?"

"I work for David Carlson, managing his sheep herds as a foreman," replied Kit.

"Big Dave! Heck I've done a lot of work for him. He's a real good hand. You're lucky to be working for someone like him."

Soon they had reached Kemmerer and filled the flat spare with air and checked it for leaks. They left the flat tire to be fixed and headed back to Chance's truck.

Chance entertained Kit with stories of really strange requests he had worked on as a blacksmith. Kit returned the favor with the story about killing the bear and finding the skeleton of a member of the Wild Bunch.

Soon they were back at Chance's truck. Chance slid out of the truck and turned to Kit. "Thanks again for your help. If you're in town tonight, stop in the White Russian Saloon and I'll buy you a beer."

"You're on," replied Kit and he headed back to Kemmerer while Chance set about changing his tire.

Kit stopped at the Safeway store in Kemmerer and filled up his grocery list. Before heading for home, he stopped at the Carlson Ranch and found Big Dave home, working on repairing some horse tack. He told Big Dave that he wanted to stay on as foreman as long as Big Dave needed him.

"Well, Kit, that's right nice of you, but I think Connor is going to need a little bit of your time for a couple of weeks and I can fill in for you till he gets done." Big Dave laughed at the puzzled look on Kit's face. "He's gonna train you just like your daddy would have and when he gets done, you ain't gonna be nobody to mess with."

Then Big Dave's tone got serious. "Are you gonna use your real name and take a chance on them jaspers from the East coming out here lookin' for you?"

"I thought about it," said Kit. "I think I may be better off letting them know I'm here and being ready for them rather than keep trying to hide and not knowing when they might figure out where I am and surprise me."

"That makes good sense, Kit." said Big Dave. "Next Friday when we meet, the four of us will work up a plan. We should have an advantage in that they think you're still some city boy egg-sucking tenderfoot. You've come a long way since I fished you out outta the snowdrift and you're about to multiply that distance."

Kit grinned, thanked Big Dave, and headed back to his new home in his old truck.

Kit quickly unpacked the groceries and put them away and then showered and changed to clean clothes. He chose a relatively new and clean denim shirt and jeans and his boots and cowboy hat and tossed a denim jacket on the seat of the truck. He did an involuntary shiver when he started the truck. One thing was for sure. When the sun went down, the temperature dropped about forty degrees almost anywhere in southwestern Wyoming.

Kit parked on the triangle in front of the movie theater and walked over to Sawaya's Dry Goods and bought two new shirts and a new pair of jeans and several pairs of light wool socks. Kit strolled back to the truck and tossed his purchases on the passenger side of the seat. He walked over to the café, got a table by the front window, and ordered the special, homemade meatloaf with mashed potatoes and gravy. While he waited for his meal, Kit had coffee and watched people walking by outside the café. On a Friday night, Kemmerer looked like a lot of small rural towns where folks came in to shop or eat or just get drunk. Kit realized what he was watching was the most people he had seen at one time since he left Chicago.

He was almost finished with his meal when he saw a group of about eight people coming into the café. He recognized three of them as Star Oil Company people he had seen in the mountains on their ATV's. Seth

Chambers saw Kit and waved at him. Sheila saw Kit and smiled, while Blair Masters did his best to ignore Kit's presence. When he finished his meal, Kit got up and went to the counter to pay his check. As he turned to walk out, he looked in the direction of the two tables the Star Oil people had pushed together, but he didn't catch Sheila's eye. Disappointed, Kit strode out of the café and headed toward the White Russian Saloon.

Kit remembered that all the bars on the triangle had a social pecking order and that the Star Bar was at the bottom. However he was not prepared for what happened as he approached the front door of the Star Bar. Just as he was about to pass by on the front sidewalk, the batwing doors of the bar burst open and a short chubby Mexican man stumbled backwards out of the bar and landed on his back on the sidewalk right in front of Kit. Protruding from the man's stomach was the handle of a knife. Before Kit could react, a second Mexican, this one taller, younger, and slimmer, dashed out and pulled his wounded friend up to a sitting position. He then proceeded to yell "Call 911, call 911" while he offered his wounded friend a drink from his beer bottle.

"Just what you need with an abdominal wound, a good shot of cold beer," said a voice behind Kit. Startled, he turned to see the grinning face of Chance Jackson.

"Shouldn't we help?" Kit managed to stammer out.

"Heck no," said Chance. "We'd just be getting in the way." Sure enough, within a few minutes the emergency response truck was there from the fire station and two

EMT's were running from the truck to treat their newly acquired patient.

"I suggest we side step this den of iniquity and head on down to a more civilized watering hole," said Chance. He took Kit by the arm and led him past the Star Bar, and shortly they were in the confines of the White Russian Saloon. They took a seat at a small table not far from the front door and before Kit knew it, Chance had ordered two beers. Kit took a look around the bar. There was the usual large wooden back bar with the obligatory mirrors and pictures. It matched the bar with some sort of dark wood finish like mahogany. The place was reasonably well lit, for a bar, and the wooden plank floor was reasonably clean. Compared to the Stock Exchange Bar, the White Russian Saloon was much nicer and the clientele much younger.

A jukebox filled the room with the sound of some country and western song about some cowboy who just got out of prison, who lost his mama, who had his pickup repossessed and who lost his dog. "We've got both kinds of music," said a grinning Chance over the din. "Country and Western."

"How come this place is called the White Russian Saloon?" asked Kit. "I don't see anything Russian about it."

"The owners are a husband and wife who came here from Russia and are supposedly White Russians," replied Chance. "Actually, I think they were the ones opposed to the Red Russians when the Czar was murdered by the commies, but I can't be sure of that."

"Well, look what the cat drug in," said a deep voice as a pair of large hands grabbed Kit and Chance by the back of their necks and squeezed them. Both of them struggled to turn and saw a grinning Thor Carlson, Big Dave's son.

"Well don't just stand there like some dumb Swede, sit down and have a beer with some real cowboys," said Chance.

"Don't mind if I do," said Thor and he flicked a chair into place with one hand like the chair was a matchstick.

It turned out that Thor and Chance had graduated from Kemmerer High School together and were old friends and drinking buddies.

"So you two have been drinking buddies since high school?" asked Kit.

"Well, not exactly," said Thor. "Old Chance here went to the University of Wyoming on a football scholarship and some idiot actually paid him real cash money to play football in the NFL for the New Orleans Saints. He played safety for three years until he managed to blow out his knee."

"Yep, those were the good old days," said a smiling Chance. "Cold beer, easy money, and easier women. I couldn't believe they would pay you that kind of money just for smacking people around."

Both he and Thor laughed loudly at that remark.

"I saved what money I could that the government didn't steal, and used it to set up my welding business and still got a little nest egg," said Chance.

"Nest egg, my ass," said Thor. "Bastard only works cause he's too stupid not to."

Kit figured out that this was an ongoing contest of one up-man ship by two old friends.

Two very attractive young ladies walked in the bar and Chance sat up straight in his chair and exclaimed, "I think I'm in love."

"You wouldn't know love if it hit you in the head with a twenty pound hammer," snorted Thor. "You're just horny."

"Ain't that the pot calling the kettle black?" retorted Chance.

"Hell, you ain't seen nothing black since you got kicked out of New Orleans," said Thor.

"The hell you say. I'll have you know I still got fan clubs made up of lovely black ladies."

"The only fan clubs you got are ones you might create on the internet," said Thor.

One of the young ladies that they had just watched walk in came over to their table. "Hey, Chance, how 'bout a game of pool?"

"My public awaits me," said a smiling Chance as he rose to his feet and followed the shapely young lass to the nearest vacant pool table.

"So I heard you shot one of them sheep killing bears," said Thor. Kit found himself giving Thor a first hand account of his encounter with the bear and his subsequent discovery of the skeleton of one of the Wild Bunch. While he was recounting his story, Kit noticed that Shelia and

Blair had come into the bar. Blair ignored Kit and promptly led Shelia to a table as far away from Kit as possible. Shelia gave Kit a small smile as she walked by their table.

"Whoa, that's a good lookin' filly," said Thor. "You know her?"

"I met her on the trail up by our camp on LaBarge Creek. She works for Star Oil with what I think is an oil and gas exploration crew," replied Kit.

"Who is that bohunk with her? He don't seem none too friendly."

"He's not. He seems to work hard at being nasty and hostile. Course, maybe that's his good side," said Kit.

Both Kit and Thor burst into laughter.

Kit got up to go to the bar to get two fresh beers as the bar had filled up and the waitress couldn't keep up with the thirsty crowd. He ordered two beers from the bartender and looked around the room while he stood at the bar. He quickly noticed Tang sitting at a table against the wall. She was with three men including the same rough looking guy he had bumped into at the Stock Exchange Bar a few weeks before. While he stood there looking toward her, Tang looked up, saw Kit and quickly looked away.

I must have this magical effect on all the women I meet, thought Kit. He got his beers, paid the bartender, and headed back go his table.

"Hey there, young fella, Howya doin'?" Kit turned and there was Andy Bain, the tow truck operator who had pulled him into town.

"Well hi there, Andy. I'm doing fine," replied Kit. "Why don't you join Thor and me for a beer."

"Love to," said Andy. "I'll be here in a minute. I'm waiting for my daughter to come out of the ladies room. With women you just never know."

Andy's daughter turned out to be a delightful addition to their small party. She had Andy's self-confidence, but must have gotten her looks from her mother. She was tall and lanky, where her father was short and stocky. She was not plain, but not pretty. She fell into that interesting and sort of attractive category. Candice was her name, but everybody called her Candy. She had fair skin with freckles and light blue eyes and dishwater blonde hair that she wore in a ponytail.

She and her brother Dan had both gone to college and returned to help their dad with his diesel repair and towing business. Candy had a mechanical engineering degree from the University of Utah and seemed perfectly content with living in Kemmerer. Thor embarrassed her by telling a story of when she was only a teenager and Big Dave had been trying to hire someone to build a line of fence. She applied and he finally couldn't think of a way to turn her down, especially since no one else had shown any interest in the job. She outworked both Thor and Big Dave and was able to lift and drive fence posts like they were made out of paper. Candy blushed at the story, but Kit could see she had broad shoulders for a woman.

They had just gotten either their fourth or fifth pitcher of beer from the bar when the jukebox began playing an old version of "Let Your Love Flow" and almost immediately everyone in the bar was up and grabbing a partner to dance to the tune. Kit sat watching with a blank look on his face as Thor pulled Candy up to dance. Thor grinned and said "This song is like the Kemmerer National Anthem. When it plays, everybody dances." And with that he and Candy were gone, heading out to the by now crowded dance floor.

As Kit looked round the bar, he saw Andy dancing with some girl half his age and then he spotted Chance dancing with a very attractive young blonde. *I knew I was out of step culturally, but this is ridiculous,* thought Kit. Dancing was not his favorite thing, no matter what song was playing.

Suddenly, out of the din of the music, Kit distinctly heard the words "You can't dance sitting down, cowboy." He looked up to see a smiling Sheila. The next thing he knew they were on the edge of the crowded dance floor mixing it up with the best of them.

"It's a cool song," said Shelia. "I can see why they all like to dance to it. How come I haven't heard from you since I saw you on the trail?"

Kit was too stunned to replay. Finally he managed to mumble some excuse about time, work, and Blair. "Blair!" laughed Sheila. "In his dreams. I work with Blair and I put up with him because he's a good engineer, but please, give a girl a little credit."

They finished the dance and stayed on the dance floor as the jukebox came up with a much slower song. Kit was beginning to enjoy himself when he felt a tap on his shoulder. He looked up to see a grinning Chance. "I'm cutting in, Kit. It's time to let this gal know what a real cowboy is like," said Chance.

Kit grinned and relinquished his dance partner to Chance. On his way back to his table, Kit carefully worked his way through the crowded dance floor. As he got off the dance floor, he felt a hand on his arm and stopped. There, standing right in front of him was a not smiling Blair. "Dancing a little above your social level aren't you, cowboy?" said Blair tersely.

"Oh, I don't' know," said Kit. "We common folk don't have much use for social levels in Kemmerer. But we don't take kindly to people putting their hands on us when they weren't invited. Take your hand off me or I'll break the arm it's attached to."

Blair scowled, but took his hand off Kit's arm and moved away.

The crowd, including Kit and his friends, continued drinking and dancing until closing time.

Kit found himself outside the bar, standing on the sidewalk with Chance and Thor. Neither of them had managed to hook up with any of the females from the bar. "I'm shocked," said Kit. "I look to you two as an example of how a man handles himself around women and both of you managed to strike out tonight."

"Tell him the statistics, Thor," said Chance

Thor turned to Kit and said, "In Wyoming there are at least two guys for every gal and when you get to the desirable single ones, the odds are probably about five to one. It's a very competitive deal."

"So, you struck out because of statistics, not your technique?" asked Kit.

"Hell, if we had any technique, we wouldn't be standing here talking to you, that's for sure," laughed Chance.

The three of them walked, somewhat unsteadily, to their respective trucks, each of them managing to complete the journey successfully.

CHAPTER TWENTY-SEVEN

Monday morning found Kit and Connor having coffee as Kit tried to get the cobwebs out of his head. They were sitting in Kit's kitchen, looking out over the landscape that stretched beyond the huge windows. Connor wasted little time in warming to his subject.

"Your father asked me to teach you all the things he taught me. Mainly he wanted you to be able to protect yourself and to be proficient with weapons and with woodcraft. Today we are going to work on self-defense."

"Before we start, I would like to ask you a few questions about my father," said Kit.

"I understand, Kit. What would you like to know?"

"I guess I'd like to know what kind of a person was he, what kind of a friend was he?"

Connor smiled. "Your father was a mean, ornery, stubborn son-of-a –bitch who made up his own rules. He was also the nicest, kindest man I ever knew. You wanted him for a friend, not an enemy. Some people are born to be weak, some are born to be strong. Your father was born to be a heroic-son-of-a-bitch. He feared nothing. He could sense what made a person tick, just by listening to them. He could smell trouble a mile away. He hated to lose at anything, even cards. He was a natural soldier. He was good with all kinds of weapons and he had the ability to almost disappear into thin air whether he was in the woods, the jungle, or the desert."

"Your father was a born leader. Men looked to him to see what to do next. When things got ugly, you followed your dad because you knew he was going to make the right decision."

"I trusted your dad with my life, and he saved it more than once. I hate being in debt to anyone, but I will always be in debt to your dad. As long as I'm able, I'll see to it that I honor my promise to him and see that no harm comes to you."

Connor paused. "That is the longest speech I ever made about anyone or anything. I hope you can be half the man your dad was."

"Are you sure he's dead?" asked Kit.

"Normally I would say yes, he's probably dead or he would have been back here within the last year. But with your old man, nothing is normal. He could be alive, but I have had no word, no messages, nothing for almost a year and a half. That's not like him, and that's why we're pretty sure he's gone. You coming along was downright spooky. You walk like he did and you even move like he did. It's really eerie."

Connor looked into Kit's eyes. "If your father is dead, and sooner or later we will find out, I can promise you that once I think you can handle yourself, I'll be gone until I find him alive or find out what happened and eliminate the people who killed him."

Connor paused and then continued. "My job is to try to teach you how to defend yourself and make your way in the world. This is what your dad would have done if he were here. I know that he would be thrilled that you are here and pleased on how you have handled yourself and how much you've grown as a man in the past weeks. You have some serious trouble looking for you, so what I'm about to teach you has real and immediate meaning and importance. I need you to focus as hard as you can on these lessons. What you learn here may save your life."

From a large bag on the floor, Connor produced a semi-automatic pistol. He explained the safety rules associated with shooting and then explained how the pistol worked, using a fake magazine to load and unload the weapon. He then did the same thing with a revolver and had Kit work both weapons until Connor was satisfied.

Connor then led Kit into the garage and into the firing range. On a table top he had arranged several kinds of pistols and revolvers. "It is important to know how to use all of them as you never know what kind of gun will be handy when you need one," he explained.

He provided Kit with a gun belt and holster. Also on the gun belt was a double magazine holder and a funny curved plastic hook that slid on the belt. After fitting the belt on Kit, Connor had Kit use an empty gun with a fake magazine and taught him how to draw, aim, and fire the weapon. Each time he had Kit cock the weapon and then draw and dry fire it without any ammunition in the chamber. He preached the need to develop muscle memory and soon Kit became more comfortable with what his hands were supposed to do.

They proceeded to the nearest firing range position, and Connor provided Kit with protective glasses and hearing protectors for his ears. He started Kit off with a 22 caliber revolver, then a 38 caliber, a 9 millimeter, a 40 caliber and finally a 45 caliber. As soon as Kit got proficient firing a weapon, Connor had him move up to a more powerful caliber until he was firing the 45 caliber with the same proficiency he had fired the little 22 caliber.

Connor looked at Kit's hands. "You're a good sized man with big hands. A 45 caliber gun is probably a good choice for a carry gun."

"What's a carry gun?" asked Kit.

"A carry gun is the one you try to keep with you at all times," replied Connor. "It's the one you'll use when you need to defend yourself."

Connor had Kit stand at the firing position with his

gun holstered and his hands in the air. When Connor's timer went off, Kit was to draw his gun and fire at the target. As the morning wore on, Kit got faster and more accurate.

They took a break for lunch and while they ate sandwiches, Connor peppered Kit with questions about things he had shown Kit to check and see if Kit remembered and understood. Kit answered the questions as they cleaned up the remains of lunch and put the dishes in the dishwasher and headed back to the range.

By the end of the day, Kit had vastly improved his speed and accuracy. Connor left about mid-afternoon after advising Kit to practice drawing and dry firing so he would be ready for the next day's session at eight A.M. Kit proceeded to clean the guns he had used and put them away. He then spent several hours reading a book Connor had given him on techniques for self-defense, several of which they had already covered that day.

By the end of the week, Kit was pleased with himself. He had become very proficient with pistols and revolvers and especially with the 45 caliber pistol. He had selected a Kimber full size model 1911 45 caliber in stainless steel with non-slip grips, customized trigger, and beaver tail. Connor had adjusted the trigger pull and the safety so that it was now second nature for Kit to handle the pistol.

Connor also taught Kit how to use pepper spray, a folding baton, and even a pencil as weapons to defend himself. In the next week they would continue with pistols, shotguns, rifles, and include knife fighting and simple hand to hand self-defense. Connor gave Kit videos of everything from knife fighting to combat shotgun use. Kit found the videos were more helpful than the books as they showed you how things were done and it was easier and quicker to learn from them.

CHAPTER TWENTY-EIGHT

By Friday night, Kit was ready for a little fun and relaxation. He showered and changed to a light denim shirt, a good pair of jeans, and his boots, which looked much better after his attempt to shine and buff them.

Kit looked at himself in the mirror and was surprised at what he saw. He was probably about twenty pounds heavier and much more muscular than when he left Chicago. He looked and felt more confident about himself than he ever had. He was physically much stronger than he had been, and in much better shape. He smiled as he thought about all he had learned in a short time and how much different his life was now and would be in the future thanks to his father and fate that brought him to Kemmerer, Wyoming.

Kit ran a few errands in Kemmerer and as he was leaving the hardware store, he almost collided with Tang. After they both recovered from their momentary surprise, Kit apologized for being so clumsy and careless and Tang's hard look softened.

"It was just as much my fault. I should have been paying more attention to what I was doing."

"Well, can I make it up to you by buying you supper at Irma's Café?" asked Kit.

Tang seemed to hesitate and finally she smiled and said, "Sure, why not. I was getting hungry anyway."

As they entered the café and made their way to an empty table, Kit noticed the usual amount of nosy folks trying to figure out what the two of them were doing together.

"No secrets in this town," he remarked.

Tang looked around and smiled at Kit. "I'm sure seeing the two of us together at supper is almost as exciting as watching *Hollywood Squares.*"

"Or maybe *Wheel of Fortune,*" chimed in Kit.

They both laughed. Tang waited until after their waitress had left with their order.

"I suppose you are waiting on me to give you an explanation," she finally said.

"An explanation about what?"

"You are smooth, I will give you that. When I first saw you I thought you were a good looking dude, but still a pretty raw dude. I was wrong. You're a lot smarter and a lot shrewder than I thought."

Kit looked down at the table and said nothing.

"After I heard about the fire arrows at the burial ground, I knew it was you. I figured that you wanted to scare us off, not arrest us. Am I right?"

Kit looked up at Tang. She was a very attractive

woman, and she seemed awfully vulnerable to him at that moment. "I'm not interested in arresting anyone or telling anyone how to run their lives. I just think stealing is wrong and tried to think of a way to put a stop to it without getting involved with the law."

Tang's face became flushed. "So you think I'm a thief?"

"Anyone who takes artifacts from public land is breaking federal law. You know it and I know it. It makes no difference if they're doing it for profit or for their own private collections."

Tang's face was red and she looked down at the table and not directly at Kit. "Do you have any idea what it was like for me to give up my career and come home to this isolated place in the middle of nowhere and try to care for my parents and keep a crappy business afloat? I did it because I love my parents, but I quickly found out my dad had been barely squeezing out a living on the station and he still had a considerable amount of debt. I worked my butt off trying to make the station profitable and I've succeeded to a point, but I couldn't also handle the existing debt load. When my dad died, the pressure to pay off the debt got greater."

"I found the burial ground by accident. No one, not even the old guys at the BLM knew it was there and I saw it as a chance to use my skills again and get rid of my parents' debt. I used illegal Mexicans to do the digging and they were good workers, but uneducated and superstitious. You scared the living crap out of them with those fire arrows. They thought the Indians had come back to life to kill them for robbing their graves. Now I can't get any of them to go back to the site, even if I offered them payment in gold."

Tang paused, waiting for Kit to respond.

A few awkward moments passed, which probably seemed much longer to both of them.

Finally Kit broke the silence. "I don't want to hurt you or make your life tougher, but breaking the law will eventually get you caught and you'll be in worse shape than you are now. If you had the money to pay off the debt, what would you do then?"

"I haven't thought about it. All I've focused on is trying to get the money to get it paid off. I guess if I had the debt paid, I'd sell the station and try to get my job back in Chicago. My mom has become quite independent and is still in good health and she has all her friends here. With a good job in Chicago, I could afford to see that she is taken care of and still have a life of my own."

"How much is the debt?"

Tang thought for a few seconds and then almost whispered, "Fifty-six thousand dollars."

"What if I were to loan you the fifty-six thousand dollars, charge you no interest, and you pay me back when you're able to?"

"You! How could you have that kind of money? You're just a hired hand. You're driving an old truck that I sold you!"

"Appearances can be deceiving," said a grinning Kit.

He went on to tell her who is father was and that he had received a sizeable inheritance and a no interest loan for fifty-six thousand dollars was not going to be much of a problem.

"But why do this for me?"

"I like you. You were nice to me, and you were helpful when I needed help with my car. I don't want to see you wind up in jail. You don't strike me as a criminal. I see you as someone who is desperate to get out of where they are in life. Besides, you never know when I might need a personal tour of the Chicago Museum of Science and Industry."

"What kind of strings are attached to this loan?"

"Only one string. You have to return any artifacts you still have to the site. I'll be glad to help you."

"You're sure about this. This isn't something you are going to change your mind about?"

"Nope. A deal is a deal," Kit said as he offered his hand to Tang. All I want is you out of the grave robbing business. You're a little too pretty to be wearing orange jumpsuits with heavy metal bracelets."

Tang blushed and smiled at Kit. "Is this just between us? Will other people know?"

"This is just between us. I'll stop by the station on Monday with a cashier's check and a note for you to sign. Do we have a deal?"

"We have a deal," said Tang as she shook his hand and squeezed it. "I can't tell you how much this means to me. I will never forget you for helping me."

"Just remember that when I need that personal guided tour."

Kit walked Tang to her Jeep. Before she opened the Jeep door, she turned and leaned up and kissed Kit on the mouth. "Thank you," she whispered in his ear and then she was gone.

Kit headed back to the triangle and his parked pickup.

CHAPTER TWENTY-NINE

Kit lay motionless on the flat rock. He had selected this site because it gave him a clear view of the slope in front of him. At the same time the overhanging rocks behind him shielded him from being seen from above and also provided some shade from the sun.

He could not believe five weeks had passed since he first started working with Connor. Kit had become proficient with handguns, rifles, shotguns, knives, and close hand-to-hand combat. At first he was amazed at Connor's accuracy and ability, but now he could occasionally outshoot Connor and was able to stay with him in hand-to-hand combat. Today was an exercise in escape and evade. Kit was armed only with a knife, although the knife was an LMF fighting knife developed in the jungles of Vietnam where his father had fought. Connor had given him the knife after asking for a coin in return to avoid bad luck. Kit had learned quickly from

Connor how to use the knife and was pleased when he had earned Connor's praise for his skill in hand-to-hand combat with the knife. Connor had given Kit a half hour head start and the objective was to make it all the way to Emigrant Springs without Connor catching him.

Kit had started out running hard and then quickly set a long distance pace he had learned from his high school cross-country team. After about an hour and a half, Kit had stopped to rest at the edge of a rockslide. Loose rocks of various sizes covered a slope that was about forty yards wide. The slide area ran about a hundred yards below Kit and went up as far as he could see. He carefully stepped onto the rocks and carefully made his way up the slide. After he had gone about one hundred yards, he worked his way to the other side where there was mostly rock and very little vegetation.

When he reached a large stable rock, he carefully picked his way, jumping from rock to rock, working his way laterally up the face of the slope to the position he now occupied. His plan was simple. He would wait until Connor tracked him to the rockslide. He felt Connor would not find any tracks on the other side of the slide and then would head up the slope on the slide trying to cut Kit's trail. Kit doubted Connor could find where he had left the slide area and would have to keep going up the slope. When that happened, Kit would backtrack and return to the starting point, hotwire the truck, and drive to Emigrant Springs.

Fifteen minutes later, Kit could see Connor cautiously

crawl out from under a large sagebrush plant near the edge of the rock slide. Kit knew Connor was scanning the area, and he lay as still as he could. Laying here on the flat rock, trying not to even breathe, Kit could hear the beating of his own heart. He was sure it was so loud that even Connor could hear it, but Connor could not hear the beating of Kit's heart. Connor began making his way across the slide area and when he reached the other side, he paused to check for sign. Finding no sign, Connor made his way up the slide, stopping about every fifteen yards to scan the area above him.

After about half an hour, Kit rose from his hiding place and carefully began making his way down the slope, moving diagonally away from where he had last seen Connor and pausing briefly when he was able to get behind a large rock that shielded him from the summit of the slope. Soon he was in the valley and running a strong pace that would take him back to the starting point. After about an hour and fifteen minutes, he burst from the trees to the open meadow where they had left Kit's truck. Kit grabbed a screwdriver from the tool box in the truck bed and opened the hood. Kit had learned how to use a screwdriver to cross the starter with the battery to start the old truck previously. To Kit's surprise, the battery was missing. The old, rusty battery tray in the engine compartment was empty!

"Missing something, partner?" Kit whirled around to see a grinning Connor stepping out from behind the tree nearest the truck. Connor stepped back behind the tree and emerged with the truck battery in his hands. "Always expect the unexpected," he said with a grin.

Two hours later they were sitting in a corner booth of the Frontier Saloon, just outside Kemmerer, drinking a cold beer. Kit wanted to know how Connor figured out he had doubled back on the trail. "Easy," said Connor. "After I didn't see any sign on either side of the rockslide for about a hundred yards, I knew you had doubled back. If you had stayed on the rockslide, I would have seen some displaced rocks. The rock and the soil under the rocks that are moved are usually slightly different in color, often from retaining a little moisture. I didn't see any such sign. Then, when I backtracked, I saw your boot marks heading down the slope. I took a couple of short cuts to beat you back here."

"You outran me back and had time to remove the battery?" said an unbelieving Kit.

"Nope, I took the battery out before I came after you. Actually I could have just removed the distributor cap, but I thought a missing battery would really surprise you."

"Well, I was really surprised to see that empty battery tray when I raised the hood."

"That was the whole idea. Sometimes you do things for the shock effect and to get the maximum surprise possible. Still, I must admit you did pretty well out there, and I had to really hustle to get back to the truck just about the time you did."

Kit smiled at the compliment and Connor ordered another round of beers.

At the same time Kit and Connor were downing their second cold beer, Tony was coming back from having lunch at a small pub a block from his office. There were nicer places on the main floor of his office building, but he liked the small, dark pub with its limited light and interesting smells that reminded him of stale beer and cooked meat. Tony hung his jacket on a coat rack by his office door and flopped down on his office chair. He had been out late the previous night with a new girlfriend. He had spent a good deal of cash to impress her and hadn't even gotten a good night kiss. Tony's lack of success with women was legendary. He used to rent the movie *The Sure Thing* to see what he was doing wrong. Naturally he did everything wrong, every time. Tony was good with machines, lousy with people.

Tony hit the computer key to check his e-mail and after a few seconds he began to sort through his messages. Suddenly Tony's eyes locked on the small screen. There was an e-mail from the Secretary of State's office in Utah and one from the same public office in Wyoming. Tony quickly opened the e-mails and printed them out and then did some searching of his own on the computer. Fifteen minutes later, Tony did something unusual, he broke out in a huge smile. "Gotcha, you little bastard?"

Tony spent about two more hours making phone calls and computer inquiries and then read and re-read his report. Still grinning he buzzed Sarah Milner, Lenny's personal secretary, and let her know he needed to see Lenny as soon as possible.

Lenny leaned back in his plush leather office chair, holding a glass of bourbon, Seated in front of his massive desk was his assistant Tony, still wearing a huge grin. "Other than looking like the cat who ate the canary, what the hell are you grinning about?" asked Lenny.

"Boss, I found the little Andrews asshole." Tony said it so fast I almost sounded like one word instead of a complete sentence.

Lenny snapped his chair forward, spilling some of his bourbon in the process. "Where is the little mother fucker," snarled Lenny.

"Well," answered a smug Tony, "I knew something would show up if I kept looking. This Andrews asshole has managed to stay hidden pretty good. I don't know how he managed to do it for so long."

"Cut the bullshit and give me the Cliff Notes," said Lenny.

"He sold his car and that triggered a title change in Utah and he bought a truck and that triggered a title change in Wyoming," said Tony with a smile.

"That still doesn't tell me where he is," yelled an impatient Lenny.

"O.K, O.K, just listen for a minute," implored Tony.

Lenny's response was a chilling silence and a grim look on his face.

Tony recognized that he was on dangerous ground and moved quickly to put himself and his story on a more solid basis. "The kid sold his Chevy to an M. Kelly in a place called Kemmerer, Wyoming. Kelly sold it to a used car dealer called Karl's Kleen Kars in Salt Lake City, Utah. The dealer, a Karl Konrad, sold the car to some lady named Sarah Wilson of Salt Lake City and she recorded the title which brought up the previous transactions. About the same time, the kid bought an old truck from the same M. Kelly who bought the Chevy from him. The title change on the truck finally came through Wyoming. The Secretary of State's office in Wyoming must be less than up to date electronically, as they do not have computer access, and I had to pay off a clerk in the office to keep looking for Andrews' name. There aren't many people in Wyoming so it was not as hard as it sounds. Utah is more up-to-date computer wise."

"And this tells us exactly what?" asked Lenny coldly.

Tony realized he still was not on safe ground, so he rushed his summary. "The kid has to be in Kemmerer, Wyoming. I can't find a listing for him for a phone, utility bill, or post office box, but I'm sure he's there."

"You mean you have no address for him?"

"No, I don't have an address, but in a small place like Kemmerer, they don't have home mail delivery. They get their mail in little boxes they rent at the post office." That seemed to satisfy and quiet Lenny.

"So, now what do we do?"

"I send a hit team to Kemmerer. By now the kid probably thinks we've forgotten all about him and he feels safe where he is. It should be easy to find him in a small town like Kemmerer. People in places like that are usually pretty stupid."

"Send Ronnie and Cotton."

"Ronnie and Cotton? I was thinking more like Duke and Big Jon."

"Duke and Big Jon are a little too expensive for some green kid who probably doesn't know his ass from apple butter. Send Ronnie and Cotton."

"OK, boss, but remember, this green kid managed to stay hidden from us for several months. He can't be entirely stupid."

"The kid was lucky. Pure blind luck or we would have found him much sooner."

"I'll take care of it," said Tony and he slipped out of Lenny's office. As he closed the door to Lenny's office, Tony noticed he was sweating profusely. His heart had not stopped pounding by the time he got to his office and sank quietly into his chair.

CHAPTER THIRTY

Dan Vanderpool was the postmaster for the U.S. Post Office in Kemmerer, Wyoming. That in itself was no big thing. Just to the east of Kemmerer and contiguous, was the village of Diamondville, which also had its own post office and postmaster. Just to the west of Kemmerer was the tiny village of Frontier, which also had its own post office and postmaster. Dan longed for the sensible day, which would never come, when the three small towns merged and had only one post office and one postmaster to serve all 3,000 some odd souls in the combined three towns. Dan was born and raised in Kemmerer and knew every single person in the three towns and most of the surrounding ranches as well. He was filling out another useless and stupid report to Washington when Zeb, one of his postal clerks, stepped into his office.

Dan looked up expectantly and Zeb, a man of few words, said "Some fellas wanna see yah."

"Send them in," said Dan and stood up as two men entered his tiny office. Dan waived them to the only chairs in the office and said, "What can I do for you?"

One of the men was heavier and broad shouldered. He had black curly hair that curled at his shirt collar and a swarthy complexion. He was dressed in dark slacks, loafers, a button down blue dress shirt, and a brand new stiff denim jacket. He looked to his partner, a slightly taller, skinny man with acne scars on his face. He had totally white hair, cut short, and was dressed almost exactly like his partner except his button down shirt was white, not blue. He too, had a brand new stiff denim jacket on.

The skinny man spoke first. "I'm Walter Krank, Mr. Vanderpool and this is my associate Samuel Jones. We have been looking for a young man named Carson Andrews and believe he may be living around here. Your clerk didn't seem to know him, but he told me you know just about everyone in this part of Wyoming.

Dan smiled at the obvious compliment. It was true that he did know just about everyone in western Wyoming.

"Just why might you be looking for this Mr. Andrews?" he asked.

"Well," replied Krank, "we're private investigators working for Mr. Andrew's father's estate. He died recently and we were hired to locate his son as his only living heir. We believe he may be living in the area, and we'd like to give him the news of his inheritance." Krank finished his sentence with a rather oily smile and a knowing wink.

"I'm sorry to disappoint you boys, but the name Carson Andrews is totally unknown to me. You say his father died recently?"

"Yes, yes, just a few months ago," said Krank.

"Well, maybe he's a drifter," Dan said. "I would suggest you stop at the police station and talk to the chief. He might know something about the young man. With that Dan stood and shook hands with both men.

"Thank you for your time, Mr. Vanderpool," said Krank, "and thank you for the tip. We'll check with the police office. Could you tell me where it is located?"

Dan gave the men directions and watched them from his office window as the two men exited from the post office and walked to their rental car with Utah plates. Dan wrote down a description of the car and the plate number. He noted that they headed the car in the opposite direction of the police station. Dan did not know a Carson Andrews, but he certainly had known Tom Andrews. Then he picked up his phone and dialed a number. "Hello, Woody, Dan Vanderpool here. I think I have some information for you."

Cotton and Ronnie drove the rental car to the nearby Fossil Butte Motel and checked in. On pure chance, Cotton checked the phone book in the room, but there was no Andrews listed. Cotton and Ronnie went over the possible sources and decided that Cotton would go to the courthouse and check all the records and Ronnie would stop at a few bars and the local grocery store.

By six o'clock they met back at the motel and neither one of them had found a thing that could be called a clue to finding Carson Andrews. There were no records of him and nobody they talked to knew him. Both Ronnie and Cotton carried a copy of a photo of Carson dressed in a business suit that Tony had managed to obtain from International Consulting, Carlson's former employer.

"I don't get it," said Cotton. "A kid like this should stick out in this hick town like a sore thumb."

"You mean like we do?" responded Ronnie. "The denim jackets were a stupid idea, Cotton. We look like cowboys from New York."

"Maybe you're right. Let's ditch the jackets and forget about trying to blend in."

"Oh, we blend, all right. We blend like a coonskin cap on a mini-skirted hooker."

"Cut the shit. Let's get some supper, and I'll e-mail Tony to see if we can get some leads from him."

Ronnie responded with a grunt and tossed his new stiff denim jacket on the floor of the small closet and pulled on his old leather jacket.

They got directions from the motel clerk for some place

several miles away called Bon Ricos and after a couple of
wrong turns, they arrived at the restaurant. There were
only a few cars in the parking lot and they were quickly
given a corner table. By Wyoming standards, Bon Ricos
was fairly upscale. To the two hit men, the restaurant was
slightly above a dump, although both conceded that the
food was not that bad. They had several drinks and then
headed for their car. The parking lot was gravel and there
were no outside lights, only the glow of light from the sign
on the one story building with a false front.

Cotton turned the key in the ignition and nothing
happened. "Shit, fucking rental car."

"What do you do now?" asked Ronnie.

"We sure as hell are not gonna get Triple A out in
this shithole," said Cotton. He got out of the car and
attempted to figure out how to open the hood. Finally he
found the catch and opened the hood, but the little light
under the hood was burned out and he could see nothing.
He leaned forward and felt with his hands to try and find
the battery.

Suddenly Cotton sensed some movement behind him
and the hood slammed down on top of Cotton's head
and arms with great force. He started to scream and then
passed out. The impact of the slamming hood alerted
Ronnie and he quickly stepped out of the car on the
passenger's side to see what had happened. As he closed
the car door, Ronnie sensed some movement behind him
and then everything went black. He was unconscious
before his face hit the gravel of the parking lot.

Three days later Manual Ramos, a bored Mexican border policeman, was checking a semi-truck load of hogs at the port of entry at Juarez, Mexico. He detested having to inspect livestock shipments from the States. The smell was always overpowering and his uniform always got dirty. With the new security cameras in use, he could no longer take a bribe from the drivers and waive the trucks through. He had to inspect every truck or he would quickly lose his job. As Manual opened up the upper hatch door at the rear of the truck trailer to look inside he witnessed an amazing sight. Taped to the stanchions above the reach of the hogs were two filthy gringos, totally naked, bound and gagged with duct tape.

Ramos lost his balance and fell backwards from the truck to the pavement, loudly screaming for his superior as he fell.

CHAPTER THIRTY-ONE

It was an ugly morning for Tony. He hadn't even made it to the office coffee pot before Lenny came bursting through the door, yelling like a banshee. Tony had never seen Lenny this angry. Tony waited for Lenny to run out of breath, as he could not quite make out what Lenny was trying to convey between the yelling, the cursing, and the screaming. When Lenny finally ran out of breath and flopped down on one of the hard plastic break room chairs, Tony wisely did not speak. Finally, Lenny, his eyes still bulging with a wild look, handed Tony a fax. Tony scanned the fax, which was a report from their contact who had provided Ronnie and Cotton.

"Holy shit," said Tony. "How the hell did this happen?"

"What do I look like, the answer man," snarled a now more intelligible Lenny. "These two idiots managed to fuck up a simple job and get a one way ride on a pig truck to Mexico."

"But how in the hell could that kid manage something like this? Either he's a whole lot smarter and tougher than we thought, or he's getting some help," said Tony.

"It doesn't matter. Whether he's a smart little asshole or he has found some help. Either way, we made a mistake and underestimated him, and so did Ronnie and Cotton."

"So, what do we do not?" whined Tony.

"What do we do now? Are you an idiot? We do what we should have done in the first place. We send in some real pros and we splatter this punk kid and any one who is helping all over some cactus in Wyoming. I don't care what we spend. We need to make an example of this punk kid. Nobody fucks with me and gets away with it. I want a plan put together, and I want you to get the best talent available. Do you understand me, Tony?"

"Yes, boss, no problem, boss, I'll get on it right away," said a cowering and frightened Tony.

Tony retreated to his tiny office and turned on his

computer. Tony was still trembling with fear at Lenny's outburst of rage and his own unfortunate proximity to that rage. Tony went to the men's room and relieved himself. He went back to the break room and after carefully checking to see that Lenny was not present, he slipped in and helped himself to a cup of badly needed coffee.

Back at his desk, Tony sipped the hot coffee and thought about how to eliminate this Andrews kid. Normally, he would send an e-mail to his contact and negotiate a deal. Usually all he provided was a timeframe and a price. Now Tony found himself on the unfamiliar ground of coming up with a plan. Tony decided to send an e-mail asking for both a replacement team for Ronnie and Cotton and a plan to eliminate the kid. Better to let the pros figure out how they were going to do their job and let them give the plan to Tony so he could pass it on to Lenny.

He went to his coded notes and found the e-mail address he needed. Soon he had composed an e-mail with the details of what happened to Ronnie and Cotton and a bio sheet on Andrews as well as what facts they knew about his presence in Kemmerer, Wyoming. Tony added a request for a top team and for details of their plan to complete the assignment.

By the time Tony had gone for a second cup of coffee and returned to his desk, his e-mail light was blinking. The entire message consisted of "Double the standard rate." Tony knew that would be the price for this assignment. He knew that was a lot of money for a hit on a young punk but, this one was proving to be very troublesome and after all, in the end it was not Tony's money. Lenny would get it from his clients, not Tony.

Tony typed in O.K. and hit the reply box.

CHAPTER THIRTY-TWO

Kit pulled on the reins and brought Dolly and the trailing mule to a stop. He had reached an open spot on the trail and swung down out of the saddle to stretch his legs. He tied Dolly to a nearby bush and lifted his canteen off the saddle horn. After a long drink of cool water, he replaced the top and slipped the canteen strap back over the saddle horn. He took his binoculars out of his saddlebag and spent a few minutes studying the area around and down from him. The aspens trees were starting to turn from green to gold up where he was resting which meant winter would not be far behind.

Big Dave had told him he could taste snow in the wind. Kit was not too sure of that, but now he felt that he could almost smell rain and snow in the air. Today there were only a few lonely clouds in an otherwise bright blue sky. Kit walked over and sat on a nearby large rock and continued to scan the open areas around him. He had taken a day off from his seemingly never-ending instruction from Connor to re-supply Odie Lone's sheep camp.

In another couple of weeks they would be moving the

sheep down from their summer grazing land in the mountains before they became impassible with snow. Tomorrow was Sunday and he and Chance were going with Woody to learn how to fly fish. Woody was taking them to a section of the Ham's Fork between the city and the power company reservoirs where the fishing was supposed to be excellent.

Before mounting Dolly, Kit checked the position of his holster on his belt. The short holster had a snap loop that covered the top of the Kimber 45 caliber pistol to protect it from falling out. The holster was on his right hip and was hidden by his long denim jacket. His Gerber LMF knife hung from his left hip, next to his double magazine holder. Satisfied that everything was positioned correctly, Kit swung up on the horse and headed up the trail toward the summit. As he neared the summit, the trail took him towards the edge of a steep drop-off. Each time Kit had made this trip he had noted how sheer and deep the drop-off was and usually did his best to keep Dolly as far to the mountainside of the trail as possible.

As Kit started past the drop-off, he looked down and there to his amazement was a huge airplane flying below him! He reined in Dolly and stared as a U.S. Air Force B-52 jet bomber flew silently below his vantage point. Kit watched as the plane flew out of sight, the roar of its engines hitting him after the plane had passed. Kit remembered Big Dave had told him sometimes the Air Force made low-level strategic bombing runs in the canyons of the mountains of western Wyoming. That was obviously what he had just seen.

Half an hour later he was unloading the mule with Odie Lone and trying to understand what Odie was saying in rapid Spanish. He felt sorry for Odie who lived a pretty lonely existence in a sheep camp in the mountains. He knew that Odie sent most of his money home to his family in Mexico. Once in a while, a letter for Odie Lone would arrive care of the Carlsons, but not very often. Kit wondered why Odie Lone's family did not write him more often, but figured it was none of his business.

After sharing some home-made rabbit stew with fresh bread from a reflecting oven for lunch, Kit headed back down to the valley. He had learned to stop at certain points on the trail to rest the horse and mule, but also to listen and observe. Connor had taught him if you took the time to be a little vigilant, you would almost never be surprised by man or beast.

Kit found himself wondering how Tang was making out in Chicago. She had taken his loan and paid off the family debts and sold the service station. Kit saw her mother around town now and then, but other than saying hello he never engaged her in conversation to find out what Tang was doing. He did get a post card from Tang about a month ago. The card had a picture of the Chicago Museum of Natural History on one side and a note from Tang saying thanks and letting him know she had her old job back as assistant curator. Since then he had gotten an envelope with a check for five hundred dollars made payable to Kit with the notation, "payment #1."

Pretty soon he could see his old pickup with the horse

trailer and he turned Dolly in that direction. As he and Dolly drew closer to his truck, he saw a second truck parked behind his. He reined Dolly to a stop and stood up in the stirrups with his binoculars to get a better look. He recognized Big Dave's pickup and could make out the figures of three men, Big Dave being one of them.

Kit pushed the binoculars back in the saddlebag and urged Dolly down the trail at a faster pace. Before long he and Dolly emerged from the trees onto the meadow where his welcoming committee awaited him. As he got closer he could make out the three men were Big Dave, Connor, and Woody.

Kit quickly dismounted from Dolly and with help from the others loaded Dolly and the pack mule into the horse trailer hooked on to his old pickup.

Within five minutes the four of them were sitting on old fallen logs in the shade of the nearest big tree, and Big Dave had produced a cooler filled with ice and beer. Kit popped the tab on his can of beer and took a couple of sizeable gulps as he felt the cold liquid seemingly clean out the dust in his throat. His initial thirst satisfied, he curiously looked over at his three guests. He was pretty sure this was not just a social visit to welcome him back from a re-supply trip to a sheep camp.

"So what brings you boys way out here?" he asked. "Not that I'm complaining about cold beer on a hot day."

Woody looked up from his beer and wiped a litle foam off his large mustache. "Well, my boy, it seems there has been sort of an incident."

"Just what kind of an incident?" asked Kit.

Woody quickly outlined the story of the two strangers and their interest in Kit and how they had found themselves unwitting and unwilling tourists to Mexico. By the time Woody had finished the story, both Big Dave and Connor were unable to keep from laughing. Big Dave managed to blurt out he was sure the two meant no harm because they were very cooperative in revealing they were concealing nothing from the Mexican border guards. With that, he, Connor, and Woody all began a new round of laughter.

"So let me get this straight," said Kit. "These two guys came to Kemmerer looking for me. You guys found out about them and managed to send them to Mexico over their protests? How did you do that?"

Woody then told the story in exact detail, pausing to let the renewal of laughter die down before finishing the story. When he had finished, Woody's face and voice took on a more serious tone. "Look, Kit, we are sure that these two were killers who were sent her to eliminate you. We're concerned that they were able to determine that you were in Kemmerer. We're also concerned that whoever sent them will not stop with this and will send more killers who will be more of the A-team variety than these two birds were."

As Kit listened he slowly began to realize that someone had actually sent men to Kemmerer to kill him. He began to appreciate that the "stories" that these three friends of his had told him about service in the military with his father were much more truth than fiction.

"One thing is for certain, Kit," said Woody. "These people are determined to spend money to see you dead. They are really gonna be pissed when they find out what happened to the two jaybirds they sent out here. They know you're here, and they'll send a much stronger team to finish the job. We can stop them and we can protect you, but you're going to have to do what we say or all bets are off on your survival.

Kit felt a chill run through his entire body. He knew his life was now in the hands of these three men who were friends of his father's and were now friends of his. He knew he would need to listen carefully to what they proposed and that following their advice might mean the difference between life and death for him.

The four of them discussed a plan of action and by the time the last cold beer had been consumed, it was decided that Kit would stay on his father's place and that Connor or Big Dave would deliver whatever supplies he needed and pick up his mail. They would do so only after calling Kit first and only after checking that they were not being followed. If they felt they were being tailed, they would keep driving to Cokeville and call Kit from there.

With their knowledge of the back-roads and their four wheel drive trucks, they were sure they could lose anyone trying to follow them. Kit wanted to continue his re-supply trips to the sheep camps and Big Dave grudgingly agreed after Kit said he would meet Big Dave at the trail head. Big Dave would bring the horses, mule, and supplies and Kit would make the trip. Big Dave would meet him at the trailhead on his return trip at a prearranged time. If Big Dave was not there, Kit was to remain in the woods at a vantage point where he could see the entire valley around where his pickup was normally parked.

Connor insisted that Kit be armed at all times. "He can handle that 45 and if they get past us, he's gonna need it."

"You mean I take it to the bathroom when I have to take a crap?" said Kit with a smirk.

"That's right, sonny," Connor replied coldly. "When you're setting on the pot, you keep the pistol in the crotch of your pants that are bunched up at your feet. More than one good man has gone to met his maker because he went to take a crap unarmed."

CHAPTER THIRTY-THREE

Dan Witte found himself staring at his notes. He was seated at a lovely walnut desk in one of the more expensive suites of the Hotel Utah in Salt Lake City. The two-room suite provided him with a private bedroom and also a living room/office. It was perfect for his job requirements and was an excellent cover for his operation. His hotel rate was $650 a day and in Salt Lake City that tended to sort out the riff-raff. The Hotel Utah was attractive to celebrities and politicians who valued their privacy and some space form the unwashed masses. The bellhops wore uniforms as did the wait staff. Even the management of the hotel seemed somehow cloned, dressed in their identical official Hotel Utah navy blue blazers and gray slacks or skirts if they were female.

The hotel was located within walking distance of the main part of downtown Salt Lake City and contained a fine restaurant that provided the hotel guests with excellent dining and more importantly for Witte was their twenty-four hour room service. Witte followed no normal routine. When he was on an assignment, he was working twenty-four hours a day and what time it was did not matter to him. His personal motto was "it takes whatever it takes to get the job done."

When he was not on assignment, Witte preferred someplace warm, with a beach and easy access to an ocean. His preference was the Pacific Ocean, usually Southern California or Mexico, but since he was originally from South Carolina, the Atlantic Ocean was a close second.

Witte got up from his desk, which was littered with notes and went to the bathroom. As he dried his hands, he stared into the mirror. For this assignment he had gray hair, worn long, a moustache, a Van Dyke beard, and blue eyes. The former was due to a hair dye and the second was due to colored contact lenses. He studied his face and was satisfied with what he saw.

His current role was that of an academic type. The gray hair gave him age and the slightly longer than necessary hair added a slightly absent minded professor effect. He wore khaki pants and a slightly wrinkled white and blue striped button down shirt. Hanging on the back of the bathroom door was his tweed jacket, complete with leather patches on the elbows. Finishing out his ensemble was a pair of older, but expensive loafers with tiny tassels.

Dan was cultivating the look of a college professor doing research and he was pleased with the result. Before returning to his notes, he pulled a slightly worn brown leather briefcase from the closet and set it on the coffee table in front of the sofa. He opened the briefcase and then pushed in hidden buttons on each side of the case and the false bottom popped open. He reached in and pulled out a Sig-Sauer P229 9mm semi-automatic pistol.

He pulled back the slide and checked to see there was a round in the chamber. Satisfied the gun was loaded, he released the magazine and checked on the spring and the bullets in the magazine. Everything was in perfect working order. He then checked the two additional magazines to make sure they were in good working order. Finally satisfied, he returned the pistol and magazines to their hiding place and closed the briefcase and returned it to the closet.

Back at his desk, Dan began to make an outline for this project and also set up a timeline. This would be one of his more complicated assignments. It was not complicated because of the subject, a young man with no training or defensive skills. Rather it was complicated because of the location. The target was located in a small town in Wyoming. Anyone new coming into town would stand out like a whore in church. Also, while the target had no skills, someone around him obviously did have skills. A smile came to Dan's face as he re-read what happened to the team that had preceded him.

That team had failed and wound up wrapped in duct tape, naked, taped to the wall of a pig truck at the Mexican border. Dan was still smiling, but the smile was grim. The stupidity of the first team was their problem. Dan did not plan to make any of the obvious mistakes made by his predecessors. He had worked out a plan and set up a team to carry out that plan. If everything went on schedule, the target would be dead in less than two weeks.

He then pulled out his laptop computer and began pulling down files that were heavily encrypted to protect the contents should the laptop fall into the wrong hands. Dan had paid for a good deal of research on Kemmerer and the surrounding area. Not all of it was usable, but some of it was very helpful. The area around Kemmerer was high plains desert. Coal was being mined by two large mining operations. One of the mines fed the needs of a nearby coal-burning power plant that supplied power to the wet coast of the United States. Just outside of Kemmerer was a sizeable national monument, Fossil Butte, which was run by the Department of the Interior of the U.S. Agriculture in the area consisted of cow-calf and sheep operations, most of which were on land leased by the Bureau of Land Management to cattle and sheep operators in Wyoming.

Dan needed a form of cover to get his team into the area without being detected for what they were and then locating the target and using the size and the solitude of the land to isolate and terminate the target. Dan had decided on creating a phony botany research group doing a survey on high plains desert plants. They were allegedly from a small college in Illinois, Sangamon State College, that no longer existed. Dan was sure no one here was going to bother to check and even if they did, such an inquiry would alert one of his team who had established a phone number for Sangamon State in Springfield, Illinois, and would provide additional phony cover.

Dan had procured two large vans and a Jeep Grande Cherokee along with three small trailers, each containing two ATV's. The vehicles were all painted white and had phony signage proclaiming them to be the property of good old Sangamon State College. One of the vans was crammed with electronics and each of the ATV's was equipped with GPS units. The other van held camping equipment, food, water, and a hidden cache of weapons and ammunition.

The plan called for Dan and four others to pose as members of the college biology research team. Finding qualified people for the assignment who could also look like college research types had proven to be a huge challenge. Dan ended up with two men and two women. Dan preferred not to use women in his operations, but in this case they made the group seem even less threatening and thus were recruited.

The sixth member of the team was also a woman. She was Mexican and spoke both English and Spanish. She would enter Kemmerer in an old rattletrap car and get a job cleaning motel rooms or washing dishes, or some other menial job no one but a Mexican would take. She would rent a room in Kemmerer and use state of the art electronic communications equipment to warn Dan if the authorities in Kemmerer suspected anything about his group. She was Dan's spy.

Dan had spent a month interviewing and checking backgrounds on his team before getting comfortable with his selections. He had scheduled a meeting in his hotel room at 7:30 A.M., a time when more people were coming and going in the hotel than usual and he felt no one would notice his five team members. Since none of them knew any of the others in the team, they would not be coming in as a group. In fact, Dan had told each of them to be there at a different time with five minutes difference in each scheduled arrival. By 8:00 A.M. all of them had arrived and were helping themselves to coffee and rolls Dan had room service provide. At exactly 8:00 A.M., Dan called for their attention. It was immediately silent in the room. Dan was pleased to see that he was dealing with professionals.

He began by explaining the overall plan and the time frame he had developed. Dan gave them each a packet of information. Each packet contained the new "identity" of the team member. Dan had each of them look over their packets. "The packet information is who you are from now on until we complete this project." He had each of them take out a name tag with their new names and put them on.

"Please use only the new names when you address each other beginning now. Get used to these names and only these names. Since none of you know each other, this should be easy. Under no conditions are any of you to tell anyone your real name. Violation of this rule will get you bounced from the team with no compensation."

Each packet also contained phony Illinois driver's licenses, social security cards, and two credit cards. "The credit cards are real and are to be used for this project. Just don't go crazy with them. Remember, we are college employees who do not make squat and are used to pinching pennies. The last item in the jacket is a DVD on botany in Wyoming. Please watch it until you feel you have some working knowledge of what it is that we are supposed to be doing in Wyoming."

Dan then turned to his computer and a power-point presentation that highlighted the plan and each person's role. Dan would be the senior member of the botany research group and would be Dr. Dan Burke, PHD. He would drive the Jeep.

Sylvia would be his assistant. Sylvia was a slender blonde in her mid-thirties. She was an expert in electronic communications and would run the communications van.

Sue was a small, dark haired Italian girl with a husky build. With her dark skin she looked like a peasant girl in her late twenties. Sue had the forearms of a weight lifter.

She would serve as camp cook. Sue was also an excellent shot with a rifle or a pistol.

Lance looked like a California surf bum. He was tall, blonde, tanned, and well muscled. He looked like a thirty year old graduate student who would rather surf than do anything else. In fact, he was skilled with a knife or any other edged weapon. He had often killed by simply breaking the neck of his target. He would drive the supply van.

Nick was of medium height, slight of build, and walked with a slight limp. He was in his late twenties and was prematurely bald. He had large ears, which were even more prominent with the lack of hair. He looked the part of a college scholar with his large wire rimmed glasses. He was actually an experienced hit-man with over ten contract kills to his credit. Nick would drive the communications van.

Dan had also hired two other men and had deliberately not told his team about them nor had he told the pair about the existence of his team. The two-man team would be set up as a diversion. He wanted to make sure that the authorities had something to chase after and take any attention way from his team. The two-man team would make a show of snooping around and asking questions, but they would take no specific action without specific approval from Dan.

After two more days of reviewing the plan and their fake identities, Dan had his team work together in loading all their supplies into the vans and the Jeep. Satisfied that everything was in order, he scheduled their departure from Salt Lake City for early the next morning.

CHAPTER THIRTY-FOUR

Kit sat on his front porch drinking coffee and watching the road leading to the cabin. In the early calm of the morning, he could hear the sounds of occasional traffic on the highway as it filtered through the pine trees that obscured his view of he highway far below. Other than a couple of magpies flitting in the trees, scolding something Kit could not see, nothing else seemed to be moving. Big Dave had called earlier saying he was coming out with Kit's new companion/bodyguard. Kit was not sure how this was going to work. He had gotten used to his new life and was feeling pretty good about his newly developed skills in woodcraft and self-defense. He was not so sure he needed a bodyguard and resented this idea more than just a little.

A rooster tail of dust coming up through the trees alerted him to the arrival of Big Dave long before he could hear the truck's engine. Soon the pickup swung into the yard in front of the house and out stepped the familiar hulking figure of Big Dave. Coming out on the passenger side of the truck was a man about Kit's age and height. He had a lanky, sort of unconnected way of walking and was dressed in old denims, just like Big Dave. He had curly black hair and was deeply tanned. He wore a set of expensive sunglasses and a sweat-stained gray Stetson cowboy hat.

Kit stepped down from the porch and Big Dave introduced the two young men. "Kit, this here is Gary

Olson. He's signed on to sort of be your partner for a while." Olson flashed a smile full of white teeth and extended his hand. Kit shook hands and noted that Olson had large hands and a strong grip. Gary looked Kit in the eyes and said, "My real name is Gary, but I've been known as Swifty most of my life."

"Swifty?" said Kit.

"Yep, I been called that since I was in the third grade. I tend to usually be in a bit of a hurry and that's how I got the nickname."

"O.K., then Swifty it is," replied an amused Kit.

Big Dave excused himself, climbed into his pickup and promptly disappeared in a cloud of dust on the ranch's dirt road. Kit led Swifty to a spare bedroom where Swifty deposited his bedroll. Then Kit took him on a tour of the house and the ranch site, including the shooting range. After a hike up to the top of the butte above the cabin, they both sat on a large flat rock looking down over the cabin to the highway.

From this vantage point they could see the sparse traffic on the highway below the cabin and to the mountains north of them. After a short period of silence, Swifty asked Kit about who he was and where he came from and how he came to be in Kemmerer. Swifty listened quietly and never once stopped Kit in his tale with a question or an interruption. When Kit had finished, Swifty had a few questions, and then explained why he was here.

"I was one of those kids who was afraid they were going to die before they had a chance to try everything in life that they wanted to try. I tried everything I could and not always with the best of results. My mama told me she was shocked that I lived to see manhood. I was a bit of a bad boy growing up, but somehow I survived without going to jail or getting seriously hurt. I flunked out of college my freshman year and wound up in the army. The army discovered that I had a real talent for some seriously bad work and I would up in an outfit called the Delta Force. Ever heard of it?"

Of course Kit had heard of the Delta Force and seen movies about it and he told Swifty so.

"Well, I spent seven years in Delta, and finally decided I had enough when I got shot on an assignment in Iraq. After I healed up, I had six months left on my hitch and I just decided not to re-up. I spent those seven years doing lots of cool, dangerous things, but I figured that the odds were starting to catch up with me and it was time to try something different. Big Dave knew from my mom that I was getting out of the service and coming home and he called me and offered me this job and here I am."

"Did Big Dave explain to you what we are up against?" asked Kit.

"He said you were on the run from some bad dudes in Chicago and they are trying to waste you so you can't testify in court against their guys. You hid out here in Kemmerer by accident and turned out to be the son of one of the great mystery men of Kemmerer. My job is to help you protect yourself. I understand you have had some pretty good training. I've heard of this Connor guy and he is supposed to be pretty damn good, for an Army Ranger, but you need to remember, I worked in Delta. Delta is an outfit I consider the best in the world. You listen to me and do what I tell you to do and we'll come out of this in one piece. You try to do things on your own and you will wind up getting killed. I can only help you protect yourself. I cannot guaranty your protection. Are we agreed on that?"

"Absolutely," said Kit, who felt a strong sense of comfort in what Swifty had just told him. Kit wanted to be his own man, but he knew he needed help in what might be coming. He had new skills and confidence, but alone he would be no match for professional hit men.

Swifty and Kit soon settled into a comfortable routine. They trained daily on the range and sometimes with Connor. Swifty increased and intensified the hand-to-hand combat training. He especially emphasized how to disarm the opponent and how to avoid being disarmed. They rode horses in to the mountains and then hiked into difficult terrain. Swifty began to teach Kit how to see the land, the trees, and the rocks as a friend, not an obstacle. He learned how to be more patient and how to blend in with his environment.

Swifty became the camp cook, Kit did the clean up work and set up the camps they made. When back at the cabin, they watched movies on television and talked about who they were and where they had come from. In a very short time Swifty and Kit were becoming good friends. They avoided town. When they needed groceries, they drove across the state line near Cokeville, Wyoming, to

Montpelier, Idaho, and shopped at a supermarket that stayed open until ten P.M. They noted that they never saw anyone they knew on those trips.

Three weeks after they met found them sitting on top of the butte that was above the cabin. They were sitting back against some large rocks, soaking in the heat of the rapidly sinking sun.

"I understand from Big Dave that you inherited some money?" asked Swifty.

"Inherit is not the right word. We don't know if my dad is dead or alive. This was money he set up in a trust for me and it didn't trigger until I showed up here. Why do you ask?"

"Well, seems to me that any young buck our age who came into some money would be driving something a damn site better than the old piece of crap you're dragging us around in."

"You don't like my truck! It's a classic. There's nothing wrong with it."

"It's a piece of crap. It's slow. It don't have four-wheel drive. It don't have hardly any power, and it rides just slightly better than an old buckboard."

"Well, it has sentimental value. It was the first pickup I ever owned, and I got it before I ever found out I was getting any money."

"Fine, keep it. Set it up on blocks in the shed with a bronze plaque on it, but use some of that money to buy something that can take us every place we want to go and still be cool enough to attract chicks."

"So you don't think it's a chick magnet?"

"Chick magnet! Hah! It's more like a chick fart. No broad worth her salt would be caught dead anywhere near that thing."

The argument continued for about a hour before Kit finally admitted that maybe it was time to get a more modern pickup truck. He did plan to keep the old truck. It seemed more like an old friend than a piece of machinery, but so then did Dolly and now Swifty, himself. Kit decided that once the trial date had passed or he was reasonably sure that he was no longer in danger of getting his head blown off, he and Swifty would go to Salt Lake City and look at trucks.

As Swifty had told Kit, "Guns, pickup trucks, and horses, does it get any better than this! Of course, we could add a good looking woman, but that's unlikely in our present circumstances."

CHAPTER THIRTY-FIVE

Dan waited until he was back in his Jeep before he opened the note he had been given with his receipt for the gasoline he'd just purchased at the convenience store in Kemmerer. Anna, his Mexican spy, was working at the convenience store as well as cleaning motel rooms for the Fossil Butte motel. Dan slipped the note into his shirt pocket and drove slowly out of the gravel parking lot. He had driven into town for supplies, and after loading them into the back of the Jeep, he had stopped for gas.

Dan waited until he reached the edge of town and then pulled over on the shoulder of the road. Satisfied that no one was following him or watching him, he opened the note and began to read. Anna had found out that their target, Carson Andrews, was in town and had been working for a David Carlson, herding sheep and then supplying Carlson's sheep camps. No one seemed to know where he was staying and no one had seen him for a couple of weeks. He was driving an old green 1949 GMC ¾ ton pickup truck.

"Well," thought Dan, "that kind of a truck can't be very common, even in this god forsaken place." He would send Lance in with one of the vans for gas in two days and see if Anna had learned anything else. So far he and his "botany" crew had run into a few cowboys, a BLM agent, and not much else. His crew was bored and frankly, so was he. They were tired of hard beds, bugs, dust, and Sue's cooking.

Jim and Hardy, his two decoys, had not lasted long. After two days of hanging around bars and asking questions nobody was inclined to answer, they came out of a bar on the second night and had four flat tires on their vehicle. They took the hint and left for Salt Lake City. They called Dan on his satellite hone and he told them he would wire them their money and to head home.

Lance returned to camp after his trip into town to gas up the van and pick up a note from Anna. Anna was turning out to be the best investment Dan had for helpful information. Anna had determined the reason the first two groups sent to Kemmerer had been pushed out so easily was that several residents, including David Carlson, Carson's employer, had previously served in a U.S. Army black ops unit that had specialized in covert operations, even during "peacetime." Anna was sure that Carlson and his group were responsible for protecting Andrews and for easily turning away the first group of hit men and Dan's subsequent "decoy" group. She did not know how many others there were in the group nor did she understand their connection to Andrews, but was working on it.

Dan reread her note and then tossed it into the cook fire. He took a can of beer from the propane-powered refrigerator and sat back in his worn lawn chair under the shade of the tarp covering the cooking area. Dan's first reaction was that he had not charged enough for this job.

He had seen the hard part of this contract as infiltrating a small town area and finding his target. He had not planned on having the target protected by professionals. He sipped his cold beer as he pondered on how to best use Anna's new information. He needed to find a way to separate the target from the professionals that were protecting him.

Big Dave Carlson strode purposefully along the downtown Kemmerer Triangle until he reached Agate Street where he walked half a block to Woody's law office. Instead of going in the front door, he walked around the small office building that once was a residence and went to the door at the back of the building and knocked. Woody answered the door and ushered Big Dave into his office where Connor was already seated.

"Boys," said Big Dave. "We seem to have run out of varmints. Them last two fellers seemed to have a real aversion to walking when their car tires plumb run out of air. Has any one seen them come back to town?"

"Nope," replied Connor. "I think they took the hint and left for greener pastures."

"I would like to be as sure as you two are," said Woody. "Still I find this has gone way too easily. I can understand the first group and they were certainly not the brightest bulbs in the box, but I figured those Chicago boys would learn from that and send us something more along the lines of the A-Team this time. These guys were too easy. I don't like the smell of this one."

"Too easy," snorted Big Dave. "You been watching too much of that trashy television where there's a terrorist behind every bush. Most of these crooks are pretty stupid."

"Maybe," responded Woody. "But I think the people who are after Kit are pretty smart and when they hire someone to do a job and they fail, then they learn from their mistakes and send out a better team that is also better prepared on what they are going up against. These last two could have just been decoys to keep us off the trail of the real killers."

"Now whose imagination is running wild!" Connor

said. "We don't get a lot of strangers in Kemmerer, and we've had damn few lately. Except for those last two yahoos, I can account for almost everyone else. We've had one or two drifters, who are now gone. We've had the geological survey team, which is also now gone. We even have some hopelessly inept Illinois college botany research group camping out in the toolies. The only other person I wasn't sure of is in the county lock-up for shop-lifting."

"You two are not giving those boys back in Chicago enough credit. My guess is that something is going on right now under our noses and we can't see it. Kit is in danger until after the trial and maybe even after that. Something is out there and we just aren't seeing it."

"So what do you suggest we do?" asked Big Dave.

"I think we keep with our routine. Big Dave patrols the town and near his sheep property and reports back what he has seen and Connor continues to work within the county. I will continue to monitor all of our electronic sources and use my network of informants. These people are out there, we just can't see them, yet."

"What bout Kit?" asked Connor. "Do we put him in hiding, do we move him, or what?"

Woody thought for a minute and then replied, "Let Kit stay where he is with his new shadow. I think he is safer there at the cabin than anyplace else that I can think of."

The meeting came to an end and Connor exited through the back door. Big Dave stayed around for a few minutes, one to squeeze a shot of good scotch out of Woody, and two to make sure that he and Connor were not seen leaving Woody's office by the back door together.

CHAPTER THIRTY-SIX

Dan smiled as he read a fresh e-mail on his laptop computer. "Nothing like technology," he thought. Dan had provided Anna with a wireless e-mail and phone device that she could keep hidden in her purse. That investment had just provided a huge dividend. Dan had known that Anna might be the best asset he had in his entire team. He knew that small town people would often clam up when being questioned by someone they perceived as an outsider. They were often suspicious of outsiders and usually with some justification. On the other hand, small town folks loved to gossip among themselves. As soon as Anna became accepted as a local, she began to hear things, some true and some false, that she would never have otherwise been privy to.

Anna had found out where Carson Andrews was living and that he had a roommate named Swifty Olson who grew up in Kemmerer, but had been gone for several years. She had also managed to get the phone number for the place Andrews was staying.

"Bingo," said Dan. He then made some calls on his satellite phone and within an hour, he had received responses to his questions. He got no information back on Swifty Olson, but he discovered that the small ranch that Andrews was living on was titled to a trust and had been for over ten years.

Dan knew that he could get copies of the drawings of the buildings on the ranch from the county, but that was likely to cause suspicion as, unlike a big city, here everyone knew everyone and was suspicious of anything a stranger did or asked for. He decided he would have two of his team attempt to covertly survey the ranch on foot.

First Dan drove his Jeep into Kemmerer and used a topographical map and the directions he got from Anna and a regular highway map to try to pinpoint the location of the ranch where Andrews was staying. After determining its approximate location, Dan drove the Jeep out of town on the highway headed for Nugget Canyon and the road to Cokeville, Wyoming.

As Dan entered the canyon, he checked for traffic and seeing none, he slowed down to try to find a side road that might lead to the ranch. After about a mile, he found a road on the north side of the highway. It was a dirt road and not in great condition. After driving by it and finding no other side roads, he pulled the Jeep off the road and again checked his maps.

Dan turned the Jeep around and headed back through the canyon the way he had come. When he got to the side road, he pulled the Jeep off the highway and onto the road. He could see nothing. The trees and the sides of the canyon blocked any view he had of where the road might lead. When he finally drove back onto the highway and headed back into Kemmerer, he tried in vain to see anything to the north of the highway. Frustrated, he headed back to the camp.

Early the next morning Dan gave Lance and Nick detailed instructions and handed each a digital camera with a zoom feature along with copies of his topographical map. Lance and Nick were to do the equivalent of a recon patrol and take pictures and make notes on the map. They were to sneak onto the ranch property at night and move into position to observe and take pictures during he day. They would pull out under the cover of darkness at the end of the day.

At dusk, Lance and Nick climbed into the van with Sue. Sue drove and Lance and Nick sat in the back. Lance and Nick were each outfitted in full camouflage gear and carried small packs with high-energy food and water bottles as well as their digital cameras, binoculars, and weapons.

Sue drove the van slowly toward the ranch letting the setting sun in the west outrace her to their destination in Nugget Canyon. Sue drove past the road turnoff and kept on going through the canyon. Once she was through, she pulled off the highway and stopped the van. After checking with Lance and Nick to make sure they were ready, she drove back through the canyon and slowed to a crawl as she approached the turnoff. Nick and Lance leaped out the door in the back of the van and quickly shut the door. They then moved into the brush lining the edge of the highway and the turnoff.

The two men began to slowly crawl through the rough terrain, carefully moving from sagebrush clump to rocks to whatever cover they could find. Other than rocks there was not a great deal of cover and since they were crawling uphill, it made the climb even more difficult. Sharp rocks and thorns caught on their clothing and in some cases tore clothing and some skin. There was just enough moonlight for them to see where they were located and to make spotting them difficult until dawn.

By dawn, they had each taken up a position that was slightly below the ranch with Nick about three hundred yards to the east and Lance about four hundred and fifty yards to the west. Each of them had found good cover in a sizeable sagebrush plant.

About six o'clock in the morning, Nick could hear doors opening and banging closed. He assumed someone was up and feeding the livestock. He adjusted his binoculars and tried to see activity. He could see the ranch house and a large barn type structure next to it. The barn had fencing attached to the west side that appeared to be some sort of corral.

Nick could not see anything of the corral, but he was sure that Lance could see the corral from his vantage point. Nick was glad he had chosen this spot. To have moved any closer would have left him exposed to even a casual observer as the ground was rocky and covered with short grass. As he studied the ground in front of him, he saw something that made his blood run cold. The sun was gleaming off what he was sure was a trip-wire. He adjusted his binoculars and looked again. Sure enough, about fifteen yards in front of him was a well-concealed trip wire.

Had he kept going during the night, he would have surely set it off. Nervously, Nick began to survey the area to his east and west and then behind him to make sure he would not accidentally set off a wire when he retreated back to the highway that night. Satisfied that no surprises awaited him downhill from his position, he turned his attention back to the ranch house. He would have liked the ability to call Lance on a radio and let him know about the trip wire, but they had agreed not to take radios as they might prove to be a source of detection. Lance would have to take care of himself.

Nick again adjusted the binoculars. The house and barn seemed to be almost built into the rock wall of the bluff behind them. The bluff rose about three hundred feet above the house and barn. Nick could see trees at the top, and he suspected that meant here was some form of water storage up there. He could make out what he was sure were birds in the trees.

Lance was cursing his choice of cover. The ground was covered with sharp little rocks that seemed to bite into his flesh. No matter what position he took, it ended up being a painful one. Because he was on the west side of the ranch house, he knew he would have absolutely no shade in the hot afternoon. Lance adjusted his binoculars and watched as someone emerged from the barn and moved into the corral. Lance could see little of what the person was doing because much of the activity occurred behind a large water tank that blocked his view.

Lance could see several horses in the corral and they were all moving toward the man, further blocking his view. "Breakfast for the animals," thought Lance. After a few minutes, the figure disappeared back into the barn and nothing but the horses appeared to move. Satisfied that no one was looking toward him, Lance ate an energy bar and drank from one of his water bottles. He carefully folded up the bar wrapper and slid it into one of his shirt pockets.

Nick was having a hard time staying awake with the hot sun beating directly down on him and was forced to drink more water than he would have liked. The natural result was that he had to relieve himself, which he did by turning carefully on his side, being careful to remain uphill from his resulting activity as he drained his bladder. He had no sooner finished relieving himself when he swore he heard the sound of muffled gunshots. He could almost feel the sound on his skin. Then it was quiet and he was confused as to what he had heard. For two hours the muffled sounds came and went. Nick decided it must be some kind of machinery in the barn. What the machinery was doing was something he could not imagine.

Lance was further away from the buildings and yet he too had the sense that he was hearing some form of gunfire, although it was quite muffled. He decided what he was hearing was hunters or kids having some form of target practice over the next ridge, and what he was hearing was some form of echo. Lance concentrated on the front windows of the ranch house and soon discovered that they were tinted with something that made any observation within the house almost impossible. As the day turned to afternoon, Lance found the heat almost unbearable and began to pray for darkness.

Nick too was hot and tired and unable to see anything that resembled human beings. He was thrilled to see the sun finally set behind Lance's position. As soon as it was dark enough and they could see lights in the windows of the ranch house, they began to crawl back down the hill to the sanctuary of the highway far below them. Both yearned for the relative safety of Sue and the van. At about nine P.M that evening Sue and the van appeared and slowed down enough for the two stiff and tired men to jump aboard the still moving van.

An hour later they had taken a field shower, changed clothes, and eaten supper. During supper, they were constantly interrupted with questions by a very curious Dan. He studied their pictures and their marked up maps and asked several questions before he finally sat down in a camp chair and opened a cold can of beer from the cooler.

It was now obvious to Dan that trying to get Kit at the ranch was not going to be successful. Dan ruled out a sniper shot because the configuration of the buildings gave no open shots and any shot would be from long range and uphill in a hot sun. Getting close to the ranch house undetected was unlikely as well. If they had trip wires,

God only knew what else they had set out to prevent any surprise visits by anyone who was unwelcome.

After finishing about half of his beer, Dan knew he would have to draw Kit out of the ranch and ambush him at a place of Dan's choosing. He then pulled out a topographical map of the area and began to study it. By the time Dan had finished the beer, he had formulated a plan. He got up and pulled another can of beer from the cooler and sat back down to work out the details in his mind.

CHAPTER THIRTY-SEVEN

Kit and Swifty had spent the day indoors. After a couple of hours on the range, Swifty made Kit clean all the weapons they had used. After lunch, they spent about two hours in hand-to-hand combat and practicing on how to disarm each other. At one point, Swifty had looked out a window in the barn when he thought he saw a reflection of light in the field below the ranch. After about five minutes of scanning the field, he decided his eyes were playing tricks on him and went back to the ranch house.

Kit and Connor had forgotten to tell Swifty about the sensors placed out in the meadow. If either Kit or Swifty had checked the control box in the mudroom, they would have known that they had some unseen and unwelcome visitors.

Kit was searching through the refrigerator for the basis of what he and Swifty were going to have for breakfast when the phone rang. Swifty was working on his first cup of coffee, and he grabbed the phone from the wall. Kit heard Swifty say, "Sure thing, Mrs. Carlson. We'll head out there right away."

Swifty hung up the phone, turned to Kit and said, "That was Mrs. Carlson. She said Big Dave asked her to call us. There's some kind of trouble up at the LaBarge Creek sheep camp and Big Dave wants us to meet him at Emigrant Springs as soon as possible."

Both men tossed their coffee cups in the sink and ran for the barn. Each of the men stopped to grab some personal gear, which they then tossed into the truck. Kit rounded up Dolly and a four-year old mare and saddled them. Kit was leading the horses into the horse trailer he had attached to his old pickup when Swifty appeared with a rucksack and two rifles. He brought Kit's 30-06 and a smaller nasty looking synthetic all black rifle with a laser scope. Swifty put both rifles on the gun rack that was attached to the back window of the old GMC truck. He tossed Kit a box of 30-06 ammunition and stuck his rucksack behind the seat on the passenger side.

Fifteen minutes after they got the phone call, they were headed down the rutted drive to the highway below them. Kit figured that Emigrant Springs was about forty-five minutes away. He kept the gas pedal down and the old truck surged forward as the speedometer needle pressed against the number seventy. Kit knew this was the high end for this old GMC. After about ten minutes, they came to the turnoff that would lead them to Emigrant Springs.

There were no longer any real springs at Emigrant Springs, just some rotting wood from the days when the springs fed water into wooden troughs. Emigrants had originally used the springs as a source of water as they come over the Oregon Trail. In later years, the springs were used by ranchers to water their livestock. Now all that remained were a few piles of rotting wood and a sizeable grove of Aspen trees. The road split at the springs, with one fork heading west and following the original Oregon Trail and the other fork heading north into the Bridger Wilderness Area.

Kit had to slow down his speed as the dirt and the gravel road was no paved highway and the ruts caused the truck to bounce high. The higher speed was causing the old pickup to slide sideways going through many of the turns. Kit turned to Swifty who was checking his pistol. "If the problem is in the camp above LaBarge Creek, why is he meeting us at Emigrant Springs? Are you sure she said LaBarge Creek?"

"That's what she said, trouble at the camp at LaBarge Creek and meet Big Dave at Emigrant Springs."

"That doesn't make any sense. If we wanted to get to the LaBarge Creek camp as quickly as possible, we'd go to the trailhead at the Ham's Fork Drainage. Starting from Emigrant Springs would take us at least two more hours to get there."

"Well, that's what she said, word for word."

Kit thought for a minute, being careful not to take his eyes off the road and trying to keep his speed up without jeopardizing the balance he needed for the pickup and the loaded horse trailer.

"Did she actually save Big Dave?"

"She sure did."

"In the past six months, I've never heard her call him anything but "Dave or David.""

"You think that maybe the caller wasn't Mrs. Carlson? I don't know her well enough to recognize her voice."

With that thought pounding its way through Kit's brain, he applied the brakes and slowly brought the truck and trailer to a halt.

Kit looked at Swifty and said, "So maybe we're being set up and there isn't a problem with the sheep camp at LaBarge Creek."

"And no Big Dave waiting to meet us at Emigrant Springs," responded Swifty.

"We could also be speculating with a little paranoia and be wrong," said Kit. "So, what do we do now?"

"We could try calling Mrs. Carlson to see if the call was real?"

"Excellent idea, Mr. Olson," said Kit as he handed his cell phone to Swifty.

"You know the little box with lines that show you how good your signal is? Well we aint' got none. No signal is available in this neck of the woods."

"So now what?"

"We proceed on to Emigrant Springs, but we go carefully. If we see anything, we stop and get out and look for any signs of an ambush and we keep our guns handy," said Swifty.

Kit felt the hair on the back of his neck go up. "I don't like the feeling I'm getting about this," he said. "Shouldn't we turn back and find a place we can get a signal to make a call?"

"Maybe we're being a little paranoid, but it has been my experience that being prepared for trouble and always expecting the worst is usually a pretty healthy way to go. Besides, if this is an ambush, we are ready and I'd rather face down these jaspers when I know what's coming rather than wait and get surprised someplace else."

Both men rechecked their weapons, including the rifles and then resumed their journey in the old pickup and horse trailer at a much more leisurely pace.

They drove carefully for about fifteen minutes and saw nothing more dangerous than a few prairie dogs that scrambled across the dusty road at the old pickup's approach.

"If I remember correctly, we should be able to see Emigrant Springs when we get to the top of this next hill,' said Kit.

The sagebrush-covered prairie was gradually giving way to clumps of Aspen. On the hills in front of them, they could see the beginnings of a sizeable pine forest that stretched out to the horizon leading up to Commissary Ridge. Just before they got to the top of the hill, Kit pulled the truck off the road and killed the engine. Both of them got out and closed the doors being careful to make no noise. Swifty led the way up the hill, and they ended up crawling the last thirty yards to the top. Just below the crest of the hill, they stopped and Swifty brought out a small pair of binoculars. He scanned the small valley below them where the springs were located.

"What do you see?" whispered Kit.

"Aspen trees and a few piles of old wood, and an empty road," replied Swifty. He continued to scan the area and then tapped Kit on the arm. "Just past the old springs, on the north fork of the road, past a patch of aspens is a white van with the hood up. I see someone leaning in over the engine compartment."

After what seemed an eternity, but was actually about a minute, Swifty whispered, "My God, it's a woman! A tall blonde woman! She looks like she's having car trouble."

"Is she old or young?" asked Kit.

"Who the hell can tell from this distance. Wait, I see some lettering on the van. It looks like it to belongs to some college, but I can't make out the name. Starts with an S, but a branch of the aspen tree between us is blocking out my view."

"You think this is legit?" asked Kit.

"I can't see anyone else around, but there could be someone waiting in the van that I can't see. Let's mosey on down there in the pickup, but let's keep our eyes peeled and keep looking around. If the blonde is a decoy she's meant to distract us, so don't just focus on her. Got me?"

"I got it, Swifty."

They crawled back to the truck and after both checked their pistols and rifles, Ki started the engine and they slowly headed up the hill and toward their rendezvous with the white van and the mysterious blonde woman.

Sylvia heard the sound of the engine of the old pickup as it cleared the hill in front of her. She spoke clearly into the microphone built into her wristwatch. "They're coming. Remember our instructions. Wait until they get out and are clear of the old pickup, and for God's sake watch your aim and don't shoot me."

Sylvia waited for a couple of minutes before she raised up out of the engine compartment as though she had just then realized that she had visitors. Sue and Nick were in the van with their weapons ready, and Lance was behind a big rock just off the road where it took the west fork. Dan was behind a pile of rocks at the base of a clump of aspen directly behind the van on far side of the north fork of the road.

Dan had set this up as a crossfire situation and created a killing ground between the van and the probable location of the old pickup. It was a very good plan and Sylvia was the bait. To complete her disguise, Dan had Sylvia smear grease on her hands and forearms and the front of her shirt and cargo pants to make it appear that she had been working on the van. To complete the scene there was a packet of wrenches unrolled on the fender of the van.

Since Sylvia had the best view, she would be the first to open fire. When she was sure both targets were in the open, she would draw her pistol from the engine compartment of the van and fire. The others would then join in to make sure nothing was left standing.

Kit brought the pickup to a stop about thirty yards from the van. He knew from his training that most people are less than accurate with a pistol beyond twenty yards. All Kit could see was the blonde girl who was now standing by the side of the van's engine compartment with her hands on her hips staring at him and Swifty.

"Open the door and step out of the truck, but do not go past the end of the door. Keep the door between you and her," whispered Swifty who had pulled his rucksack from the floor and into his lap.

"Hello there," said Kit.

"Thank God you came along," said Sylvia with a big smile on her face.

Kit opened the truck door and stepped out onto the ground. The truck door remained between Kit and the blonde. "What seems to be the trouble?"

"I don't know. The damn van just quit on me and I tried to call for help, but the batteries in my radio are shot and my cell phone can't pick up a signal," said the blonde.

Kit still saw no one else and neither did Swifty who remained silently sitting in the passenger seat of the pickup.

Kit started to walk around the truck door and moved towards the blonde and the van. "Well, let's have a look at the van and see if we can . . . ." The next words froze in Kit's throat as he saw the smiling blonde reach down into the van's engine compartment and pull out a revolver. She was swinging the revolver up to point at Kit, who had frozen in mid-stride and could not seem to make his hands or feet or any part of his body move. Just as the blond brought the muzzle of the gun up to point it at Kit, a small dark hole appeared in the middle of her forehead, just above her nose. Simultaneously, the roar of a gun shot arrived and the blonde seemed to fly backwards without moving her feet and collapsed on the ground in front of the van.

"Get down, Kit, you idiot," screamed Swifty who was now standing outside the pickup on the passenger side with the door between him and the van. Swifty was holding a small deadly looking weapon with a short barrel and a squat ugly scope on the top.

Kit's control over his muscles arrived just in time for him to dive back behind the truck door before Sue and Nick began firing from behind the doors at the back of the van. Two rounds hit the door in front of Kit, but did not penetrate. Luck was on Kit's side as both rounds came from 9mm pistols, and they lacked the power to penetrate the old truck's heavy doors. The old truck had about twice the amount of steel in the door as a new modern truck would have had. These details added up to helping save Kit from the first volley of gunfire.

"Get down, get under the truck," yelled Swifty as he began to direct his fire at Sue and Nick behind the van. Kit dropped to his stomach and crawled under the truck.

He was crawling toward the back of the truck toward the horse trailer when he felt a bullet flash by his head, close enough to hear it and feel the wind it created. A second round hit the left rear tire on the truck and caused it to make a loud pop and then a loud hissing noise as the trapped air escaped.

Kit turned on his belly and peered out from behind the flattening tire, trying to figure out where the shots were coming from. Another round slammed into the sand just to the left of Kit's head, causing him to pull back behind the flattened tire like a frightened turtle. After waiting for a few seconds, Kit slowly peeked out around the right side of the tire and looked out. He could see nothing. He took off his hat and moved it to the let side of the tire with his left hand while he continued to look out from the right side. A bullet slammed into the hat and tore it out of his hand. Fortunately Kit had continued to focus on the area in front of him, and now he saw the shooter clearly. A large blonde man was behind a big rock located just past the fork in the road that went to the south.

The shooter had a good view of the left side of the truck, but he obviously could not see Kit unless he exposed himself above the rock. The rock seemed to give the shooter very good protection until Kit noticed there was a large pile of rocks a few yards behind the large rock and that gave him an idea. Kit waited until the shooter exposed himself slightly and then Kit took steady aim with his 45, being careful to brace his hands around the frame of the big pistol and then taking a deep breath and letting half of it out. His shot was a little high and to the left of the shooter, but it obviously was a surprise as the shooter quickly ducked out of sight.

"How does it feel when someone shoots back, asshole," thought Kit. Then Kit fired two consecutive rounds just above the rock where the shooter had disappeared, aiming for the rock pile right behind him. Kit was counting on the bullets ricocheting back against the big rock the shooter was hiding behind. He could hear the whine of the bullets ricocheting followed by loud cursing and then the reappearance of the shooter who began to blaze away at Kit's position behind the truck wheel.

Kit had been waiting for just such a moment and just as the shooter fired for the third straight time, Kit fired and hit Lance high on the right shoulder with one shot. Unlike smaller caliber weapons like the 9mm and even the 40 caliber that the would-be assassins were using, the 45 caliber bullet has a great deal more impact power. The bullets that Kit was using were powerful hollow points. The impact of the bullet hitting Lance's shoulder spun the large blonde man around and knocked him to the ground, while his weapon went flying into the rocks.

The sound of more gunfire brought Kit back from the shock of seeing his bullet knock down a real person. "How we doin', Kit?" yelled Swifty who was still firing at the van from the right side of the truck.

"There was one in the rocks to the south and I winged him," Kit yelled back.

"Good shootin'. Let's slide back to the horse trailer

and get the horses and ride the hell out of here. They made a sieve out of the truck radiator. It ain't goin' nowhere."

Kit quickly retrieved his hat and crawled over the passenger side of the truck and he and Swifty crawled their way back to the rear end of the horse trailer. All during this maneuver they were taking fire from Sue and Nick who were still at the back of the van.

Dan swore at himself. His position was blocked from the truck by the rocks and aspen stand in front of him. He had been shocked to see Sylvia cut down by Swifty and amazed to see Lance go down from Kit's gun. He knew he needed to move to his left and come up and flank the two targets, shooting them before they knew he was there. He scanned the terrain in front of him and picked out a sheltered route that would take him behind the truck's location.

He had no sooner started out for the first position, a large rock, when he was forced to dive for cover when a burst of small arms fire riddled the trees he was standing next to. "What the hell was that?" he thought just as two horses and riders burst through the aspen grove to his left and disappeared into the timber to the north. Dan swung around on his knees and fired two quick shots at the rapidly vanishing figures.

"Shit," swore Dan as he scrambled to his feet and ran back to the van to assess the damage. He quickly took stock of the situation. Sylvia was dead and Lance had a shoulder wound that looked worse than it probably was. Lance could still help, but he was probably not going to be able to hit anything with a gun because of his shoulder. Dan grabbed a first aid kit out of the back of the van and tied a quick bandage over Lance's wounded shoulder. Sue and Nick were unhurt, but surprised at the ferocity of the firefight and in a little bit of shock over Sylvia's death. The van was riddled with bullets from Swifty and what was left of the engine coolant was dribbling out into the dirt under the radiator of the van.

"Leave Sylvia and let's get to the ATV's" yelled Dan. Like all of them, Sylvia had no identification on her body and nothing to link her to Dan.

Dan led the three other killers back about fifty yards to a clearing in a heavy pine grove where they had hidden the five ATV's. Before they started their engines, Dan had them go through a checklist that included weapons, ammunition, portable radios, GPS units, water, and food as well as full gas tanks. After a quick inventory of each ATV, Dan led the three others out of the clearing and in pursuit of the two horsemen.

Kit and Swifty had ridden about a mile before they halted. Swifty got off his mare and checked her over carefully. He ran his hand over her left flank and lifted it up in the air for Kit to see. The hand was covered in blood. Dan's two quick shots had not missed entirely.

"How bad is it?" asked Kit.

"She's still able to walk, but she is bleeding badly and she won't make it much further. What the hell do we do now?"

Kit thought for a second and dismounted from Dolly.

He walked over to where Swifty was standing and looked at the wounded mare. Kit turned to Swifty and said, "You take my horse and make your way back to the nearest ranch and call for help. I'll take the wounded mare a little further and then leave her and go on foot. That will put me high enough in the Bridger Wilderness to make it rough on them, even with me on foot."

"That is the dumbest idea I ever heard of. How can I protect you if I run off and leave you?"

"Look, it's me they're trying to kill. You're just in the way. Unless you get help in a hurry, they're going to track us down and kill both of us. There are at least four of them all heavily armed, and I bet they have ATV's or 4x4's and are on our trail now. If you can get some help, I'll lead them up by lower LaBarge Creek. Remember that hidden box canyon with the cave I told you about. Well, I'll lead them up the creek, lose them, and hide out in the cave. Big Dave knows where it is, and I'm sure these killers don't. Remember, they are the outsiders up here and they shouldn't be that hard to lose. Besides, I still have my pistol."

"You do make a mighty good argument, Kit," said Swifty. "I should be able to get to the Wilson place in a little over an hour. I can call from there. You sure you can outrun them and lose them in the trees?"

"Does a bear crap in the woods?"

"Very funny. I'll hide out behind that aspen grove over there and brush out my trail. You better get going. That mare is not gonna last long."

"I'm going, but I have a question. What the hell were you shooting at them with?"

"Swifty laughed and pulled out the short nasty looking weapon from his rucksack. "This, my friend, is the Delta Force's best buddy, the H&K SP5 sub-machine gun. I'm almost out of ammo. It tends to use it up pretty quickly. Now git before I decide to shoot you."

Kit grinned, mounted the wounded mare, and set out heading north into the Bridger Wilderness.

Swifty led Dolly back behind the aspen grove and tied her to a tree and then broke off a large spruce tree branch and used it to sweep the ground clear of both his boot prints and Dolly's hoof prints.

Swifty then held Dolly's head in his arms with his hands over her muzzle. About ten minutes passed and he heard the sound of small engines that seemed to resemble a swarm of very loud bees. Another five minutes went by and the first of four ATV's burst past the spot where Swifty and Kit had paused to talk. Swifty held his breath until all four of the ATV's had disappeared into the tree cover to the north. Swifty took a compass bearing and checked his GPS. Then he mounted Dolly and headed her to the east. As soon as they were on a well-worn game trail, Swifty applied the heel of his boots to Dolly's flanks and urged her on. He knew he was truly in a race for life or death.

Kit had heard the sound of the engines of the ATV's and knew the killers were in pursuit. After about ten minutes, he knew they had passed Swifty's hiding place and were continuing on after him. He tried to take what he felt was the shortest route to the LaBarge Creek drainage, but also headed into places that would be a lot tougher for an ATV to traverse than a horse. He could feel the mare's strength draining as her pace began to slow.

Kit had just cleared the crest of the ridge he had been climbing and was descending down the other side into the LaBarge Creek drainage when his horse just seemed to give out on him and slid to the ground. Horse and rider slid down the side of the ridge for about twenty yards on a ground cover of dried leaves and pine needles before coming to a halt. Kit had kept his toes in the stirrups as Big Dave had taught him to do so he was able to pull his feet out when he felt the horse begin to fall. In doing so he did not wind up trapped under the horse.

Even so, the fall knocked the wind out of him and it took him a couple of minutes to recover. Kit then got to his feet, retrieved a canteen and his GPS and compass from the saddlebags along with a box of ammunition. He checked his pistol, and it was still secure in his holster along with his knife in its scabbard on his left side. Kit also had two extra fully loaded magazines in his jacket pocket.

Kit checked on the mare. She was still alive, but breathing heavily and she was still losing blood from the wound on her flank. It was unlikely she would survive, but Kit couldn't risk shooting her to put her out of her misery. The sound of the shot would draw the killers to him like flies to honey. Kit took a compass bearing and headed on foot at a fast pace toward LaBarge Creek.

Kit found himself jogging down the side of the ridge toward the creek and he tried to pace himself and keep the panic he felt rising from taking over his body. He knew he had to pace himself if he were going to lose the killers in the drainage and get to his hiding place in what he had so recently come to know as "The Wild Bunch Canyon."

He finally reached the creek and began running northwest along the banks. Before long he found an old game trail that mostly paralleled the creek and stayed on it. The trail was narrow and winding and would be tough for an ATV. Kit came to a shallow place to ford the creek. He crossed the creek and went up about thirty yards on the other side to a rocky area. Then he walked backwards, staying in his original footprints, returning to the creek. Then he waded downstream about fifty yards and climbed up the bank where it was low and returned to the game trail. "That should slow them up," he thought.

Dan halted the procession of ATV's at the site of the dying mare and pointed to the wound in the flank. "I knew I hit something when they surprised me. I wonder if I shot one of them? They must be riding double now. That'll slow them down."

Nick had dismounted his ATV and was studying the ground around the dying horse. Soon he was walking north of the horse, moving in small, but ever widening circles.

"What the hell are you doing, Nick?" asked an irritated Dan.

"Looking for sign, boss. I don't see any sign of another

horse. I think I see footprints, but it looks like only one set. I think we were chasing only one horse and rider. The other one must have slipped past us."

"Shit!" exclaimed Dan. "That means one of them went for help. Which one are we chasing?"

"I'm not sure, but these prints look more like some kind of hiking boots than cowboy boots."

"I'll bet these belong to the Andrews kid. The other guy, the one with the damned machine gun, looked like the real cowboy type," said Sue.

"How the hell did he get a machine gun?" asked Nick. "It scared the shit out of me."

"Shut up, all of you," yelled Dan. "It doesn't matter who did what. We have a job to do and so far we've botched it. Sue, you take your ATV and back track and pick up the trail of the other jerk. Take Lance with you and make sure the cowboy is dead long before he can get to any help."

Both Sue and Lance nodded their agreement and they mounted their ATV's and took off back in the direction they had just come from with their small engines roaring like hungry chainsaws.

"Nick, you follow these tracks. We'll take it slowly to make sure we don't lose him. On foot he can't outrun our ATVs and we should catch him within an hour." Nick mounted his ATV and slowly turned it north towards the creek with Dan right behind him.

Sue and Lance made good time retracing their trail and almost went by Swifty's previous hiding place without noticing it. However Lance had decided to move out about twenty yards from the trail and just happened to cut the track of Swifty and Dolly. He immediately signaled Sue, and they then went to almost full throttle in their pursuit of the obvious horse and rider trail.

After almost twenty minutes, Swifty heard the buzzing of their motors and realized they had picked up his trail. He rode Dolly through a fairly narrow cut in some rocks and then doubled back. He stopped to tie Dolly off in a small grove of Aspen trees. Swifty removed the lariat from the saddle and ran back to the cut in the rocks. He went to the far side of the cut and tied off one end of the rope to a sturdy pine tree next to the rock cut and draped the rope across the narrow cut and over to the rock on the other side. Then he went back across the cut and threw leaves and pine needles on the rope to hide it. Swifty moved to a spot behind the rock and ran the rope around a tree just behind the rock. Finally he crouched down where he was safely hidden behind the rock, holding the end of the rope in his gloved hands.

In just a few minutes the two ATVs approached the cut between the rocks and headed right through it, one ATV following right behind the other. Swifty pulled hard on the rope and it suddenly became a clothes-line about neck high and knocked first Sue and then Lance off their ATVs. The ATVs, suddenly rider-less and rudderless quickly crashed into the nearby trees. Swifty jumped from behind the rock with his pistol in his hand and shot a sitting upright, but stunned Lance right between the eyes.

Sue was laying on her side on the ground where she had been slightly stunned by the fall. She saw Swifty shoot Lance and she lunged for her pistol which had ended up on the ground about three feet behind her. Swifty shot Sue in the back of the head, twice, just to make sure. After checking both bodies to make sure they were dead and finding no identification, Swifty ran to where he had tied off his horse. He took a GPS reading and then mounted Dolly and continued his race to get help for Kit.

CHAPTER THIRTY-EIGHT

Kit had stopped to rest as he leaned against the trunk of an aspen tree. His lungs were burning and his legs felt like he had been running in sand. He checked his GPS and estimated that he had about four miles to go before he got to the cave. He hoped that Swifty had gotten to safety and found some help. He had faith in Swifty. After what he had seen today, he would rather have Swifty on his side than the entire Wyoming National Guard. The guy was a one-man army. Big Dave had been right about choosing him to help Kit.

Kit paused to listen. He could hear an occasional bird, but so far no sound of the buzzing ATV engines. He willed himself to his feet and resumed his now painful jog toward the hidden canyon.

Dan sat on his ATV and cursed. Nick was walking

slowly around in circles over a large rocky patch of ground. They had lost the trail and Nick was having trouble finding it again.

"Well, which way did he go, damn it? The dumb bastard didn't just fly off or vanish into thin air."

"Boss, after we crossed the creek he headed up on this rocky area and here I can see no tracks. I'll need to check the perimeter of this rocky area to try to cut his trail."

"Jesus Christ! Stop blabbering and get to it. He's on foot. He can't be far away."

"You know, boss, you could get off that thing and help me."

"Okay, okay, I'll help. What do you want me to do?"

"We'll cut the area in half. I'll go to the left and you go to the right and we'll meet on the other side. If you see any tracks, yell out."

In fifteen minutes, they met on the other side and neither of them had seen any tracks.

"Now what do we do?" growled Dan.

"We go back to the creek and see if he might have backtracked on us," answered Nick.

They crossed back over the creek and searched the trail north, past where the tracks had turned to cross the creek. Finally, Nick found the new tracks about fifty yards further up the path. "Damn that boy is smarter than we thought," said Nick.

"I don't give a shit about how good a Boy Scout he is. Our job is to find him and kill him and I want it done now!"

By the time Dan and Nick had picked up Kit's rail, he had made it to the mouth of the canyon. He stopped to rest and thirstily drank out of his canteen. He then refilled it from the creek and used his knife to cut a good-sized branch off a pine tree. Kit then walked about a hundred yards past the canyon opening and walked quickly into the surrounding pine trees like he was changing direction.

Kit then backtracked to the creek. He walked into the creek, using the branch to brush out his footprints. He walked up the creek to the canyon entrance and then walked up the bank and into the canyon, using the pine branch to brush out his foot prints.

He stood at the entrance to the canyon after brushing out any trace of his prints on the ground from the creek and then stood quietly, listening. He could hear the normal sounds of day time in the canyon. He could hear a few birds and rustle of the wind in the trees. He looked up and could see a hawk floating on the air above the canyon. "Probably looking for lunch," Kit thought.

He studied the canyon and decided that the area on the north side of the hidden cave was sloping enough that he might be able to crawl out of the canyon that way if he had to. He looked at the steep slope of the canyon and shivered. Kit hoped that he wouldn't have to try that climb. Then he walked to the hidden cave and stooped to enter it after carefully brushing out his tracks with the pine branch.

Kit awoke with a start as his head bobbed forward. He was quickly awake and afraid. How could he have fallen asleep? How long had he been asleep? Kit checked his watch and the luminous dials showed he had been asleep for about an hour and a half. He checked his surroundings. His canteen was next to him. Both his pistol and his knife were on his belt. He had bullets, his GPS, his compass, two loaded magazines, and his fire starter kit in his pockets.

He took out his handkerchief and wiped his eyes and face. Then he sat still and listened. He could hear nothing. He crawled closer to the entrance of the cave, being careful to stay in the shadows that lined the floor of the cave, illuminated by the narrow streams of sunlight that got past the rock wall in the front of the cave. Again he stopped to listen. He could hear nothing, nothing at all. Then he realized that they had found him or a least had found the canyon. Haring nothing at all meant he did not even hear the birds that he had heard just a couple of hours before. The birds were silent because of the presence of something they feared. Kit was pretty sure it was the killers.

A few minutes passed and then Kit could swear he heard footsteps. They were moving slowly, cautiously, and their boots were making noise as they were slowly crunching down on the rocky floor of the canyon. Kit checked his pistol and pushed the release button, carefully dropping the magazine into his hand. He had four of the normal eight rounds counting the bullet he extracted from the chamber. He carefully reached into his pocket, pulled out four loose bullets and reloaded the magazine.

He then inserted the magazine back into the pistol as quietly as he could mange. He carefully and slowly pulled back on the barrel of the pistol, retracting the slide until it cocked the hammer back and then slowly released it, forcing a new bullet into the chamber.

Satisfied, Kit sat back on his heels to wait.

Kit could hear the sounds of footsteps on the loose rocks in front of the cave, and they seemed to be getting closer. He held his breath, afraid to make any kind of a sound. The footsteps seemed to go past the cave and then they became softer as though the walker was moving away from the cave entrance. Then the footsteps stopped. Kit could almost see the person turn and then start walking back toward the wall in front of the entrance to the cave.

The sunlight that had illuminated part of the front of the cave had seemed to dim and the illuminated floor area was much smaller than he remembered. Kit then realized that the sun was going down in the west and as it went down behind the west wall of the canyon, there was less light getting to the cave. He looked at his watch. It was almost seven o'clock. He was sure that he and Swifty had been ambushed about ten o'clock in the morning. Had nine hours really passed since then?

Kit decided on a plan of action. Since this much time had passed, either Swifty and help were not coming or they were very late. Kit knew he was on his own. He also knew he was trapped in the cave, but they had to come in to get him and when that happened he would have a fighting chance of survival. He was also pretty sure that there were only two of them based on the sounds that he could make out.

Kit moved to a spot in the cave that gave him the best angle of fire to the cave opening that was outlined by the remaining sunlight. He sat on the floor with his legs crossed and his body leaning slightly forward, holding his pistol in a combat stance.

Suddenly the small area of sunlight on the floor was blotted out, and Kit could make out a large shadow between the rock wall and the front of the cave. He waited until he could see more than a shadow. His eyes were adjusted to the semi-darkness. Someone coming in from the outside would not be able to see the interior of the cave until their eyes adjusted, unless they had a flashlight. A light seemed to erupt in the cave and Kit was temporarily blinded. Then he saw it was a flashlight beam and it was slowly panning the sides of the cave, working from the right side of the entrance to the left. Kit waited until his eyes adjusted and then sighted in his pistol on what he was pretty sure was the center of the chest of the shadow holding the flashlight. Just as the light was about to reveal Kit's position on the floor of the cave, Kit pulled the trigger. With the small area of the cave confining the sound of the shot, the noise was magnified so much that it almost left Kit unable to hear. The flash of the shot lit up the interior of the cave for a second and Kit could just see the face of his target before the flash temporarily blinded him.

A loud scream was followed by a thump as the flashlight hit the cave floor and bounced. The shadow seemingly flew backwards out of the entrance to the cave.

Kit then heard "God damn, I'm hit. I'm hit. The sonofabitch shot me. Shoot the bastard."

Kit then flattened himself out on the floor of the cave as he heard several shots and at least two bullets flew into the cave and ricocheted off the walls. Several more shots followed, but none of them found their way past the outside wall and into the confines of the cave. Kit could hear more screaming and moaning. He had obviously hit the target, but he had not killed him and now they knew where he was. Kit was trapped in the cave. He crawled forward and retrieved the fallen flashlight and turned it off. Then he crawled to the back of the cave.

Several minutes passed and there were no more shots. Kit could still hear sounds of movement outside the cave, but none that were close to the entrance. He could hear the occasional moan and curses that he was sure were coming from the killer he had wounded. Then he heard sounds he could not identify. He heard the sound of something scraping against the outside of the cave or the cave wall. The sounds came and went and were repeated several times. Finally they stopped.

Kit listened carefully and again heard some footsteps moving toward the front of the cave. He carefully crawled to the left side of the cave by the entrance, the opposite of where he had been waiting the first time. He carefully peered out past the entrance and could not see through the opening that should have been there between the front of the cave and the wall. Then his heart sank as he saw why.

They had piled grass and sagebrush into the opening. They were going to light the pile and try to burn him out. With the cave having no other air source, he would run out of oxygen or be overcome by the smoke pretty quickly.

Kit was no coward, but he was definitely afraid. He didn't want to die and certainly not like this. He decided to take the offensive. If he ran out shooting before they started the fire, he might take them by surprise. However, he didn't know where the killers were in the canyon, and he could wind up a sitting duck.

Kit decided to let the killers light the fire and come out as fast as he could when he had smoke as cover. The fire would quickly turn to smoke and the smoke would rise up the canyon wall, as well as into the cave. If he could get out of the cave and then try to climb the north slope of the canyon, he might be able to use the smoke for cover. The killers could not see any better in the smoke than he could and he knew that one of the two was probably not able to do much accurate shooting. It might not be the best plan, but it was better than dying of smoke inhalation or worse.

As Kit waited, all he could think of was a scene from the movie, *Butch Cassidy and the Sundance Kid* where the outlaws made a run for their horses from a small building, right into the rifles of several hundred Bolivian soldiers.

Kit tried to shake the image from his mind and readied himself for the desperate run for the canyon slope.

Kit heard a hissing noise and then heard something hit the side of the rock wall and almost immediately smoke began to rise into the cave. Staying low to the floor of the cave where there was less smoke, Kit rushed the entrance of the cave and pushed his way through the burning grasses and sagebrush.

There was smoke everywhere, and he tried to hold his breath and get past it. As soon as he cleared the wall in front of the cave, he scrambled to climb up the rocky slope of the canyon. With each step he expected to feel the impact of a bullet in his back. He had gone up about fifteen feet when his foot slipped on a rock and he slid down about three feet, jamming his knee into a small crevice in the rocks.

Kit heard gunshots and waited for the impact as they tore through his body. But nothing happened. They couldn't have missed at that range. Kit turned to look through the now diminishing smoke. About twenty feet from him were the two killers, both sprawled on the ground. Both had been shot in the head, their guns lying on the ground beside them.

Kit painfully pulled his knee out from the crevice in the rocks and made it to his feet. He then carefully slid down the rocky slope to the canyon floor. He looked around the small box canyon again and all he could see were the two dead killers. He could hear nothing. He slowly walked toward the bodies and cautiously looked around.

"Well hell, better late than never," came a voice from up high above Kit.

He looked up at the south wall of the canyon. Standing up and holding their rifles were Big Dave, Woody, and Connor. Big Dave gave Kit a wave, and then they disappeared from sight.

"You throwing a bar-b-q and not inviting your friends?" said a smiling Swifty as he walked into the canyon from the hidden entrance. "Awful damn smoky place you got here. Must be downright unhealthy for a young feller like you."

Kit hobbled over to Swifty and hugged him. "Hey, I told you I'm not that kind of guy," protested a laughing Swifty.

"What the hell happened?" Kit managed to get out.

"Well, those two yahoos tried to catch me on them little go-karts, so I used an old lariat trick and I dumped them on their ass. Then I had to shoot them for being impolite and trying to shoot me. Old Dolly and I high-tailed it to the Wilson ranch and called big Dave. He had me meet him, Woody, and Connor here outside the entrance to the canyon. After we figured out that you were in the cave and the two killers were in the canyon, we decided to use you as bait to get those dummies out in the open.

Big Dave and the others went up the south wall of the canyon to get the high ground and cover the canyon floor. My job was to cover the entrance in case they tried to run out. After the two killers set the fire and you came running out, they moved out into the open to try to see you through the smoke. That was a bad choice on their part. I think those three old coots hit both of them at least three times. By the way, looks like you hit one pretty solid in the shoulder. He sure sounded pissed then. Course, that don't mean much to him now."

"You used me as bait!" exclaimed Kit.

"Actually smoked bait might be a better description," laughed Swifty.

A few minutes later they were joined by Big Dave, Woody, and Connor. They each took turns hugging Kit and exchanging insults with Swifty.

"What do we do with the bodies?" asked Swifty?"

"I think they need to just disappear," said Big Dave. These are bad people nobody will miss. I know a few places where we can stash them so they can be recycled just like Mother Nature would want. I think it best they just disappear so neither we nor Kit need to talk to any authorities about what happed here. Connor and I will take care of all five of them and their vehicles. We'll also tow Kit's truck back to the ranch."

"What about the people who sent them," said Kit. "Won't they come looking for them?"

"Oh, I think we can find a way to send them a convincing message and discourage them from any future attempts to harm you, Kit," said Big Dave. "Woody has been doing some snooping, and it seems some sleazy attorney in Chicago may be behind all of this. We plan to make him an offer he can't refuse to leave you alone."

CHAPTER THIRTY-NINE

Two days later.

Anna had figured out that not being able to contact Dan on her wireless after two days was not a good sign. The final decision to get out of town came after she overhead a conversation between one of the county deputies and Andy Bain, the tow truck driver. They were buying a couple of cold drinks while she was ringing up Andy's gas purchase.

"I'm telling you there is something funny about the van you're having me haul in" said Andy.

"What's funny about a wrecked van we found in a ravine?" asked the deputy.

"The front of that van is full of holes and they look a whole lot like bullet holes."

"Oh, Andy, that's just probably some kids or hunters using it for target practice. Happens all the time."

"Maybe, but there is one line of holes that looks like it came from a submachine gun and that ain't from no kid or no hunter."

Anna looked outside and let out a short gasp. Loaded up on Andy's flatbed wrecker was one of the two vans that Dan had been using. The van was badly wrecked. Later that day, when her shift was over, Anna packed up her things and left Kemmerer on the first bus to Salt Lake City.

Three days later.

Emelio could hardly believe his luck. He looked up and down the darkened street to make sure no one was watching. The street and the sidewalks were empty in this older commercial area of Salt Lake City. The neighborhood consisted mainly of old warehouses. There was a white Jeep Cherokee parked by the curb with the keys in the ignition. Attached to the Jeep was a small trailer with two like new ATV's, also with the keys in their ignitions. Emelio checked to make sure no one was inside the Jeep. The Jeep was empty. The interior of the Jeep was empty and clean, like someone had carefully cleaned it out. After again checking the street in front and behind him, Emelio slipped behind the wheel of the Jeep, started it, and drove off, being careful to drive within the speed limit and not draw attention to himself.

One week later.

Lenny was both surprised and slightly intrigued. He was looking at a box of cigars on his desk. This was not just any box of cigars, but a box of expensive Cuban cigars. They had just arrived by courier wrapped in a shiny gift-wrap with a small card containing his name and address, but no return address. Lenny could not image who would send him cigars. Most of the crooks he defended and took care of were cheap bastards who had to be reminded repeatedly to pay their "legal" bills to Lenny.

Lenny leaned over the box as he cut the seal on the lid with a letter opener and opened the box. Lenny screamed and fell back in his desk chair. There in the cigar box were five pairs of human ears, covered in dried blood! Under the lid of the box was a small envelope contained in a plastic waterproof bag taped to the lid. After he recovered from his initial shock, Lenny used the letter opener to pry the envelope loose. Once the bag was free of the box, Lenny cut open the bag and then the envelope. Inside was a small card made from very expensive bonded paper. On the card was printed this message:

> "Stay out of Wyoming or your ears will be next!"
> The Commanches

Lenny's body went limp, and he felt himself wetting his pants.

Two months later.

Ms. M. Kelly, assistant curator of the Chicago Museum of Science and Industry, was in her office having her morning cup of coffee and reading the morning edition of the *Chicago Tribune.* One of the lead stories was about the murder trial of the two Sabatini brothers. The headline read "Eyewitness testimony buries Sabatini brothers!"

Ms. Kelly smiled to herself as she read the rest of the article. The police had taken the position that Kit had been placed in "protective custody" out of state in Wyoming as a key witness in the murder trial. It read a lot like the spin-doctors in the prosecutors' office had been very busy since Kit's surprise return to Chicago. She finished the article and then reached over and read the article she had found in the *Casper Star Tribune* over a month ago. She had developed the habit of looking up the Casper paper each day on the internet to keep up with what was going on in southwestern Wyoming. The article had caught her eye, and she had printed it out and kept it on the corner of her desk.

"Mystery surrounds a van found wrecked and abandoned in Lincoln County." The story went on about the van being found in a gully by a rancher looking for a lost cow. "The van was white with Sangamon State University painted on the door. A check by the local sheriff's office of the serial number of the van found it to be titled to Sangamon State University in Springfield, Illinois. However, a check with Illinois authorities revealed that Sangamon State University went out of existence in the late 1980's and the school's records are now maintained by the University of Illinois in Springfield. A search of their records revealed no evidence of any ownership of the van. Authorities in Kemmerer, Wyoming, have ended their search for the owner and are holding the van in a salvage yard until such time as an owner comes forward. The wrecked van appeared to be perforated with bullet holes."

As she put the article back to it's resting place on the corner of her desk, Ms. Kelly took another sip of coffee and tried to keep from laughing out loud. "Now, just who does this sound like?" she thought to herself.

Her next sip of coffee was interrupted by the voice of her secretary on her intercom.

"Ms. Kelly, there is a gentleman to see you, but he doesn't have an appointment."

"Did he say why he needs to see me?" said Ms. Kelly.

"No, Ms. Kelly, but he did say something about collecting on a promise."

"Please send him in."

Tang rose to her feet and stepped out from behind her desk. She smoothed out an imaginary wrinkle in the skirt of her light green business suit and looked up as the door to her office opened.

Almost filling the doorway was a tall, broad shouldered, dark haired young man dressed in a navy pinstriped suit, with a gold tie and a blue button down dress shirt. The only thing that seemed out of place was a Stetson cream colored cowboy hat that he held in his left hand and the black Tony Lama cowboy boots on his feet.

"Good morning, Ms. Kelly. I came to collect on that promise for a personal tour of this world famous museum. I hope you can accommodate me on such short notice."

Tang's response was very un-professional as she ran forward and threw herself into Kit's waiting arms. Kit scooped her up as though she were weightless and kissed her full on the mouth. Tang looked up at him with her sparkling green eyes and said, "What brings you to Chicago, cowboy?"

Still holding her tightly in his arms, Kit smiled at her and said, "It seems I've been having some trouble with that pickup you sold me."

THE END